Nicole ✿ 'Dell
SWEPT AWAY
Interactive Fiction for Girls

Other books by Nicole O'Dell

Dare to Be Different
Risky Business

Nicole 'Dell

SWEPT AWAY

Interactive Fiction for Girls

BARBOUR
PUBLISHING

HIGH STAKES

DEDICATION

Logan, Megan, and Ryleigh, at not even two years old, the three of you have so much life ahead. Your eager young minds and sweet spirits bring joy to me every moment of every day. I pray you stay little as long as possible and grow up slowly in the loving embrace of your Savior, Jesus. Someday, when you're ready, you can read these books your ol' mom wrote and know that all I want is for you to make wise choices. With God's help, your dad and I will uphold you through all that life throws your way. I love you with all my heart.

—Mom

Chapter 1

OUT WITH THE OLD

"You might have to get out and push."

Amber groaned and rolled her eyes. "Very funny, Dad. The scary thing is, one of these days, it's going to be true."

Dad chuckled. "Ah, she hasn't failed us yet." He rubbed the faded steering wheel.

"Well, there's a first time for everything." Amber sulked down in the cracked vinyl seat and covered her eyes with her forearm. Her friends all had fancy new SUVs or expensive sedans. But no, her parents never wanted a car payment or—*gasp!*—a lease payment. Nothing but a complete waste of money when they already had a perfectly reliable vehicle—or so they said. If she had a dollar for every time they'd explained the horrors of a lease agreement. . .

The brakes squealed as Dad pulled the twelve-year-old Toyota into the garage. He smiled and patted the dashboard. "You did it, girl." He'd somehow ignored the *putt. . .sputter. . .putt* sounds the car had made all the way up the driveway.

"Yeah, Dad. We made it home. But what about tomorrow? What about the next day? When will we ever be able to get a new car now that you lost your job?" Amber squeezed her eyes shut, holding back the tears that threatened to spill.

"Now, Amber."

Amber steeled herself against the coming speech that she knew by heart and caught the sigh before it escaped her mouth.

Dad's lips moved in what looked like prayer for a few moments. He took a deep breath and turned her chin with his hand until she lifted her watery eyes to meet his. "God has always provided everything we've ever needed and much, much more. I have no reason to think He's going to stop now." He let go of her face and rubbed her arm. "Sweetie, give Him a chance."

"Yeah, yeah. I know." Amber rolled her eyes and fought the urge to point out that God had provided that stuff—which wasn't excessive, by any means—before He *unprovided* Dad's

job. She climbed out of the car and paused a
moment to give the rusted hood a few little
pats—like paying respects at a funeral. *Sigh*.

Amber had one foot in the door when she
heard three light honks. *Brittany!* She let her
book bag slide off her shoulder. It landed on the
garage floor with a thud. She jogged out to the
driveway to greet her best friend.

The window on the driver's side of the
brand-new, silver Lexus SUV slid down and
Mrs. Kim leaned her head out. "You girls be
good and have fun. I will come to get you
tomorrow afternoon." She spoke in halting but
precise English.

"Okay, Mom. Thanks." Brittany waved her
tiny hand as she came around from the other
side and joined Amber on the driveway.

As the girls walked toward the house, Amber
rested her forearm on Brittany's shoulder.

Brittany shook her head and laughed. "You
know, one of these days that's going to get old."

"Nah. You love it and you know it." They
walked through the garage toward the house, and
Amber bent to pick up her schoolbag then opened
the door to the dated kitchen. "Don't mind the
cracked tile and stained countertops. I promise
they're clean." Amber flicked away a crumb.

Brittany laughed. "You give me the same little speech every time I come here. You'd think after ten years, you'd know I don't care about tile and countertops."

"Easy for you to say. Your dad got promoted to Chief Something-or-Other the same week my dad got laid off from teaching. Your house is perfect. Mine. . ." Amber waved her arm. "Well, not so much." She slumped as she pulled open the refrigerator door to see what they could snack on. *Ooh! Leftover frozen pizza.*

"Yeah, I'm really sorry about your dad's job." Brittany picked a few pieces of nonexistent lint from her sleeve.

"It's pretty bad timing with college next year and all." Tears burned at her eyelids again. Amber blinked them away before Brittany could notice.

"But your grades are perfect. You'll probably get a scholarship. I thought that was the plan anyway." Brittany threw her hands up. "We've talked about getting scholarships and going to college together since we were little—we've got to get out of small-town Gwinett."

"Yeah, I know. But if I don't get one, I probably won't be going away to school. I'll have to get a job and go to the community college part time." Amber shrugged. "It'll be fine.

Right?" She finally turned around to look at Brittany.

"Fine? That would not be fine. Not at all. You can't stay trapped in this valley dungeon forever, surrounded by nothing but mountains. And you *will* get a scholarship. You'll see."

"Thanks. I do love the mountains, though." Amber couldn't risk getting her hopes up.

"Well, everyone loves the mountains. But there's so much world out there." Brittany pointed out the window.

"Yeah, well. . .anyway. . .enough of that." Amber held up the pizza. "Cold or heated?"

"Definitely cold." Brittany grabbed a piece as big as her face.

How did Brittany pack away so much food? She could eat twice as much as Amber. Where did she put it all? "Sounds good to me. Grab some more if you want. Let's go downstairs." Amber inspected an ivory porcelain plate for chips or cracks before she handed it to Brittany. She reached in the refrigerator to grab two cans of Coke. *Nope.* In its usual spot, she found an imposter, the store brand. She grimaced and held it up for Brittany to read the logo. "Hope cola's okay."

Brittany smiled and reached for the can.

"Hey, works for me."

"This cutting corners stuff is starting to get on my nerves." Amber shook her head, took her plate, and hurried from the kitchen.

The girls went down to the basement, which Amber's parents had let them turn into a hangout a few months back. They'd put a big rug down on the cold cement floor and brought Brittany's plush, gray sofa over when her parents bought a new leather set. Amber reached for the television remote but put it right back down, opting for music instead. She flipped on the stereo and turned up the volume.

"So, what do you want to do tonight?" Brittany plopped down on the couch and took a bite of her cold pizza.

"I'm open to whatever." Amber pushed a stray crumb back into her mouth. "Make some suggestions."

"Well, we could shop, go see a movie, check out Kyle's birthday party. . ." Brittany counted each idea on a finger.

Amber sighed. "All I hear is money, money, money."

Brittany shifted her legs as her eyes glazed over in apparent irritation.

Oops. I'm being a drag. "But I wouldn't mind

12

helping you shop. And Kyle's party—well, we'd have to think of an inexpensive present. He is my cousin, but it's not like we buy gifts for each other every year." Amber stood up and started for the stairs. "Let's go get ready."

"Great." Brittany jumped off the couch and brushed the crumbs off her pants before following. "We can find a gag gift for Kyle— something creative and funny that won't cost much."

Amber stopped abruptly and whirled around to face her friend, almost knocking her over. "Wait a sec. How're we going to get around? You don't have a car with you, and neither of us wants to be caught dead in my dad's car."

"Oh, come on, your car would be fine. But let me call my dad and see if there's another possibility—he should be home from work by now. Hang on." Brittany pulled out her sleek new smartphone and touched the screen in a few places. One more light tap and the speakerphone turned on.

Amber could hear it ringing.

Click. "Hello?"

"Hey Dad, it's me."

"What do you need, Brittany?"

Amber giggled at his halting speech. Like

Brittany's mom, Mr. Kim spoke nearly perfect English even though he'd been raised in Korea. Amber thought his accent sounded cute.

Brittany glared and put her finger to her lips. "Dad, I was wondering if you and Mom have plans tonight?"

"We are going out to a restaurant in one hour. Your mother is getting ready now."

"Since you're home now and Mom's done shopping, would you mind if Brittany and I came by to get a car? We want to go to the mall and to a birthday party."

"That is okay. But I can drop off car to you. It would be a long walk."

Brittany winked at Amber. "That would be so great, Dad. Thanks!"

"Welcome, Brittany. See you in one hour."

Brittany slid her phone closed and gave Amber a triumphant look. "There. We've got good wheels and good plans. Now we need. . ."

"Good outfits! Now *that* I can help with. Let's go." They scrambled up the stairs to Amber's room and hurried to her closet.

"It's a good thing you have on great jeans, Britt. Mine would be huge on you."

"Yeah, these are my favorite ones anyway— they're new." She twirled to look at her body in

14

the mirrored closet door.

After about fifteen minutes of sorting through tops, they settled on a couple of long-sleeved, burn-out tees over lace-trimmed camis. "I'd like to wear the amethyst one, it goes with my green eyes." Amber held the purple shirt up to her chin and batted her long eyelashes.

"Good. I wanted to wear the red one anyway." Brittany grabbed the hanger out of Amber's hand.

Satisfied with their choices, they dressed quickly and turned back to the mirror. Brittany hardly ever wore makeup, so it surprised Amber when Britt started rifling through the makeup drawer. She applied some pink blush to her cheeks and some mascara to her dark eyelashes, which helped open her eyes a bit. After a swipe of lip gloss, she ran a brush through her silky hair and then plopped on the bed to wait for Amber.

They heard a soft knock at the door. "Come in." Amber turned to look. "Hey, Mom. What's up?"

Her mom stood in the doorway wearing her typical tracksuit and wiping the sweat from her forehead.

"You just get back from a run?"

"Yeah, I did four miles—on the treadmill, though. I didn't go out." She paused to catch her breath. "But I wanted you to know you left all of your dirty dishes down in the basement."

"Oops!"

Mom swiped at the sweat dripping down her red face with the towel hanging around her neck. "You promised, when your dad and I let you convert that space into a hangout, that you'd keep it picked up. If you can't, you won't be able to take food down there. We don't want to wind up with an ant problem—or worse."

"I know. I'm sorry, Mom. We got excited about our plans. I'll take care of it before we leave."

Brittany winced and offered a hesitant smile. "Yeah, I'm really sorry, Mrs. Stevens."

"It's okay. I already cleaned it up this time. Just make sure you pay more attention next time." Mom turned to leave the room. "Oh, one other thing I almost forgot. You left the kitchen light on, as well as the light on the basement stairs and the two lights in the basement. That's a lot of wasted electricity. That costs money."

"Sorry," Amber mumbled. Couldn't she just let it go? As her mom left the room, Amber glanced at Brittany, hoping she hadn't paid too much attention to the lecture. Amber silently buckled her belt and pulled on a pair of brown knee-high boots, then smoothed the leg of her jeans around her ankles.

Approaching the mirror, she cheered up when she saw the new hairdo she'd paid for with her birthday money last week. It still shocked her when she caught a view of herself. Going from a cute shoulder-length bob to a shorter choppy layered cut with big chunky highlights made her feel more spirited, fun—edgy. Amber rubbed her fingers in a tub of pomade and then used them to piece her style into more spiky chunks. One last ruffle achieved the desired messy look. Satisfied with the results, she sprayed a light aerosol mist of hairspray and then shook her head to make sure her hair still bounced—just like the hairdresser had taught her. *Perfect.*

Now for makeup. She stared at the mirror for a second.

Brittany snored loudly from the bed.

"Very funny!" Amber grabbed a pillow from the floor and threw it at her. "Hey, perfection takes time."

Brittany grinned. "Yeah. Yeah. Just get on with it."

Amber turned back to the mirror. Now,

what had that makeup lady said about plum eye shadow? Wasn't it plum that contrasted and highlighted green eyes the best? *Okay, here goes.* Amber swiped some along the lower part of her upper lid and out from the corner. Then she added some dark eyeliner and lots of mascara to her long lashes.

"Ugh. I'm so jealous. Your eyes look beautiful." Brittany moved back to the mirror. "If I put that much makeup on, I'd look like a clown or a little girl playing dress up."

Amber laughed. "I'm sorry. But I can't disagree. Your sweet little face would look silly with all of this on it. Be glad you're so gorgeous you don't even need it." She added some blush and some rose-tinted lip gloss. She snapped the cap back on the tube and slipped it into her pocket for touchups. "I'm ready. You all set?"

"Yep. As soon as my dad gets here with the car, we can leave." At that moment, the doorbell rang and the girls packed up their things and scurried down the stairs.

Amber beat Mom to the front door and pulled it open. "Hi, Mr. Kim." She tried to sidle around her mom to get out of the house in a hurry. Mrs. Kim was moving from the driver's seat of the Volvo to the passenger seat of the

SUV. Couldn't let Mom figure out that Mr.
and Mrs. Kim brought them the extra vehicle
because Amber didn't want to be seen in their
own car. "Gotta go, Mom." Amber kissed her
on the cheek and stepped onto the porch. "We'll
be back by eleven."

"Where are you g–?" The front door clicked
shut on Mom's question.

Oops. Amber froze on the porch step. Would
her mom open the door to finish her inquiry?
After a few seconds, Amber figured Mom had
let it go. *Phew.* She waved at Mr. and Mrs. Kim
as they drove off in the Lexus and climbed into
the black Volvo where Brittany already waited
in the driver's seat. Rubbing the tan leather
upholstery, Amber leaned her head back on the
luxury headrest. She reached up and pushed the
button to slide open the moon roof and flipped
on the satellite radio. "Now, this is the life."

❀

"Are you mad we left early?" Brittany gripped
the steering wheel.

"Not really. I just don't understand the
problem."

"I didn't feel comfortable." Brittany glanced
at Amber and then to the road. "People kept
going in and out of that one bathroom and

locking the door."

Amber laughed. "Don't people usually lock the door when they go into the bathroom?"

"Two or three people at the same time?" Brittany shook her head. "No. There was something going on in there. Besides, Paula Markham told me that some people were doing drugs."

"Hah. Paula is the biggest gossip in school. I don't believe a word she says." Amber rolled her eyes. "And Kyle does *not* do drugs. He's too smart for that." Who did Britt think she was, accusing her cousin like that?

Brittany sighed. "I didn't say for sure that Kyle was doing drugs or that he even knew about it. But something didn't feel right."

"All right. Let's drop it." Amber rested her forehead on the cold window and watched the darkness fly by. "I was ready to leave anyway." Would she have stayed longer if she'd gone alone?

Chapter 2

A GRAND PRIZE

"Amber Stevens and Brittany Kim, you're both needed in the office," the faceless voice droned from the crackly loudspeaker.

"Oooooh, you're in trouble!" Several boys in Amber's class teased her.

"You guys are so immature. Are you sure you're seniors? Really?" She clucked her tongue and grabbed her books and purse. They quickly scooted their desks so close together that she had to turn sideways to squeeze between the desks on her way out of the room, giving the boys the perfect opportunity to try to trip her.

Ugh! Grow up! She scowled and rolled her eyes as she stepped over their outstretched legs.

Amber saw Brittany a little bit ahead of her in the hallway. "*Psst.* Britt!" She hissed through her teeth.

Brittany turned and waited for Amber to catch up. "What do you think they want us in the office for? We can't be in trouble for anything. Can we?"

"I have no idea. But we haven't done anything wrong that I can think of." Amber shrugged. "I guess we're about to find out." She pulled open the office door and they stepped inside.

Mrs. Reely, the principal's secretary, glanced up from her computer and smiled. "Hi, girls. Have a seat." She gestured to the orange plastic chairs that lined the windows to the hallway. "Don't mind me. This computer is acting up again." She peered over her half-framed glasses at Amber. "I don't suppose computer genius runs in your family, too? Or should I call Kyle to come help me?"

Amber laughed. "You'll have to get Kyle for that. I don't know the first thing about them."

The secretary looked at the schedule, then picked up her phone and placed it between her ear and shoulder while she rifled through her Rolodex.

Brittany slumped down and shrugged toward the window behind her chair. "I hope no one sees me."

"Oh, who cares? We didn't do anything

wrong, Britt." Amber laughed it off. "Besides, they all heard our names on the announcement."

Mrs. Reely drummed her fingernails on the desk while she waited. "Yes, Mrs. Pasterning, when Kyle Stevens gets back inside from gym, would you please send him to the office?" She replaced the phone in its cradle and spun her desk chair away from her desk.

"Why no public announcement for Kyle?" Brittany whispered.

Before Amber could respond, Mrs. Reely's phone buzzed twice and she turned to the girls. "Principal Warner is ready for you both. He's waiting in his office. Go right on in."

Amber shuddered in mock horror.

Brittany put her hand over her mouth, stifling her giggles.

Principal Warner smiled at them and gestured to the orange and blue padded chairs opposite his desk.

Brittany sat on the edge of her seat. She wrung her hands together and tapped her foot.

Amber plopped down and quipped, "Hey, Prince Warner. What's happening?" He had a reputation of being a fun principal who enjoyed bantering with the students. Amber knew he wouldn't find her disrespectful, but she also knew her parents would be horrified if they had heard her say that.

His eyes twinkled at the nickname. "Oh, nothing much. I have something I wanted to discuss with you two." He pulled two files from his desk drawer and stared at the contents of the top file for a moment.

Hmm. What's this all about? Amber fidgeted in her seat for a few moments, then she glanced at Brittany and had to choke back her laughter. Brittany was as white as a ghost—Amber wondered if she might pass out. *Poor thing.*

"So," Principal Warner said, smiling. "You two know your grades are near perfect and you're exemplary students. You've also never missed a day of school. Right?" He leaned forward.

Amber's shoulders relaxed. This should be a fun meeting. "Yep. Now you're going to tell us we both got awarded full rides to Princeton, right? Get it? Prince Warner. . .*Princeton*. . ." Amber waited for a chuckle or a laugh that never came. *Ooh, tough crowd.* "Not funny? Okay, I'll stop."

Brittany's eyes shot daggers.

Amber knew it drove Britt crazy when she acted like this—which was probably why she

24

did it so much. People—grownups—always liked her, so she didn't worry. *"Too familiar with adults. . ."* That's what Mom and Dad always said. Amber considered the possibility. *Nah. No such thing as too familiar—if you can pull it off.*

Principal Warner's blue eyes still twinkled. "I do get it." He chuckled and shook his head. "Actually, I wish that were my news. But hey!" His eyes brightened even more. "I've got a second best for you." He pulled a sheet of paper from his stack and skimmed it as he paraphrased the words. "Dave Druthers of Druthers Ford Dealership made an offer to the student body over eight years ago. He offered a new car to the student who graduated with straight A's and perfect attendance for all four years of high school. The problem is, it never happened until this year. . .and now. . ."

"Now, it's happening twice." Brittany shook her head.

"Wow! That's amazing." Amber stood up and paced the room. "I can't believe it. We need a new car so bad."

"Well, here's the thing," Principal Warner hesitated. "I double-checked the details with Dave Druthers today. He's offering a brand-new Ford Focus sedan." He turned his computer

25

monitor toward the girls so they could see the car.

"Wow. It's beautiful!" *Never thought I'd have a car like that.* Amber sat down and stared at the screen with the pearly white car pictured driving down a country road. "It's so pretty in that color, too. And four doors? Stereo system? It's a real car!"

"Yep, it's a real car. That's for sure." Brittany smiled. "Would you believe that is the exact car—different color—that my parents considered buying me last year when I got my license? They decided I wasn't ready for my own car, though."

"I remember you test driving it now that you mention it." Amber bounced on the edge of her seat. "You said you loved it."

"Well. . ." Principal Warner turned the monitor back around to face himself. "Even though it looks like you could both qualify for it—which is an amazing feat—there's only one car to give away."

Amber deflated like a blown-up balloon that slipped away before the end got tied. "What do we do now?"

Principal Warner seemed uneasy. He hesitated and looked at his computer screen. "We're going to have to make it a contest between the two of you. I mean, it would be open to anyone who had a chance, but since there's no one else in the school with perfect attendance, let alone the grades, it will just be you two."

Amber collapsed in her chair, deflated even more if that were even possible. She looked at Brittany and offered a wry grin. "There's always a catch, isn't there? We can't compete against each other."

Brittany's dark eyebrows knitted together. "What do you mean? Why can't we?"

"Sure you can," the principal interjected. "You didn't even know this was on the table until I told you just now—so you haven't lost anything. Just don't either of you count on it, and then you won't be too disappointed if you don't win. But you should both definitely work toward it. It will be a lesson in good sportsmanship, however it turns out."

"Sure. We can do this. It'll be fun, actually." Brittany smiled. "No matter what, one of us will win a car. That means we'll have a car to share when we're away at college."

Amber shook her head. "No guarantees for me and college. You know that, Britt. And neither of us better come down with typhoid or tuberculosis or some other horrible disease that causes us to miss a day of school. But you still make a good point." Amber considered the possibilities as she toyed with the choppy ends of her hairdo. "Okay, I'm in. I'm going to give you a run for your money, though." Amber winked at Brittany.

"I wouldn't have it any other way." Brittany nodded once, sealing the deal.

Looking at the notes he had written, Principal Warner cleared his throat. "Okay, like I said, the deal is, if either of you misses a day of school or slips below a 4.0 GPA, you're out of the running and the other will win the car at graduation. If you both keep the record you have going, it will come down to actual grade percentages. Right now, averaging all of your classes, Amber, you're tracking at a 96.5 percent and Brittany, you have a 96 percent."

Amber made a fist and punched the air. "Yes!"

"Obviously, you're so close, it's anyone's game. One or two questions on one test could change the outcome. You've got to work really hard if you want to win that car."

Amber sat up, stretched her arms over her head, and cracked her knuckles. "Well, I guess I've got some studying to do. I thought we'd be able to skate through the last half of senior year. Guess not." She stood and collected her things.

Principal Warner laughed good-naturedly. "Ah, that was my plan all along. Got to keep you girls on your toes."

"Thanks for everything, Principal Warner." Brittany pulled the door shut behind them.

Amber groaned at Brittany. "Why do I feel like no good can come of this?"

"Oh, it'll be fine. Don't even worry about it. It's just a little healthy competition." Brittany waved her hand.

Easy for her to say, with a fleet of fancy cars at her disposal. "Yeah, I guess you're right. We'll just have to make sure we don't take it too seriously."

❀

"You mean they're going to give you a car?" Dad's fork froze in front of his face and his jaw dropped while Amber told the story over dinner that night. "You see?" He dropped his fork on his plate and pounded on the table. "I told you to give God a chance. I told you He wouldn't let us down."

"Hang on. Before you get all excited, let me finish the story. There's a catch."

His face fell slightly, but he quickly recovered. "Still, this is clearly a God thing no matter what."

A little chink in the armor, Dad? Amber shook her head to clear her negative thoughts. *It's not his fault, after all.*

Mom reached over and covered the top of his hand. "Let's let Amber explain before we get carried away."

Amber resumed her story and spared no detail. She finally stopped to take a bite of her untouched dinner, then continued. "Plus, not only do I have to compete with Brittany, but we wouldn't get the car until the end of the school year. So, I don't see how this can be much help for us. Our car isn't going to last that long."

"Well, don't be too sure about that last part, Amber." Dad pointed his finger at her. "Our car will last as long as the Lord wants it to. Not a day longer, nor a moment shorter. That's a guarantee." He looked thoughtful. "Besides, this would be your car. It would go to college with you. God's still going to take care of your mom and me."

"And as for the competition," Mom jumped in, "that's part of life. Your friendship should be strong enough to withstand that after all these years."

"But what if Brittany wins the car?"

"Then you'll be happy for her, sweetie."
Mom winked and gave her a knowing smile.

"I'm not sure I'll be able to do that. She
doesn't need the car like we do, Mom." Amber
picked at her food.

"Trust that God knows what we all need,
and let Him sort it out." Mom stood to put
some dishes in the sink. "And you think you
wouldn't be happy for her, but I promise you
would be. You love her."

"Yeah, I suppose you're right." Amber gazed
out the window at the sun setting over the
mountain range. "No. I know you're right. What
was I thinking? Of course I'd be happy for her.
I lost myself in the dream for a little while. But
I've got it together now." She nodded and took
one last hearty bite before she put her plate in
the sink.

"Good. I'm glad to hear it." Dad rose from
the table and grinned. "Now go study!"

Laughing, Amber headed up the stairs to
call Brittany. Halfway up the stairs, she had
second thoughts and ran down to grab her book
bag. Studying might not be a bad idea. But she
had time for a phone call first—always time for
that. Besides, if she kept Brittany talking on the

phone, then Britt couldn't be studying either. *Distraction—there's a plan!* Amber chuckled out loud as she dialed.

Chapter 3

HIT THE BOOKS

"Come on girls. We're going for a run *slash* hike." Amber's mom bounced into her bedroom dressed in one of her lavender warm-up suits. "You two need a break from all this studying. You've been at it all day. Enough's enough. Your Saturday's going to be over before you even know it."

Amber flopped back on her bed and groaned. "A break makes sense, Mom. But a run? That's not quite what I had in mind. Do we have any Oreos?"

Brittany's eyes widened. "Oreos sound good to me. I ran on my treadmill this morning."

"Nope. No cookies in the house. Besides, you two have been inside sitting on your duff for weeks—you used to run all the time. You need fresh air, activity. . .and so do I. It's going to be way too cold to hike in the mountains in a few weeks—so come on, let's go." She checked their feet. "Brittany, I see you have your running shoes on already. Amber can loan you some warm clothes."

Brittany stared at her Nikes.

Amber could read her mind. She knew Brittany wished with everything in her she'd worn high-heeled shoes that day. Why, oh why, had she worn running shoes? Across the room, Mom had her foot up on a desk chair, stretching her calf.

It's no use. "We'd better get this over with, Britt." Amber shook her head and laughed. It had been a long time since she and Mom had gone running together. Maybe it would be nice to get out and stretch a little. "How far are we going to go?"

"I want to jog the Hidden Falls trail. You remember? The one that runs along Jenny Lake and overlooks the cascade."

"Mom, that's got to be five miles long!"

"We'll go up two and a half miles and then return the same way." She laughed. "You can do it. We used to go much farther than that. We'll take it slow and walk when we have to."

"Okay with me, Mrs. Stevens. Sounds kind of fun, actually."

Amber shot Brittany a look. What changed her mind? Oh well. Maybe it would be fun.

They collected what they needed and headed to the garage. Amber scurried barefooted, carrying her running shoes, across the cold cement garage floor and climbed into the car. While her mom drove them to their starting point, she pulled on her socks and tied her shoes.

Brittany pulled her hair into a ponytail.

Finally ready, Amber relaxed and watched the beautiful, familiar terrain out the window. Immediately, a sense of peace washed over her. *Why would anyone live anywhere else?* "We should go skiing this weekend. There's enough snow at the higher elevations. And with Christmas next month, the slopes are going to get busier soon."

"Not a bad idea. We had better get as much use as possible out of our season passes—I doubt we'll be able to afford them next year."

Sigh. Thanks for the wet blanket, Mom.

"Here we are." They pulled over outside the park entrance and got out of the car. The echo of three doors closing shuddered through the mountains.

The sharp, crisp smell of the evergreens awakened Amber's senses. Amazing how a few short miles up the mountain completely changed the air—changed everything, actually. She inhaled a few times, clearing her lungs and her mind with every breath.

They stood beside the car and stretched their muscles. "Ready?" Mom sounded eager. "Let's go."

They set off in a jog up the mountain trail, the pine needles crunching beneath their feet. The frigid air felt much colder than their home in the valley.

Her breath making little white puffs of smoke, Amber said, "This really does feel good." *Gasp. Puff.* "I forgot what fresh air could do for me." *Gasp. Puff.*

"It sure doesn't sound like it feels good." Brittany laughed as she easily kept pace.

They jogged along the western shore of Jenny Lake in silence except for the rhythmic *crunch. . .crunch. . .crunch. . .*of the evergreen needles beneath their feet. The air got thinner as they started the slight rise up the mountain— going downhill would be so much easier. Suddenly, big, white snowflakes started to fall around them. The flakes filled the air and swirled in front of their faces, landing on their cheeks and melting into little droplets of water.

No one broke the silence. Amber figured her mom was praying—she had that look on her face—and Amber could understand why. They couldn't feel closer to God than the Wyoming mountains, especially when it snowed. Amber closed her eyes for a brief moment. *Can You still hear me, Lord? Or have I wandered too far from You?*

She shook her head to clear her thoughts and took a deep, raggedy breath to fill her lungs with oxygen. "I think I need a break."

"No you don't. Push through it." Mom smiled. "Keep putting one foot in front of the other. Wait for that second wind."

They continued on. And on. They trudged up the slowly rising elevation toward the cascade in what Amber would call a jog, but was probably more like a fast walk. It happened just like Mom said it would. After a few minutes, Amber fell into a pattern again, able to keep up the rhythmic pace. She glanced at Brittany, who jogged alongside her on the right. Not even a tiny huff or puff. *Well, if I were that small, I'm sure it would be easy for me, too.*

They reached the end of the trail at an elevation of almost seven thousand feet. Trying to catch her breath, Amber staggered over to the guardrail and peered over the cascade at the treetops below. Beautiful. Not a care in the world. It felt good to rise above the trials of life.

Mom's soft smile assured Amber she wasn't worried about a thing—not that her faith ever wavered. Brittany's face didn't give away her thoughts, but her relaxed posture comforted Amber enough that she could stay in her own peaceful reverie and not worry about anything —a real rarity for Amber.

"Anyone need some water?" Mom took a bottle of water out of her jacket. Everyone took a thirsty drink—but not too much. They still had a long way to go to get back to the car.

One more gaze out over the valley revealed the setting sun in the western horizon. Mom must have noticed the same thing. "I think we'd better be on our way, girls." She stretched her quadriceps by raising her foot and grabbing her ankle behind her leg. She gave it a few squeezes and then hopped in place for a moment to work the kinks out of her ankles. "Going back is downhill, so it should be faster. It's harder on your shins, though. So, be careful."

They set off on a nice, steady gait, enjoying the ease of the sloped terrain. The falling snow slowed with their descent and stopped completely when they made it about halfway to the car. The light feeling of being up in the mountains gave way to the pressures of life in the valley, the weight of the lower elevation evident both physically and mentally.

❀

"I hope you girls aren't too upset that I pulled you away from your studies and made you exercise." Mom handed them each a bottle of water from the refrigerator.

Amber easily unscrewed the top of her water bottle—the seal had already been broken. Lovely—a used bottle that had been cleaned and refilled with tap water. She watched carefully, hoping her mom had the foresight to give Brittany a fresh bottle.

The seal on Brittany's bottle snapped as she screwed off the top, then took a long drink of the cool water.

Amber breathed a sigh of relief and glanced at her mom with silent thanks.

Mom's chin lifted slightly and she winked. She got it—most of the time.

"No, Mrs. Stevens." Brittany leaned to the side with her arm over her head, her long, sleek, black ponytail swinging as she stretched. "I

didn't mind at all. I think it was a great move—
we needed it."

"Yeah, Mom. We haven't done that in a
while, and I don't think ever while it snowed.
Cool." Amber took a swig and leaned against
the counter.

"We'll have to do it more often, then." Mom
grinned.

"Now, it's back to the books for us." Amber
held one arm out toward the doorway and
waited for Brittany to join her.

"Oh, I don't know." Brittany's face fell. "I
think the break is doing us good. Let's take the
rest of the night off."

"Really?" Amber checked the clock. It did
feel nice to take some pressure off. They had
studied for four hours straight before the run.
And Brittany looked so hopeful. "Okay, Britt.
We'll quit for the day."

Brittany grinned. "What do you want to do?"

"First? Sustenance. We'll collapse and die if
we don't get food. Then we'll talk plans."

Brittany laughed. "Such a drama queen."

Amber had already pulled the doors open
so she could dig through the kitchen cabinets.
"Aha! I knew it!" She triumphantly pulled out
a half-eaten package of Oreos. "Milk!" Amber

pulled the milk from the fridge while Brittany got two glasses.

Amber unscrewed her cookie and scraped the filling off with her teeth. She dunked the chocolate cookie part into her milk and held it there for a few moments.

Brittany dropped an Oreo into the milk and let it float there until it started to sink. She used a spoon to retrieve the milk-logged cookie and popped the whole thing into her mouth. It barely fit, and milk dripped out of one of the corners. She leaned forward over the counter and held up a cupped hand to catch the drip.

"Here, silly." Amber laughed and handed her a napkin, then they polished off the cookies in the bag. "Okay, now that I've had enough sugar to last the whole week, we can talk plans. What do you want to do tonight?"

"I think a movie. My treat." Brittany casually threw that last part on the end.

"Okay. I'll treat next time." Amber hoped she'd have money next time.

"Deal!"

❀

"Amber, we're leaving for church."

She rolled over in her bed and mumbled good-bye to her parents. Barely awake, she sensed movement in the room. *Brittany!* For a moment she'd forgotten Britt had spent the night. Amber pried one eye open and peeked across the room where Brittany stood fully dressed, tying her shoes. Amber bolted up to her elbows. "You leaving?"

"Yeah, I told you my parents would be picking me up." Brittany picked up the brush. "Your parents left already. Don't they want you to go with them?" Brittany hesitantly asked.

"Want me to? Sure. But they don't force the issue." Amber lay back down and pulled the covers up around her. "They're trying to let me find my own way."

"Hmm." Brittany smoothed her hair in the mirror.

Amber tilted her head. "Ah, I can hear the disapproval in your *hmm*."

"Well, I think church would be good for you. If I were your mom and dad. . ."

"Oh, I know. You'd be a slave driver." Amber threw her pillow at Brittany and they both laughed.

Brittany peeked out the window. "They're here. Gotta go!" She grabbed her things and started to leave the room. "Next week, come with me. Okay?"

42

"Your church is so far away," Amber whined.

Brittany laughed. "It's downtown—thirty minutes away. You'd drive farther to go shopping. You're coming."

"We'll see, Britt." *We'll see.*

Chapter 4

BE MY GUEST

"How can you make popcorn without a bag?"

"Are you serious?" Amber stared at her supposedly brilliant best friend. "You've really never seen popcorn made on a stove in a pot?"

"Nope, I've only had the microwave kind—oh, and the kind at the movie theater."

"What do you think people do with the jars of popcorn kernels they sell at the grocery store?"

Brittany shrugged. "I just assumed they put them in some sort of special bag and popped them in the microwave."

"Really? I can't believe it." Amber turned away briefly to face the stove, then spun back around. "Wait! I have a question. What about before microwaves? Where did popcorn come from then?"

"I guess I never really thought it through. We don't have popcorn at home very often—it's not really a Korean delicacy, you know." Brittany shrugged her shoulders.

"Well, okay then. I guess you get to learn how to make *real* popcorn now." Amber reached for a pot from the cabinet under the range. "Trust me, once you taste this stuff, you'll never want microwave popcorn again." She poured oil into the bottom of the tall pot on the stove. "The key is to put in enough oil so every kernel is submerged, but not so much they'll drown in it when they pop." She poured two pieces into her palm. "Now, the next step is important. You only put two kernels into the pot. Wait until they pop, then add the rest."

"Why?" Brittany peered through the glass lid.

"That way you know it's hot enough to pop the rest of the corn."

"Yeah, but I mean, why only two? Why can't you put it all in there? The oil would still get hot, right?"

"Um, well, yeah. I guess so." Amber's forehead creased as she wondered why. "But anyway, that's how it's done."

"Ha! You don't know." Brittany grinned and crossed her arms triumphantly on her chest. "But whatever. We'll do it your way. Two kernels."

Pop. Pop.

"Okay, now we're ready for the rest." Amber lifted the lid and poured in the popcorn. "And. . . now we wait."

Brittany peered through the clear glass lid of the pot.

"A lot of people will tell you to shake it the whole time once it starts popping. But really, the trick is not to. If it's the right temperature, it will pop fast enough that the popped kernels will rise and the unpopped ones will stay on the bottom."

They stood at the stove, leaning over to watch the bubbling oil heat the corn kernels inside. A few early responders popped into big, white fluffy clouds while the rest simmered longer.

"Hey, I've been meaning to ask you something." Brittany hesitated.

"What's up?"

"My church is having a Christmas concert next Thursday, and I wondered if you'd like to come—"

"Aw, Britt. You know I don't really like to go to church. Don't make me. . .pleeeease?" Amber stuck her bottom lip out in a pretend pout.

"It's not church, though—it just happens to be *at* a church." Brittany stood over the steam coming out of the sides of the pot lid. "What could be wrong with a concert?"

Amber opened her mouth to explain the vast numbers of things that could be wrong with it, but closed it when Brittany held up her hand.

"It's White Horse." Brittany's eyes gleamed.

Ooh. She got me. "Why didn't you say that in the first place? I'd love to see them! You should have said: 'Hey, Amber, let's go see White Horse!' It wouldn't have mattered where they were playing—I'd have agreed to go without all the begging."

"Oh, I know," Brittany admitted, her eyes twinkling. "But that wouldn't have been nearly as much fun for me."

Amber snapped the dish towel at Brittany's leg. "Oops! We're about to burn this popcorn." The lid rose as the popped kernels pushed it up from its secure spot atop the pot and started to spill over. She poured as much as she could fit into the extra-large red plastic bowl Brittany held.

"Um, I think we're going to need a bucket. That's a lot of popcorn." Brittany reached her hand into the bowl.

"Wait! Not yet." Amber grabbed the salt. "We need to put the finishing touches on it." She sprinkled the salt over the top and then jiggled the bowl to mix it up, careful not to spill any, and then stuck a kernel in her mouth. She repeated those actions several times until her taste tests confirmed perfection.

"What about butter?"

"Never butter. It's much better like this. Just the right amount of oil, plenty of salt. You'll see." Amber tasted another kernel and grinned. "Go for it." She held the bowl out.

Brittany stuck a few pieces into her mouth and chewed for a moment—her eyes growing wider and wider. She grinned and nodded, reaching for the bowl again. "That's so much better than at the movie theater or out of a microwave. Wow." She took a handful. "I could be ruined for the other stuff forever."

Grinning, Amber reached for a couple of Cokes. Oh, right. Make that generic cola. They headed to the basement where two movie rentals waited.

❦

Amber and Brittany stood side-by-side, swaying in rhythm to the White Horse ballad. The rich harmonies swelled through the auditorium as the instruments trailed off leaving the most beautiful a cappella sound Amber could have imagined. After the first half of the concert had pelted the audience with high-powered rock music, the sweet ballad comforted her ringing eardrums.

As the song came to an end, Pete Starr, the lead singer, stood at the microphone and waited until the room grew silent as the audience took their seats. He kept his eyes closed until the shuffling ceased. His gaze roved the large room, skillfully appearing to look at each of the five thousand people right in the eye. "Many of you are here tonight because you like our music."

He held his hand up to quell the thunderous applause. When it died down, he continued. "We appreciate that so much. Many of you, though, don't really know why we do what we do. So, if it's okay with you, I'd like to tell you." He leaned his electric guitar on its stand and picked up his acoustic guitar. Then he reached for a stool that had been placed by his side. "Do you mind if I get comfortable while I tell you a little story?"

The crowd roared its approval as the lights dimmed and the rest of the band sat on the floor on the darkened stage.

Spotlight shining only on him, Pete Starr sat on the stool and placed his guitar on his lap. He closed his eyes and began to strum a familiar tune.

Amazing Grace, how sweet the sound
That saved a wretch like me
I once was lost but now I'm found
Was blind but now I see.

He changed keys and continued, blending the tunes into one fluid song.

Jesus loves me this I know,
For the Bible tells me so,
Little ones to Him belong
They are weak but He is strong.

Amber couldn't take her eyes off the singer. The simple songs and simple messages she'd heard many times before somehow made sense to her for the first time. Maybe the atmosphere and mood of the crowd had softened her, but she'd never felt so connected to God as she did right in that moment. She wanted to—tried to—shake her head to break the pull she felt, but the pounding in her heart remained.

When I survey the wondrous cross
On which the Prince of glory died,
My richest gain I count but loss,
And pour contempt on all my pride.

She sensed only stillness around her—no movement, no whispering, no one making their way to the restroom. Many people cried real tears as the age-old songs touched them.

Through many dangers, toils and snares
We have already come
'Twas Grace that brought us safe thus far
And Grace will lead us home.

Pete jumped to his feet, the stage lights came on and the brightest lights drenched the band— light shone right up from the midst of them and down on them from above. The drummer gave a loud crash of the cymbals and the rest of the band joined in to sing:

When we've been there ten thousand years,
Bright shining as the sun
We've no less days to sing God's praise
Than when we've first begun.

Amber couldn't look at Brittany. She had too many thoughts running through her mind, and she feared her emotions would show. How had she crept so far away from God that simple old songs could make her feel so lost and needy?

The song ended, and Pete took the microphone from its stand. "I see you all appreciate those songs much like I do. Do you realize, in a few short verses of some old songs, we heard about the grace of God that saves sinners like all of us, the gift of Jesus who came to heal us, forgive us, and love us, the promise that Jesus will be with us through the trials of life, and the blessed assurance of our eternal future with God? It gets to me every time."

He paused and closed his eyes for a brief moment before he opened them to make piercing eye contact. "We're going to continue with our concert in a moment, but first I want to give you each an opportunity to respond to the Holy Spirit if He's knocking on your heart's door."

He looked up and down the rows, engaging as many as he could. "Maybe you're hearing this for the first time and you'd like to know more, or maybe you've wandered away from the God you knew in your youth. Whatever your circumstances, if you're touched by what you've heard tonight and you'd like to pray about what you've heard, stand to your feet and come forward."

Pete waited. "I want you to come to the front of this stage where you'll be met by one of our prayer counselors." Teenagers streamed into the aisles of the dark auditorium.

Amber's feet rooted her in position. She wanted to respond—needed to respond—but she couldn't move. She watched as people went forward for prayer. A magnificent sight. She knew they felt changed. She wanted that experience, too, but she stood paralyzed. Praying by herself worked just as well, right? Then why didn't it feel just as good?

As quickly as the opportunity presented itself, it ended. The concert resumed with an upbeat rock song Amber recognized from the Christian radio station. She shook her head to clear her thoughts and tried to get into the concert again. After the song ended, she finally dared to look at Brittany, who stared back at her, searching with her eyes. How long had she been watching?

Amber just smiled. What else could she do?

Brittany returned the smile, but she couldn't mask the hint of disappointment in her expression.

She'll see. I'll find my way back on my own.
She'll see.

❁

Sandpaper in her throat, a hammer pounding on
her head, Amber drew the covers tight around
her shivering body. Was there a window open?
The room felt like a freezer. She tried to roll
over, but every muscle in her body ached. Even
her toes screamed their soreness. She opened
one eye to peer at the clock. Five minutes until
the alarm went off. She pulled the covers over
her head and willed herself to feel better.

For every second of those five minutes, she
didn't move a muscle, but then the alarm went
off and she had to reach out from the covers
to hit the snooze button. That tiny movement
exposed her body to the cool air and sent her
into another fit of trembling. Her shoulder
ached from the reach, and her fingertips tingled
when she touched the clock. She needed
medicine, but it was so far away.

Amber stumbled to the bathroom and
fumbled through the cabinet. Feeling weak, she
leaned against the counter and reached for the
Tylenol, knocking over a few other bottles. Just
then, Mom came around the corner and saw her.

"What on earth is wrong with you? You

look horrible!" She hurried to Amber's side and felt her forehead. "Sweetie, you're burning up. Go on. Climb in bed, and I'll bring you some water."

"No way, Mom. I have to go to school." She stood up straighter, preparing herself for battle.

Understanding dawned on her mom's face. "Oh no. You're not going to school like this. You need to be in bed—maybe even at the doctor's office. You're sick, honey."

"Yes. I've been sick before, and I'll be sick again. Mom, you can't make me give up this contest. Not now. Not after how hard I've worked." Amber sat on the edge of the bathtub, tears burning her feverish eyes. "Besides, Mom, it's Friday. If I can get through today, then I can sleep all weekend."

Mom sighed. "Okay. Make sure you use lots of sanitizer and wash your hands often. You don't want to start an epidemic. And you have to promise if you get any worse, you'll call me to come get you. Oh, but your dad will have the car. He has an interview." She left the bathroom shaking her head and muttering. "I don't like this one bit."

Amber reached for the shower knob and then decided soaking in a hot tub would feel much better on her freezing skin. While the tub filled, she brushed her teeth. The thought of the long day looming ahead of her made her shiver again. Her skin tingled and her stomach churned as she climbed into the water. Thankfully, the Tylenol had started to take the edge off the headache, but the flames in her throat just burned hotter.

She sank lower into the bath and closed her eyes. A few minutes passed and she sat up, startled—she must have drifted off to sleep. Hurrying out of the tub as fast as her sick body would allow, she checked the time. Only fifteen minutes left until she had to leave for school or risk being late. Looking pretty didn't matter, but late was not an option. Amber threw on a sweat suit and went to the kitchen at the speed of a dying turtle, the best she could do.

Mom had some dry toast and juice ready. The toast looked good but her throat refused it. She'd have to do without. *Just make it through the day. One day.*

"Come on. I'll drive you." Mom bit her lip and shook her head.

Amber eyed her mom on the drive to school. *I hope she doesn't decide to make me stay home. I need to win this car. We need it.* Trying to save her strength, she put her head back on the headrest and dozed until they pulled into the carpool lane at school.

"Baby, I'm going to be praying for you today." Mom patted her arm.

Amber climbed from the car and winced at the weight of her book-bag strap on her shoulder. "Thanks, Mom. I'm going to need it." She trudged up the stairs to the school entrance and made her way to class, bones aching and creaking with every step.

The bell rang for first period. Second period. Third period. The day passed in a fog. Amber navigated the halls and attended each class, but she remembered none of it as thoughts of her bed danced in her head.

The school day finally over, Amber lumbered into her house and poured herself into bed. Mom popped her head in and asked her a few questions. . .she thought. Amber mumbled her answers. . .she hoped. But she could concentrate on nothing but her pillow. She laid her head on its cool surface, her feverish skin tingling at the brush of her long eyelashes on her cheek. She fell asleep instantly and dreamed of nothing as her body healed.

Chapter 5

A BIG FAVOR

"Britt, winter's going to be over before we know it." Amber gestured out the dining room window at the receding snow. "Well, I take that back. Winter's been near its end for a while. It's ski season that I'm worried about." She craned her neck to try to see up the mountains beyond her backyard. "We've only been three times this whole winter. There's still good skiing up there, I hear. We should go this weekend."

"Hmm?" Brittany put down the pencil she'd been gnawing. "Ski? Is that what you said?" She closed her book and stood from the table. She stretched her arms far above her head and leaned deeply to each side. "We could go tomorrow, I guess."

"Saturdays are busy on the mountain, but

I think it's worth it. Let's do it." Amber went to her closet. "I got this new ski outfit back at Christmas—they bought it before Dad lost his job—and I've only worn it once." She pulled out an eggplant, green, and cream three-in-one jacket and off-white ski pants and held them to her body while she swooshed in the mirror. "Besides, like Mom said, we might not have season passes next year. I've got to get one more use of this."

"Oh, I have my same old ski stuff from last year. I'll probably have to wear that for another couple of years." Brittany stood in front of the mirror and turned to look at her body sideways.

"I'm sure if you just asked, you'd have a whole new wardrobe before you could snap your fingers."

"It's not like my parents are willing to throw money away." Brittany shook her head. "Even they would say the old one fits fine and I should get more use out of it."

"Yeah, right. Whatever." Amber rolled her eyes. "Guess you'll have to wear what you've got, poor girl." She winked at Britt, zipped her new jacket, and preened in the mirror. Not exactly top of the line, but the color made her eyes pop and the fit showed off her figure. *Nice.*

❀

Swoosh. Swoosh.

Amber kept her skis in a perfect parallel as she gracefully swished her feet from side to side. Nearing the end of the run, after the last steep grade, she tucked her poles behind her hips and brought her body in tight and low to gather speed for the long stretch to the bottom of the mountain. She pushed off with her right ski and then her left, enough to gain momentum for a strong finish. The wind whipped through her hair while the snowflakes pelted her cheeks and clung to her eyelashes as she whizzed past the trees and wove between the other skiers.

Ah, freedom. Speed.

Arriving at the bottom of the mountain, she swiped her feet to the side, whipped her skis ninety degrees to the left, and then dug them into the snow for a complete stop. She turned to look up the fluffy, white mountain for Brittany.

There. A brand-new, top-of-the-line pink snowball taking her time to come down the mountain. Amber shook her head. *Guess I was right. All she had to do to get a new outfit was ask.* Amber liked her own outerwear better, even though it cost about a third of what Brittany wore. *Why did cost even matter, though?* Brittany looked adorable, but Amber knew she did, too. Why couldn't she be happy for her friend?

Brittany gracefully made her way down the mountain. Amber smiled at her hesitant style. She arrived near the spot where Amber waited and slowed to a safe and steady stop.

"One more time, then lunch?" Amber didn't want to quit yet.

"Sure, I'm up for another run. But I am getting hungry." Brittany shook the snow off her cap and put it back on her silky head.

They waited in line for the ski lift and then sank onto the bench as it came up behind them and pressed against the backs of their thighs. It carried them high above the treetops as they made their way slowly up the mountain. So serene—yet powerful—to be up above the trees, looking down on the snow-covered evergreens. The snow started to fall again, lightly at first and then big heavy flakes that absorbed the sound all around them. Like a fairy tale.

"It feels so good not to be thinking about school," Brittany whispered, closing her eyes.

Well, it had. Amber wished Brittany hadn't brought it up. But since she had. . . "Speaking of school, Britt, I've been thinking." She hesitated and scraped the snow from one ski with the razor-sharp bottom of the other. "We really don't need to push ourselves this hard." She waited, hoping Brittany would catch on without making Amber actually say it.

"How could we not? We need to do the best we possibly can." Brittany's eyebrows raised in the middle as the outsides furrowed in confusion.

"Well. . .I mean. . .yeah, we do need to do our best unless. . . Oh, never mind."

Brittany turned on the seat as much as she could without falling, and looked at Amber. "No. What were you getting at? Tell me."

"Oh, I was just thinking. . .you know. . .you don't really need a car. . .oh, forget it, really, never mind. Really." *Please let it go.* Amber could feel her cheeks turning red. She should never have even thought about suggesting Brittany let her win. Why had she opened her big mouth? *How awkward.* Amber stared at Brittany, willing her to let it go.

Brittany stared back for a moment, still confused, and then the light dawned on her face. She averted her eyes and adjusted her gloves. When she turned back, she graciously let Amber back out of her fumble. "Well, you can quit studying if you want to. But I wouldn't suggest it." She winked.

Relieved, Amber said, "Okay, then. Game on."

They arrived at the top of the mountain. Amber adjusted her goggles, then they skied off the lift. The snow had picked up, and the run down the mountain felt much more frigid than the one before. Lunch would be a welcome reprieve.

They skied silently. Amber decided to stick with Brittany on this run rather than tear off ahead and wait at the bottom. When they reached the bottom of the mountain, they clicked off their skis and set them against the ski rack. On their way into the lodge, they unzipped their jackets and tucked their hats into the pockets. Right away, the warm damp air of the lodge became too much for them, and they started peeling off layers. They clomped over to a wooden table and staked their spot with a pile of coats, sweaters, goggles, and face masks, then headed over to the cafeteria line.

All without a word.

Clo-clomp, clo-clomp, clo-clomp. Their ski boots pounded an unsteady rhythm on the painted concrete floor. Stepping in line, they scanned the menu board and hungrily waited to order. Cheeseburgers and fries for both of them—two burgers for Brittany. "Seriously?"

Amber laughed, breaking the awkward tension. "You're going to eat two cheeseburgers?"

"Sure! I'm famished!" Brittany forced her flat stomach into an imaginary potbelly and rubbed it.

Phew. Everything had returned to normal. For the moment.

❁

"Come here." An unseen assailant pulled Amber into an empty classroom on Friday afternoon.

She stumbled through the doorway and struggled to regain her footing. "Hey!" She spun around to face her attacker. "Oh. Kyle. It's only you."

Kyle opened his mouth wide in feigned horror, exposing his shiny new braces—replaced as a second attempt after he wouldn't wear a retainer the first time. "Wait a minute. You looked like you were going to kill someone when you turned around. Now you look disappointed. What do you mean *only* me?"

"Oh, I didn't mean anything by it." She brushed him off with a wave of her hand. "I just meant. . .oh, never mind. What's up, anyway? Is there a reason for this attack?"

"I need to talk to you." Kyle poked his head out of the classroom and peered in both directions down the hallway like a spy in a movie. "Before I say anything, though, I need to make sure you're cool. I mean, I know you're cool—you are my cousin after all." He nervously ran his fingers through his chestnut, shoulder-length waves, then stuck his hands in the front pockets of his khaki cargo pants. "But, you know. . ."

"No. Not really. I have no idea what you're talking about." Amber lifted her wrist and spun her silver watch around so she could read the time. "My bus leaves in ten minutes. You better make it quick."

"Okay. Fact is, I want you to win that car—I think I can help."

"How can you help? I'm already studying more than humanly possible." She sighed. "But so is Britt."

"That's the thing. You need an edge." Kyle looked expectant, waiting for agreement, perhaps. When none came, he shrugged then continued. "You need something your *competition*"—he wiggled two quotation-mark fingers on each side of his head—"doesn't have."

Why did she feel grateful he kept it impersonal by not using Brittany's name? Something didn't feel right. "What did you have in mind?" Amber crossed her arms on her chest as if to ward off the possibilities.

"I've been working in the computer lab lately. I'm reprogramming some of the older computers in a last effort to salvage the old systems before the school has to replace them."

"Right, in exchange for some extra credit. I know all that. What does it have it do with me?" She pulled her arms tighter.

"You pretty much know I'm a computer genius. Right?" Kyle's blue eyes twinkled from behind the stringy hair hanging in his face.

"Yeah, everyone knows that. You're seriously going to have to move this along. I've got to go." She held her watch up to Kyle's face. "I'm about to miss my bus."

"Okay." Kyle shot a quick glance toward the door, then lowered his voice to a whisper. "Deal is, I can get you copies of your midterms. You can study right off the tests themselves, and—"

"Whoa. Whoa. Stop right there." Amber held up a hand and started to back out the door. "I want no part of anything like that. Brittany's my friend, and cheating is wrong. That's not how I want to win." Amber turned to hurry away. "I'm going to pretend we didn't have this conversation."

Kyle grabbed her arm as she stepped through the door. "Just remember my offer. She can't be too much of a friend if she's willing to fight so hard to take something you clearly need way more than she does. Think about it."

Hmm. Could he be right?

Chapter 6

HEARING VOICES

"Well, well. Don't you look lovely?" Mom sipped from her coffee cup, leaning forward carefully so she wouldn't spill on her church clothes—JC Penney knit separates in coordinating mauve and olive green.

Why doesn't she get new clothes? Amber wondered, shaking her head at her mom's dated and over-worn outfit. Visions of an eggplant ski bunny swooshed in her head. *She could have had three outfits for the price of my new ski clothes.*

Dad came into the kitchen as Amber spread butter onto her almost-burnt toast. He winked at Amber. "What's the occasion?"

"I'm going to church." She held up her hand to ward off the onslaught of questions and squeals of excitement. "Brittany's church."

Mom deflated a bit, but almost immediately perked up. "That's great, honey. What brought this on?"

"I just decided to go. No big deal."

"Sounds good, sweetie. Have a good time." Mom put her cup in the sink and grabbed her out-of-season-and-style white purse.

"Have fun." Dad tucked his Bible under his arm and held the door to the garage for his wife.

That's it? Shocked they let it go, Amber hurried to the dining-room window where she could see into the open garage. Her mom and dad stood beside the car giving each other big grins and a huge high-five. Dad made two fists and clenched tightly. Amber could read the *Yes!* on his lips.

So predictable. With a smile, Amber returned to the kitchen, shaking her head while she poured cereal into a bowl and added milk.

She hoped the service wouldn't be too painful and would pass quickly—they planned to go shopping afterward. Brittany had originally offered to pick her up *after* church for the shopping part. Why hadn't she agreed to do it that way? She could have slept in and avoided the whole church thing.

She must be feeling guilty for almost cheating.

No! Why would she feel guilty? She told Kyle no, and she meant it. *But I considered it.*

Nope! Amber shook her head to clear it of the raging inner battle.

Glancing at the clock on the microwave, she dumped her milk into the sink and rinsed out her bowl. She dried her hands on the towel next to the sink and glanced out the kitchen window just in time to see the silver Lexus pull into the driveway. The horn lightly sounded. She grabbed her purse and pulled the door shut behind her, checking to make sure she'd locked it.

She slid into the backseat next to Brittany. "Hi, Mr. and Mrs. Kim. Thanks for picking me up."

"Is our pleasure, Amber." Mrs. Kim looked into the backseat and smiled warmly. "We go to church, then Brittany take us home so you go shopping. We take a nap."

Mr. Kim laughed along with his wife and turned on the radio. *What nice people.*

Amber finally turned her attention to Brittany, adorable in a new black cashmere sweater with a tiny turtle pattern. She also had a hot-pink scarf draped across her shoulders—it looked long enough to reach her knees—and a matching pink, black, and green slouchy hat over her silky hair. She had on the coolest jeans—stylish and nondescript, but Amber could tell by the perfect fit and the luxurious denim they were just as pricey as the rest of her outfit. Brittany always found the cutest clothes in those specialty boutiques she went to with her mom.

"Love the scarf." Amber reached over and picked up one end and flung it over Brittany's other shoulder.

"Thanks. It's new." Brittany laughed and repositioned the drape. She opened her slouchy, bright green Balenciaga bag and turned it discreetly toward Amber, and motioned for her to look in.

Amber leaned over so she could see inside the bag. Right on top laid two credit cards. The gold one sparkled. She looked up at Brittany. *Huh?*

Brittany pointed at Amber and back at herself. "Sky's the limit," she whispered and pointed both thumbs to the sky. "Dad got another raise."

"Congratulations." Amber tried to look happy for Brittany. She didn't want Brittany to do without just because she had to—did she? And really, what did she have to do without anyway? Visions of her mom in her decade-old knit separates flashed through her mind.

"So, we have the gold card and permission to

use it freely." Brittany grinned, still whispering.

"We'll see." Amber didn't like the idea of using Mr. and Mrs. Kim's credit card for things her parents couldn't buy her. How would Mom and Dad feel about that? But maybe they didn't even have to know about it.

They arrived at the church for the contemporary English service even though there was a Korean service immediately following it. The Kims thought it helped them with their own English, and they enjoyed the music—they called it worship.

Amber considered her parents' church. It didn't have music, and the service reminded her more of a ninety-minute Bible study. What's the word? *Stifling*. Much of it rose above her head, and she couldn't be bothered trying to figure out all of the Greek mumbo-jumbo. At least Brittany's church broke things up with music, soloists, instruments, and sometimes even little skits. Kept things interesting—as interesting as church could be, anyway.

As they walked into the sanctuary and found seats, Amber wondered if she could find God somewhere other than at church. There had to be other ways. She gazed around the auditorium and wondered what church looked like back when Jesus walked the earth. They probably didn't have volleyball and basketball teams. Pretty sure there weren't potluck dinners and Christmas plays. But what if this was the only way now? *Scary thought.*

The congregation rose to their feet as the band started to play. Some people raised their hands into the air; others clapped along to the music. Many people swayed along with the beat. They sang every song three times, at least. Why did they have to do that? Didn't they know enough worshippy songs to do more of a variety rather than sing the same ones over and over?

Amber didn't want to stare at Brittany, but—dying to know if she joined in on all the hoopla—she cast a subtle glance out of the left corner of her eye without turning her head at all.

Brittany sang along with the music. In fact, she knew the song well enough to sing along with her eyes closed. That must mean they did the same ones every week, too. *Sigh.*

The pastor took the microphone and invited people to come forward if they needed prayer for some reason. Amber stared openmouthed when Brittany's mom scrambled over the feet of at least eight people to get to the other side of their seating section. She went down the aisle and stood before the pastor with the other hopefuls. Amber counted two women wearing hats, three men in ties, two kids she knew from school, one little boy with his arm in a cast, and an elderly man in a wheelchair being pushed by a bent-over woman—likely his wife. What did they all expect God to do for them? What *could* He do for them? It was different than the prayer time at the concert. This time the lights were bright, and people were just looking around like it was no big deal.

Amber checked her fingernails, then counted the lights hanging from the ceiling while the pastor prayed for the people up front and the band continued to play and sing soft repeats of the choruses they had already sung. The music finally ended, the pastor prayed again, the offering baskets passed from hand to hand, then, finally, sermon time. Half down, half to go.

Amber wished she'd mastered the art of sleeping with her eyes open. But wait. She wanted to try to take it all in, didn't she? *I want to find God, right?* She sat up straighter and popped a piece of gum into her mouth hoping the sugar would perk her up.

". . .still small voice that He uses to call

out to you in your life." Pastor Johnson paced across the stage while he spoke. "It always seems like the devil, our enemy, shouts at us with temptations, taunts, sarcasm, while the Holy Spirit of God whispers through the storm. You see, He's one classy guy. He doesn't need to shout, beg, or make deals with us. He just speaks truth, quietly. He knows we'll hear it when we're ready to listen for it." He paused and looked around at the people.

He's right. Those voices, those battles she'd been having since the White Horse concert came to Amber's mind. Why did the wrong things always look more appealing, more fun, but the right choices were quiet, difficult, and not nearly as shiny? *I thought I was the only one who felt that way.*

Pastor Johnson continued. "There is not one thing new under the sun. This isn't any surprise to God, and it shouldn't be any surprise to us. The Bible tells us how our enemy operates. It also tells us we need to shut off his access to us by not giving him an ear. Learn the sound of the voice of God, and meditate on His truths so you can't mistake an imposter."

The rest of the service moved swiftly, and they stood for the last chorus before Amber knew it. *Time for shopping.*

After they dropped Mr. and Mrs. Kim off at home, Brittany turned the car in the direction of the mall. "So?" She looked at Amber, her eyes big with hope. "Did you hate it this time?"

"Surprisingly, no." Amber shook her head and thought hard about her answer. "In fact, there were a few things I'll have to think about." She didn't want Brittany to get the wrong idea, though. "But, Britt. Come on, the music and stuff? That's a little much for me." She shook her head. "It's like my mom and dad's church goes to one extreme and yours goes to the other."

"Yeah, it probably seems that way. You'd get used to it in time and eventually start to enjoy it, I promise." Brittany looked thoughtful. "Hey, speaking of your parents' church—between the two, which do you prefer?"

"Oh, no contest. If I had to choose, yours! Hands down." Amber feigned horror at the thought. "That's like asking if you prefer a funeral or a baby shower." Both girls laughed.

Amber turned toward the window and realized they had passed the mall. "Where are we going? I thought we were going shopping."

"We are. We're going for the good stuff on Mom and Dad—forget the mall." She pulled into the parking lot of a high-end strip center.

"Britt, I can't let your parents pay for clothes for me. I don't really need anything, anyway." Amber reached for the door handle. "I'm calling this a window-shopping trip for me."

"Come on. Don't be silly." Brittany waved the gold card in the air like a dangling carrot taunting Amber.

Amber laughed and shrugged. "We'll see."

They wandered through the stores, felt the rich fabrics, and tried on several outfits. Then they saw them. The perfect pair of Lucky Brand jeans—long, dark, just-right wash. Perfect.

"Amber, you need to try these on. They'll never fit me." Brittany shoved the hanger at her.

Amber lifted the price tag, then peered at it through one squinted eye. "One hundred dollars? You have GOT to be kidding. There's no way." She started to return them to the rack.

"Don't look at the price. Try them on." Brittany grabbed Amber's shoulders and steered her toward the fitting rooms.

Against her better judgment, Amber slipped on the jeans. *Ahh.* Second skin. Made for her. "Well, you were right. They are perfect. But I'm not getting them."

"Sure you are. Take them off."

"Did you hear me, Britt? A hundred bucks! I'm *not* buying them."

"No, you're not buying them. I am. End of discussion."

Amber got dressed quietly. She wanted those jeans—badly—but felt awkward having Brittany buy them for her. *I guess that's what friends are for, right?*

By the time she'd finished dressing, Amber had decided to let Brittany buy the jeans for her if she really wanted to.

On the way to the cash register—Brittany with a small pile in her arms, and Amber with her pair of jeans—they passed the Donna Karan section. Amber stopped short at the sight of a mannequin wearing an emerald green pintucked blazer, black slacks, and a white blouse—the kind of outfit that never went out of style.

"I wish I could buy my mom that outfit right there." Amber pointed at the mannequin.

"Well, get it for her. I told you, sky's the limit."

"No way! I'm not letting you buy something for my mom. I was just saying. . ." Amber checked the price tags. "Besides, it's twice as much as my jeans. No way."

"Seriously, Amber. If you don't, I'm going to have to come all the way back here and get it later. Save me the trip." Brittany winked.

"No. Really. You can't." Amber pleaded with her eyes. "Mom would be really embarrassed. She'd never be able to take it and enjoy it. I'll save up for it and get it for her birthday or something."

"That's a lot of money to save for a birthday present." Brittany gave in but shrugged her shoulders. "It's already March. Isn't her birthday in August?"

Amber gazed out the storefront window. "Mom doesn't care much about that stuff anyway." *She's happy with what she has.*

Chapter 7

INDIFFERENCE

"Wouldn't you rather go to a wedding than a funeral, Mom?" Amber ran her fingers through her hair, fighting the urge to pull it out.

"Come on, now. Our church is not like a funeral. Not even close." Mom dried her hands on the dishrag as she walked past Amber. "I don't know how you can even say that." She left the kitchen, but a few seconds later, poked her head around the corner. "And I suspect Brittany's church—or is it yours now, too?—isn't much like a wedding, either." Apparently having said her last words on the subject, she left for real.

Dad lowered his newspaper and pursed his lips. "Amber, I don't understand what you have against our church. It teaches good, solid, biblical doctrine. It forces you to think. It takes you to a higher level of understanding."

"I know all about it, Dad. I went there for years and years, remember?" Amber tapped on her chin, deep in thought. "In fact"—she held up a finger—"I went there every week until you decided I could choose for myself where—or even if—I wanted to go at all. Remember?"

Dad nodded slowly.

"Well, that's what I'm doing. I'm exercising the right you gave me to make up my own mind—find my own way."

Dad eyes drooped with his frown as he turned his saucer and watched his milky coffee swirl in the cup.

Amber didn't mean to hurt his feelings. "Dad, your church. . .they're good people. They mean well. It's just—"

"What?" He looked up with heat in his eyes. "What could you possibly have against good Bible instruction and well-intentioned scholars?"

"That's just it, Dad. I don't want Bible instruction—at least not right now."

"But—"

She held up her hand. "Hold on. Please let me finish."

He softened his expression and sat back in his seat.

81

Amber exhaled the breath she'd been holding. "If I go to church, I want to learn how to really know God, how I'm supposed to live, and how to actually do it. I don't care one bit about how many horsemen are in a legion, or how many cubits long the wall around Jericho measured, or that the Greek word for baptism is *baptizo*."

Dad's eyebrows rose, and his jaw dropped.

Amber laughed at his expression and rocked her chair on its back two legs. "Yes, silly. I remember some things. Probably more than you think I do. But I need more than that right now . . .or less. . .maybe just different. I don't know." She let the front legs of the chair fall forward on the once-white linoleum with a thud. "I need heart, not facts and figures. I want. . .um. . . relationship. I guess that's the word."

"You want that?" Dad asked softly.

"Well, I mean. . .I don't know what I want, really. But if I did search for God, that's how I would do it." Why did she find it so difficult to be honest about this? Because if she told them about her spiritual search, they wouldn't leave her alone about it, that's why. But then again, if she confided in them, maybe they could help her find her way. No. . .one look at her dad's eager-Labrador expression confirmed her initial fears. She'd have to keep it to herself for now.

Amber heard a honk in the driveway. She dumped her dishes in the sink and hurried to grab her purse. Would she need a jacket? The weather had started to warm up some, but the springtime dew from the mountains still lent a chill to the air at times. She reached in the hall closet by the front door and grabbed a pale-green nylon Windbreaker before rushing out the door—didn't want to keep Mr. and Mrs. Kim waiting.

Seeing Brittany in the driver's seat, Amber approached the passenger side. Puzzled, she opened the door. "Where are your mom and dad?"

"They weren't feeling well this morning, so they stayed home."

"Oh." Tasting the bitter exhaust fumes, she climbed into the car.

Neither girl said anything for a moment, suddenly presented with an opportunity. They looked at each other. Amber didn't want to suggest it first—then they both smiled.

"You want to?" Amber decided to make the first move.

Brittany didn't even try to pretend she didn't know what Amber suggested. "Breakfast? Shopping?" She grinned.

"I'm game." She tried to sound excited, but why did she suddenly feel disappointed about not going to church? She couldn't prefer church over eating and shopping. Could she? "I even have money today. I babysat this week, plus mom gave me forty dollars for new shoes." She chewed her bottom lip. "But I mean, we could still do all of that if you wanted to go to church first."

"Oh, sure. I know. But everyone needs a break now and then."

"Okay. Fine with me. I was just saying." Amber felt a twinge of regret for arguing with her mom and dad and then deciding not to go at all. Oh well, they would never even know.

"Besides, if we wait until the churches let out, we'll never get a table anywhere." Brittany put on her turn signal and made a U-turn at the next intersection. She turned the car toward the strip-mall entrance where their favorite breakfast spot, Egg-static, had a corner position. "We haven't gone here for the Sunday breakfast buffet in a long time."

"I know. It's so yummy, and it's only $5.95." Amber patted her belly. "If they knew how much you could eat, though, they'd probably charge more—at least double."

"Ha-ha. You're funny." Brittany grinned and

rubbed her tummy. No secret how much food she could pack away.

Cars filled most of the spots in the lot outside the restaurant, so they pulled into one at the bank next door, and then walked over to the entrance. They groaned when they saw the long line at the door. The sweet cinnamon smell of the baking rolls and the sound of the sizzling bacon made Amber's stomach rumble.

They shifted impatiently as they stood in the slowly whittling line. Finally, the hostess called their name, then took them to a small booth at the back of the room. They slid onto the green vinyl seats next to the windows and ordered coffee and orange juice.

"Hey, this is really nice." Amber poured two packs of sugar and two creams into her coffee, then took a sip.

"Tell me about it. It really is." Brittany tapped her fingernails on the table. "But I'm famished. I'm getting a plate."

They wove among the three buffet bars and piled their plates high. Amber picked up the ladle of oatmeal, but let it plop back into the steaming vat—too lumpy. She settled on some of the cheesy bacon-and-egg quiche, some fresh fruit, a few slices of bacon, and a small cinnamon roll.

Brittany's plate had a few scoops of scrambled eggs, hash browns, a few pieces of sausage, and a cinnamon roll. She also carried a bowl with two biscuits and a huge dousing of sausage gravy. She put it all on the table and slid into the booth. "Wow. I don't know if even I can eat all of this."

"Five bucks says you eat it all and then go for some fruit." Amber blew on a bite of the hot quiche.

"You're on!"

They tore into their breakfasts, mouths too full to speak for the first few minutes. Finally, between bites, Brittany opened her mouth, as if to say something, and then closed it right away.

"What were you going to tell me?" Amber prodded.

"I wanted to ask you something, but I hate to bring it up." She stirred her hash browns in the pool of ketchup then took a sip of her coffee.

Amber waited, knowing Brittany would eventually spit it out.

"Awhile ago, you mentioned something. It's kind of bothered me since then. I haven't wanted to say anything. But. . .I sort of feel like if I don't say something now, I never will and it'll keep bugging me." She kept her eyes down.

Amber put her fork down and waited. "Well, if something's on your mind, Britt, you should talk to me. Just say it."

Brittany looked her in the eyes. "It's about something you said on the ski lift."

Amber's heart sank. She thought Brittany had forgotten about that. "What did I say?"

They waited while the waitress set down a basket of their famous toasted-almond biscotti and refilled their coffee cups.

"It's not really what you said, it's more what you were going to say. Remember?"

"Sorry, I'm going to need more details. That was a long time ago." Amber cut off a bite-sized piece of quiche with her fork. She moved it around on her plate and then just let it lie there.

"You started to kind of hint that you wanted me to let you win the car." Brittany almost whispered the words. She took a bite of her cinnamon roll, and then sat back against the booth, chewing slowly, as though she couldn't swallow past a lump in her throat.

"Oh. That?" Amber waved her hand in the air. "It didn't mean anything. Really. It was a stupid thought, and it hasn't crossed my mind since." She dunked the end of a biscotti into her coffee and held it there to soak.

Brittany peered at her with one eyebrow raised.

"Really, Britt." She took a bite of the softened cookie as though it somehow sealed her point.

"Well, I have to tell you. It kind of bugs me that you ever even said it. Momentary lapse or not." Brittany shrugged. "I'm being honest. I don't think it's fair you even had those thoughts."

She's not going to let it go. Amber sighed.

Brittany twisted her napkin and tied it into a knot. "I mean, am I supposed to forfeit the contest just because you need a car more? Does anything in life work that way? The lottery? Job interviews? The Oscars or the Emmys? Nothing works like that."

Amber opened her mouth, but Brittany hadn't finished.

"Besides. . ." Brittany put her napkin down. "The contest isn't only about the car. It's a huge honor to win it. It'll mean a lot on transcripts and everything. Why should I forfeit that?"

Amber didn't look at Brittany while she formulated her words. "Look, Brittany. I shouldn't have said it. It had been kind of a tough week for me personally. I'd been worried about my family—my dad had some interviews that didn't go anywhere—and thinking about my future. It was selfish, and I wasn't thinking about anything but the car."

"You know. . .it's not my fault your dad got fired."

Amber's head reeled as if slapped.

Brittany's eyes immediately flashed with regret, but it was too late to take the words back.

"I can't believe you said that. My dad didn't get *fired*. He got laid off. And no one ever suggested you were at fault. That's ridiculous. Like I said, I was only thinking about the car—which you *don't* need, by the way—I wasn't thinking about the other benefits of winning." She took a few breaths to calm her fuming nerves. "Wait a second. You mentioned transcripts." Amber narrowed her eyes. "We found out weeks ago that we both got awarded full scholarships. So, how does this contest help with that? What do our transcripts have to do with it anymore?"

"I meant that at the time you brought it up, it might have mattered."

"No, it really wouldn't have. This is a made-up, local contest that wouldn't have been over by the time colleges made their decisions. We would still have the perfect attendance and the grades, even without the contest. So, I'm not buying that argument. It all comes down to the car."

"Are you saying our friendship comes down to the car?" Brittany's eyes welled up with angry tears.

"No! I didn't say that. You did. I said the *contest* comes down to the car." Amber closed her eyes and took a few ragged breaths, hoping to collect her thoughts enough to find a way to fix things. "You know what? If you'll remember correctly, that day in the principal's office, I said this contest would lead to no good between us. Remember?"

"I guess that's because you know yourself well enough to know you couldn't handle the competition." Brittany's eyes grew cold.

"That stung, Britt. I hope you don't mean it. I hope this whole conversation is because of the pressure you're feeling."

"According to you, *I've* got it easy. *You're* the only one with pressure, Amber."

Amber stared at her best friend for a moment. What had gotten into her? "I've never seen you like this. I don't know what to say. This really hurts my feelings."

"Now you know how it feels."

"Look, I said I was sorry. I said I made a mistake—had a judgment lapse. If you can't forgive me or understand it, I can't help you. But I'm not going to sit here and take this. You're acting so cold. I don't know where this is coming from." Amber bit her lip. "Maybe you should drive me home."

"Probably a good idea." Brittany stood up and dropped a few dollars on the table for a tip and headed for the door.

Amber added two dollars and followed her out.

The ride took about fifteen minutes, but in the silent car, it went on for ages.

"We've never argued before. I don't know how to do this with you." Amber gazed out the window.

"I'm sure we'll get over it. I just need some time. I have to focus on my studies right now. It's hard because I know in the back of my mind you don't want me to win. It's hard to know your best friend would prefer that you fail."

"What? I don't want you to fail—I just happen to want to win. Same as you."

"No, that's where you're wrong. Not the same as me." Brittany pulled into the driveway.

"Not at all." She stared straight ahead. "If you won, I would be just as happy to see you sit in that car as I would be if I won it myself. Not so with you. I don't know how to deal with that. I'm sure I'll figure it out, though."

Amber wondered if she could be right, but shook her head in denial. "I'm sorry, but you're dead wrong. But whatever. I can't convince you. I'll leave you to your books. Call me when you figure things out." She jumped out of the car and shut the door with more force than necessary, then hurried into the house without even a backward glance—she didn't want Brittany to see her tears.

Stomping up the stairs, muttering to herself the whole way, Amber couldn't get to her room fast enough. She flung herself on her bed and let the tears flow. How had everything gotten so messed up? How could Brittany have accused her like that? What if she were right? But how could she be so cold and mean about it? Besides, Brittany sure hadn't taken a break from studying since the contest started, either. *She wants to win just as much as I do.*

Amber sat straight up on her bed and grabbed her phone. Before she could change her mind, she dialed Kyle's phone number.

It rang three times before he answered. "Yo."

"Kyle? It's Amber."

"Hey, Cousin A. What's up?"

"Well, I'm calling because I want. . .well. . . could you. . ."

"Spit it out. I don't have all day," Kyle said in his typical teasing manner. "What do you want?"

Amber took a deep breath and said the three magic words that could change her life.

"Hook me up."

Chapter 8

FINAL, FINAL, FINAL

"You're sure, now?" Kyle held up three papers he'd printed from the office computers. He reached up and waved them back and forth above Amber's head. One answer key for each of her three major final exams—the scary ones anyway. Calculus. History. English Literature.

She crossed her arms on her chest, refusing to reach for them. "Would you please stop being so immature?" She looked around the schoolyard teeming with students to make sure no one could hear them. "Besides, how do I know we won't get caught?"

"I can't explain all the technical computer stuff I did to fix the access dates on the file and erase the printing record—you'd never understand it all anyway. Funny *you're* the one getting a scholarship."

Amber rolled her eyes. "A little homework goes a long way."

"Eh. No time for homework. Anyway, you're going to have to trust me." Kyle smiled. "I'll be honest with you. They could have the hard drive examined by a professional, and *could*"—he wiggled his fingers in the air—"find the information. But they'd have to know what they were looking for, they still wouldn't know for sure I did it, and it would cost them a couple of thousand dollars per hard drive—ain't gonna happen."

Amber exhaled the air she'd been holding and reached for the papers. Hesitating one more time, she considered her options. Once she held those papers in her hands, there would be no turning back. But she still had time to go the other way. She'd studied hard, after all—might not even need to do this and still win the car. Even if she didn't, the car wasn't the most important thing in life. Right?

The car. She had to win that car. Besides, Brittany had pretty much accused her of ruthlessly going after it. Might as well go all-out since Brittany assumed the worst of her anyway. Cheating sure wouldn't help Amber find the way back to God, though. *Nope, don't go there—*

not now. Before she could change her mind, she shut off the good voice and grabbed the papers. "Thanks, Kyle. I've got to go." Amber turned and jogged off.

❀

"Brittany's here for you," Mom called up the stairs toward Amber's bedroom. "I'm sending her up."

What could Brittany want? Amber jumped off her bed and scurried to hide the answer keys she'd been studying. She lifted her mattress and slipped the papers under it, trapping them between the mattress and box springs with only seconds to spare before the knock sounded at the door.

"Come in." Amber sat at the desk with an open schoolbook in front of her. She tried to calm her racing heart and trembling hands. She didn't look up.

"Amber, can we talk?" Brittany's soft voice didn't hold even a hint of the rancor of last weekend.

"Okay." Amber sighed and shut her book. She turned to look at Brittany, raised her eyebrows, but didn't smile.

"I'm so sorry." Brittany's eyes welled up with tears. "You were right. You apologized for your comment. You explained it was your mistake. I should have forgiven you and forgotten about it completely."

No, you should have dropped out of the contest. Amber shook her head. "It's okay. I totally get how it would have been frustrating to think I expected that of you. It's fine. Can we forget it now?"

"Absolutely." Brittany grinned and reached out to hug Amber who stood up to grab her tightly. They clung to each other. Flaws or not, trials or not, they loved each other—that much Amber knew for sure. After a bit, they lay back on the bed and watched the ceiling fan rotate into a blur.

"So, what now? What do we do? We have finals this week." Amber thought of the answer keys she'd hidden directly under the spot where Brittany lay.

"What do we do?" Brittany sat up, crossed her legs, and bounced once, grinning. "We take our tests, we cheer each other on, and we see what happens."

Amber nodded.

"I'll tell you what. I'm even going to pray for you at the start of each class period during finals. Will you do the same for me?"

"I don't know." Amber laughed. "That's not

such a good deal for you, Britt. I'm sure God's more likely to answer your prayers than mine."

"I'll take my chances, silly."

"It's a deal, then." Amber held out her hand and they shook on it. "For now, want to study?" She held up the mammoth Literature book. She could at least help Brittany study. Maybe she should offer to share the tests with her, or not use them anymore herself.

No. She'd keep her eyes on the goal.

"I thought you'd never ask." Brittany grinned. "Only best friends could help each other study with so much on the line."

"Yeah, best friends. That's us."

❀

"Take out your number-two pencils, put all of your books and personal items beneath your chairs, and get ready. We'll start the test as soon as the bell rings."

Amber looked across the room at Brittany who pretended to bite her nails and tremble in nervousness. They both laughed, and Brittany put her hands together in a sign of prayer. Amber nodded and closed her eyes for a brief moment. Being quite sure God didn't want to hear from her after what she'd done, she didn't pray. Brittany would probably be better off without her prayers anyway.

The calculus teacher watched the clock on the wall as it ticked the final seconds off until the bell rang to signal the official start of the class period. "Okay, students. You may begin your exam."

Silent except for the rustling of papers, everyone opened their test booklets and readied their scratch paper and calculators. Amber flipped through her test and realized for the second time that day if she hadn't studied off the sheets Kyle had gotten for her, she'd never have been able to get the grades she needed. Some of the formulas on the test had barely even been discussed in class.

Amber glanced at Brittany—her eyebrows furrowed as she looked down at her papers and chewed on her eraser. Since they had studied together almost daily over the past months—except for the one week they weren't speaking—Amber knew all of Brittany's strengths and weaknesses, and knew she'd have a tough time with the test they had in front of them.

Regret and relief mixing like oil and water, Amber took a deep breath and began to solve her first problem. One by one she answered the questions and then double-checked her work.

With fifteen minutes to spare, she closed her exam booklet and cracked her knuckles. Several students shuddered in disgust at the sound of her popping joints.

"Sorry," she whispered.

Engrossed in her own work, Brittany never glanced her way. She didn't look happy.

Lord, help her. The impulsive prayer filled Amber's mind and made it all the way to her heart. She watched Brittany finish her test and thought back over the study session they'd had the night before. She had known full well what would be on the test, but she steered Brittany in other directions. The lump in her chest grew larger with the memory.

With her head down on her arms, Amber thought of Brittany's comment the night before. "I really think this will probably be on the test." She'd stopped at a difficult chapter when they flipped through the book one last time.

Amber wanted to kick herself for replying, "No. Why would it be? We didn't spend nearly enough time on it in class." One thing to cheat on a test—that was wrong enough by itself— but to steer your best friend down the wrong path so she wouldn't do well. . .how could she? A better question would be how to fix it.

But there would be no going back. Too late to change a thing. *What's done is done.*

The bell rang, and several students groaned and slammed their tests shut. Brittany sat frozen, staring at her paper with no expression on her face. Finally, she peeled herself from her seat and made her way among the other zombie-like students to the front where she handed her paper to the teacher. Britt's face paled and her shoulders slumped forward in defeat as she headed for the door.

"Don't forget your stuff." Amber pointed toward Brittany's desk.

"Oh. I almost forgot." She hurried to pick up her stack of books and met Amber at the door.

"Don't ask." She shook her head in reply to Amber's questioning eyes, the color returning to her face. "We'll talk about it later. I need to put this behind me. There's still one more test."

"I have History now. You have. . .what? Oh, yeah, Lit." Amber hesitated. "Hey, I already took that test—it's not too hard. Want me to tell you some of the questions?"

"No way!" Brittany came to life and shook her head. "Besides, even if you did, I know what I know, and there's no room in my head for anything else. I'm on overload."

They parted ways and headed to their classrooms on opposite ends of the senior wing. She should feel better now that she'd offered to help Brittany, but Amber only felt worse. Now, not only did Britt know Amber would cheat if she had wanted her to, but she also thanked her for it as though Amber were some great friend. *If she only knew the truth.*

Amber took a cleansing breath. "One more exam. Only one," she said out loud to herself. A couple of students passing by looked at her like they thought she lost her mind. Maybe she had.

Sitting at her desk in her history class waiting for the teacher to pass out the tests, Amber thought back over the year. All in all, it had been a good one. A lot of pressure, a lot more studying than she had intended to do in her senior year, but still good. She smiled softly at the memory of the day she and Brittany both received their acceptance letters to the University of Wyoming. They knew they'd get in, but the scholarships made it much more exciting. A full ride. What more could she ask for?

A car would sure be nice.

Focus, Amber. Focus. The moment of truth. The final test of the final week of the final year of high school. She opened the test booklet the teacher had laid before her, and read through the questions on the first page.

Thank God for Kyle.

Chapter 9

WE HAVE A WINNER

"Amber Stevens and Brittany Kim. Could you please come to the office?"

This is it. With only four days left until graduation, she and Brittany had been on edge, waiting to find out who won the contest. Grades hadn't been released yet, so they had no clue. They met up in the hallway, exactly as they had almost seven months ago when they got called into the office to first learn of the contest. Had it really been seven months since then?

The walk down the hallway and any conversations along the way blurred as Amber's thoughts raced and swirled. Within a few minutes, they sat in Principal Warner's office, waiting for the final verdict.

He pointed to the phone resting between

his shoulder and his ear, and motioned with five fingers that his call would only take a few more minutes.

Could she still back out? What if she put a stop to the whole thing right then? But she couldn't. She had a fifty-fifty chance of winning a brand-new car for herself—for her family— and would find out, one way or another, in a few minutes. But what if she didn't win? Amber wanted to be happy for Brittany—she really did. But she feared she wouldn't be able to find it within herself. Of course, she never thought she had it in her to be a cheater, either!

"Okay. Thanks so much. I'll be in touch." Principal Warner hung up the phone and turned to the girls, smiling from ear to ear. "Amber, Brittany." He nodded at them both. "I first want to say I am so very proud of you both. You have been exemplary students in every possible way. I understand you both got accepted to the college of your choice?"

"Yes, sir." Brittany wrung her hands together in her lap and took several deep breaths. Was she about to pass out? Poor girl wore her emotions on display.

Poised only on the outside, Amber patted Brittany's arm. "We're both going to UW on full scholarships."

"That's wonderful, girls. How exciting."
He paused, his eyes glimmering. "UW is close
enough to drive home once a month or so, right?"

"Well, sure. If we had a car, that is." Amber
teased back, trying to look cool and unfazed in
front of Principal Warner.

"Okay. This much you already know: One
of you will own a brand-new car before you
walk out of this office today. But knowing how
close you two are, you'll probably be sharing it
at college and to get you both back and forth
for visits. So the outcome should be exciting no
matter what." He leaned back in his chair with
his hands behind his head. "Before I tell you the
results, you need to know how very impressed
I am. You both deserve to be commended
for the way you acted during this race. You
both worked hard, but you stayed true to each
other. You took the high road and relied on
honesty, hard work, and friendship as the most
important things."

Amber never felt smaller.

"But alas, you're not here for all of that.
You're dying to hear the outcome, aren't you?"

Both girls nodded.

"Okay, after calculating everything, it came
down to the final exams. Either of you could

have won at that point. But the exams pulled out a clear winner. The winner, after your scores were finalized and confirmed, is. . ." He paused for effect, and then shouted, "*Amber!*"

Amber looked at Brittany, stunned, her mouth hanging open.

Brittany threw her arms around Amber and squeezed. "Oh, Amber. I'm so, so happy for you. You worked so hard for this. This is how it was meant to turn out—I just knew it."

"Can I call my mom and dad?" Amber words squeaked out. Her throat was so dry and her heart beat so hard, she wondered if they could hear it.

"First, let's go outside and take a look at your new car. Okay?"

Amber nodded, unable to speak.

The three of them walked out to the commons area. As soon as they turned the corner toward the front door, they saw it: the most beautiful new pearly white car parked right in front—with a big, red bow tied around it and her parents standing right beside it, beaming with pride. Could it get it better than that? She turned to Brittany, and her heart sank again. Not because Brittany looked sad—not at all. In fact, that would have made it easier. But what killed her was how Britt's face glowed. Her eyes radiated true joy at the sight of her best friend winning such a great honor. Amber reached over and hugged her. They clung to each other.

"Congratulations." Brittany squeezed her tightly. "I'm so glad it's over."

"Me, too." Amber laughed. "Believe me."

Principal Warner shook Amber's hand. "There will be someone here from the newspaper to take your picture with Dave Druthers by the car after school. You can drive it home today, but there'll be a ceremony at graduation where Mr. Druthers will formally present you with the keys and the title." He grinned. "Congratulations."

Amber didn't know what to say. It would have been so much better if she'd won it the right way. But still. . .

"I hate to break up this love fest, but there are classes going on." Principal Warner checked his watch. "You two need to get back to class."

"All right. Give me a few minutes with my mom and dad, okay?"

Brittany walked into the school with Principal Warner, leaving Amber outside with her parents.

Mom stepped forward and embraced her.

"We're so proud of you, sweetheart."

Dad wiped his eyes. "We've never been more proud of you than we are at this moment."

❀

"I really need to talk to you." Kyle hopped into the passenger seat when Amber pulled her new car into a parking spot. "Mmmm. I love the smell of a new car." He rubbed the dashboard.

"Me, too. What's up?"

"We have a problem."

Amber's face whitened, and her eyes opened wide. "What kind of problem?"

"We're about to get caught." He held up a finger. "I should say, they're about to find out someone cheated."

"H-h-how? W-who's about to find out?" Amber started to tremble. She'd never been in trouble before—especially not like this.

"Don't panic. I set it up so we won't get blamed for it." He shuffled and his eyes darted side to side—definitely hiding something.

"Okay, then who will?" Amber's heart sank, instinctively afraid of the answer.

"It had to be Brittany, kiddo. It's how it had to be."

Amber turned white and froze in place. "You framed Brittany for this? How could you do that?"

109

"Well, actually, it was quite easy. I hacked her password—*bkim*—and made the access on a day and time when she really was in the computer room—at least according to the sign-in log."

"I didn't mean how *did* you do it. I meant, how *could* you do it? I mean, it's bad enough I cheated against her, but it's so much worse now that she's going to get in trouble for it." Amber pounded her forehead on the steering wheel a few times.

Amber noticed students streaming into the school, so she assumed the bell rang. In a huff, she grabbed her bag from the backseat and almost slammed the door, but managed to hold back. As they hurried toward the front entrance, she hissed at Kyle, "Fix this!"

"Fixing it means you take the rap, kiddo. Your call. I'm not doing it." He took off in the other direction lighting a cigarette—apparently not attending school that day.

As she headed toward her class, the intercom squeaked. "Brittany Kim, please come to the office immediately."

Amber wanted nothing more than to get in her car and drive away from the school as fast as she could. She slumped into her classroom

110

and tried to focus, but she couldn't concentrate on anything but the thought of what could be happening in the office. At that very moment, Brittany faced sheer heartbreak—and Amber was completely to blame.

Part of her wanted to run right down to the office and put a stop to it, but the logical side of her brain reminded her they'd take away her car and her scholarship if she admitted to cheating—no way could she allow that to happen. But as things stood, Brittany was in trouble. How could she watch her best friend lose everything because of her? What kind of person could do that?

But her whole life depended on that scholarship and her family needed that car. *What have I done?*

Class ended, and then another one started and ended. No word of Brittany. Finally, as she walked toward Calculus, busybody Paula Markham grabbed Amber's arm, pulling her to a dead stop.

"Did you hear the news?" Paula's eyes bugged out with excitement at the gossip.

"What news?" She tried to act nonchalant, but dread coursed through her veins.

"Brittany got busted for cheating." Paula

whispered and looked both ways.

Yeah, right. You can't wait to tell them all.
"How do you know that?" Amber tried to look
surprised.

"I went to the office to get a Band-Aid."
She held up her bandaged finger. "I heard the
secretary calling her parents."

Oh no. "Oh. What a bummer. I have to go."
Amber turned away without another word.

In her math class, she sat in back, near the
window. Hopefully her teacher would chalk her
lack of focus up to end-of-the-year boredom.
Only two days remained until graduation, after
all. Would she be there? Would Brittany?

Distracted by movement in the parking lot
outside the window, Amber turned her head just
in time to see a shiny Lexus pull into a parking
spot—right next to her brand-new car. Mr. and
Mrs. Kim climbed from their car looking white
as ghosts, like they'd had the wind knocked
out of them. They hurried into the school with
looks of such dread—like they marched to their
doom.

Amber's inner battle continued to rage. She
couldn't let Brittany suffer like this. But *she*
couldn't take the fall either. She could blame
Kyle. No. She shook her head. That wouldn't

work. It's not like he operated with a super-high moral compass. He'd surely rat her out. She deserved it anyway—didn't she? *Oh no. What do I do? What would Brittany do? She'd never have done this—that's what!*

Exactly thirty-four minutes later, the Kims walked down the sidewalk toward their car with a shell of their daughter following behind. She carried a box, presumably with the contents of her locker, and her bag slung over one shoulder and across her chest. Her shoulders slumped forward as if to shield herself from the stares and the reality of the horrible nightmare she'd woken up to. Finally, Amber looked at her face: her skin chalky white, her eyes sunken and dim, and her cheeks moist from crying. The tears had stopped flowing—she must have run out.

Brittany climbed into the backseat of the Lexus. Her mom shut the door and got into the passenger side. Mr. Kim got into the driver's seat, but didn't even reach for his keys. No one moved inside the car, and no one's lips moved— they just sat there as if pulling away from the school would seal Brittany's fate.

Amber looked at the clock. Class neared its end, and the hallways would soon be filled with students. She could still fix this. All she'd have to do is run out and stop them from leaving. Then, they'd go to the office, and she'd tell her story. Simple. It's what would come after that that froze her in her seat. Amber glanced out the window at her car—her prized possession, the symbol of her adulthood, her freedom, her success—her cheating.

The Kims still waited for something, as though they could sense the battle going on within her. Then she saw Mr. Kim had his eyes squeezed shut, but his lips slowly formed words. Brittany and her mom sat in their seats the same way—eyes closed, lips moving. *Ah. They're praying.* That realization hit Amber like a punch in her gut. Such good people. They didn't deserve this.

But I have so much to lose.

Now or never.

The time has come to make a decision. Think long and hard about what you would really do if you encountered the exact same circumstances Amber is facing. It's easy to say you'd make the right choice. But are you sure you could admit your wrongdoing and risk everything— graduation, scholarship, and a new car—and disappoint your parents so badly? Especially if your family had such a great financial need and your friend's family did not. . .would that make a difference in your choice?

Once you make your decision, turn to the corresponding page to see how it turns out for Amber—and for you.

Turn to page 116 if Amber decides to turn herself in and clear Brittany's name.

Turn to page 152 if Amber decides she has way too much to lose to admit to cheating.

❀

The next three chapters tell the story of what happened to Amber when she decided to admit to cheating and clear Brittany's name.

Chapter 10

HOLD EVERYTHING

That's it! Amber jumped out of her seat and scrambled over her backpack and purse in the aisle. "I'll be back. I have to. . .go. . ." She saw her teacher staring openmouthed as she ran from the room, leaving the door open behind her. She couldn't take the time to close it. They'd be pulling out of the parking lot at any moment—it might already be too late.

Tearing down the hall at full speed, Amber saw the doors looming ahead of her. It felt like she moved in slow motion—like running through quicksand in a dream. She chanted with every step. *Please wait. Please wait. Please wait.* She slowed down a bit where the hallway intersected with another one—good thing, because she almost ran right smack into Kyle.

He grabbed her arm. "Whoa, whoa. Is someone chasing you?"

"Can't talk now." She shrugged off his hand and picked up speed as she approached the door.

From behind her, Kyle called, "Don't do anything stupid, Amber."

She ignored him.

Panting, she pushed the crash bar on the door and spilled out onto the steps. She looked toward the parking lot on her right. Still there. Mr. Kim had turned in his seat and appeared to be talking to Brittany in the backseat. Amber approached the driver's side window and knocked.

Mr. Kim whipped around, his tie tucked across his left shoulder. He buzzed his window down with the flick of a switch. "Miss Amber? Is something wrong?"

She tried to catch her breath. "Mr. Kim, Mrs. Kim, if it's okay, I have something I need to say to Brittany—to you all. Could you maybe step out of the car?"

"Is okay, Amber. Wait a minute. We get out." They climbed from the car and stood before her.

Amber cleared her throat. "I have no idea how to say this except to just do it." She took a deep, ragged breath.

"What's going on here?"

Amber closed her eyes and sighed at the familiar voice of Principal Warner. She slowly turned around to face him. "I have something I need to say to the Kims." She stared at the ground. "It's good you're here. You need to hear this, too."

Principal Warner's face had turned a blustery red. "Amber, I heard you left class without permission and then tore through the hallways like you were on fire. Now this? What's going on?"

"Give me just a minute. You'll understand." She took a deep breath, wiped her sweaty hands on her jeans, and then looked at the principal. "It wasn't Brittany. It was me."

She turned away from his confused expression toward Brittany, who had her arms crossed on her chest. "You know you didn't cheat, it seems like your parents know you didn't cheat. And I *definitely* know you didn't cheat. How do I know? Because I'm the one who did it. I had help getting copies of the exams, then without me knowing, my *help* framed you for it."

Brittany glared at Amber and shook her head. The glare quickly dissolved as she looked her mom and started to cry.

Mrs. Kim reached a protective arm around her shaking daughter.

After a moment of silence, Mr. Kim directed

his stern attention to Principal Warner. "I'm sure this will be fixed right away." He faced Amber. "Miss Amber. I know you did wrong. But took a lot of. . .uh. . .guts to do what you just did. We all make mistakes in our life. Is part of life. You made right choice when important."

Brittany snorted and shrugged her mom's arm off her shoulders.

Amber steeled herself for the onslaught she'd been expecting.

"I am so angry and so hurt. . .I don't even know what to say to you, Amber." Brittany shook her head and glared at the sky. "I guess I'll have to give you points for coming clean. Why did you do it, anyway?"

Amber looked down at the ground. "Why did I cheat? Or why did I admit to it?" Her voice came out barely a whisper.

"I guess I know why you cheated—your faith is dead. You have no faith in anything, not even in yourself." Brittany pulled her arms tighter across her chest, her face as cold as stone. "But why did you admit it now when you were pretty much assured of getting away with it?"

"I saw you, Britt. I saw you walking to your car, beaten down, sad. I couldn't be the cause of that." She opened her mouth to continue, but decided that some things were better left unsaid.

"You had to know I'd be furious."

"Having you mad at me, as bad as that is, is better than knowing I ruined your life. This was all my fault—"

"Obviously."

"—and I'll do anything to try to fix it. I want things to be right between us."

Principal Warner stepped closer to the group. "Folks, I think it would be best if we took this to my office. The bell is about to ring, and students will be all over the place."

They silently made their way to the front office, entered the conference room, and took seats. Amber played with the dial on her silver watch. Brittany stared out the window. Mrs. Kim tapped her fingernails on the table. Mr. Kim—always the stately professional—sat still and straight. No one said a word.

Principal Warner came into the room. "I called your mom and dad, Amber. They'll be here shortly."

Amber slumped lower in her seat.

"So, we'll save any talk about your situation for their arrival. How about we fix things for the Kims so they can be on their way?"

Everyone nodded.

"Well, I wish this could be under different circumstances so you could truly enjoy your victory, Brittany. But you did earn this." He reached an open hand to Amber, who placed the car key into it. He took the key and put it into Brittany's hand and closed her fingers around it. Then, Principal Warner clasped his hands around her fist and squeezed. "You deserve this, Brittany. You worked hard. You've been a stellar student. Please enjoy your reward."

Brittany wiped the tears from her eyes. "It's just. . .well. . .I wish. . ."

"I know. The win is bittersweet." Principal Warner released a deep sigh.

Brittany turned away from Amber, toward her parents.

Amber couldn't let the moment pass without one more attempt to reach out to her. "Brittany." The tears fell like waterfalls down her cheeks. "I'm so sorry. I don't think I've ever really understood what it means to be sorry until now. I wish I could change things. Please, please forgive me."

Brittany stared at her, appearing to listen to what Amber said.

Amber flinched, shocked when Brittany reached out one hand and placed it lightly, gently even, across her cheek. Brittany gazed at her with sadness. No, not really sadness. . .pity. Without a word, Brittany left the room.

Mrs. Kim hurried to Amber's side. "Dear Amber, is okay. You make mistake. We love you like our daughter. Brittany will turn around and forgive you. She loves you, too. She a good girl. You'll see." She started to leave the conference room, but stopped. "One more thing. Brittany is right. You have no faith. If you had faith in Jesus, you would have trusted Him enough that you didn't cheat. If you had faith in yourself, you'd have known you not need to cheat. If you had faith in your parents, you'd have known they didn't want you to cheat to get a car. Find your faith, Amber. Go to church. Okay?"

Amber nodded, Mrs. Kim's words resonating in her mind. Those might have been the most words she'd ever spoken at one time to Amber, but they proved she knew her well, perhaps better than anyone.

Mrs. Kim walked through the doorway where Amber's mom and dad stood waiting to enter. She patted Mom on the arm and gave her a sympathetic look, but didn't speak to her.

Amber wished she could disappear. She couldn't think of a single place on earth that would be worse than where she sat at that moment. The middle of the lion cage at the zoo right before lunchtime—better than this. The operating-room table without anesthesia—much better. A burning building—she'd take it. But no, her immediate fate was inescapable. She'd have to sit there and face her parents.

The plush, vinyl conference chairs let out a *whoosh* as Amber's parents sank into them. They looked at the principal, pale, speechless. They hadn't said anything, yet. What could be said?

"I'm really sorry we had to call you here under these circumstances. . ."

The principal's voice droned on like a buzz in Amber's ear. She couldn't listen to the facts being recounted again.

What have I done? No more college scholarship. No more car. No more trust. No more perfect high-school transcripts. *Wait a second! Will I even graduate with my class?*

"Wait!" Amber interrupted Principal Warner.

"—came running out to stop them from leaving." He finished his sentence, then looked at her. "What is it, Amber?"

"What about graduation? Am I going to graduate?" Amber's heart, like a lump in her throat, beat wildly.

"We're about to talk about all of that. So, hold on one second with those questions, okay?" He looked at her with kind and compassionate eyes and then turned back to her parents. "Do you have any questions so far?"

"No, I think we pretty much get the picture." Dad squeezed his eyes shut.

Mom sat forward. "I have one question. What about whoever helped her cheat? Is that going to be pursued?"

"Of course. In fact, I have a pretty good idea who it was. I felt this was a separate circumstance and will deal with that later."

"Okay, I'm sorry. It's not that I want someone else in trouble—oh, I don't know what I want." Mom rubbed her temples with her fingertips.

"I understand. Believe me."

"Can we move on to the consequences? I don't see a need to drag this out endlessly." Dad shifted in his chair.

"Sure, Mr. Stevens." Principal Warner took out a yellow legal pad and began to write as he spoke. "I haven't had a chance to clear any of this with the school board, yet. But this is what I think will happen. Obviously, the car goes to Brittany, and she wins the contest by default."

"Yes, obviously—rightfully so." Mr. Stevens shook his head at Amber.

"We'll have some issues to figure out with the car title over the next few days." The principal cleared his throat. "As for college entrance and your scholarship, that's going to be up to your college. I am under no obligation to report this incident to them—although I probably would have if you had gotten caught but hadn't come forward. It would be a matter of honor as a principal. But I believe the fact that you came forward on your own deserves to be distinguished from other situations. You will have to submit a final transcript to the school, though—it will be up to them what they do with it."

Principal Warner swiveled to look out the window. "Here's my dilemma, though." He turned back around and peered at them through squinted eyes—obviously deep in thought. "You cheated on three exams. That means you receive an F on those tests. Two of those teachers have a class policy that also requires you to be dropped from the class. Mrs. Tillman, your History teacher, doesn't require an automatic drop, and you pass that class even with the F on the exam. So we'll put that class aside, for now.

Calculus and Literature are my concern."

He shook his head for a moment, rubbed his forehead, and lifted his eyes toward the ceiling.

Amber held her breath. *Think of something, please.*

"You have to make up those two classes to graduate—you'll have to retake them in summer school. But even still, your grade point average will be affected by the Fs. I guess that's part of the price you'll have to pay."

"It sounds more than fair, Principal Warner." Mr. Stevens leaned forward to shake his hand. "Can you tell me, though, in your opinion, what you think UW will do?"

He leaned back in his chair and tapped his fingertips together. "I'll shoot straight with you. They'll let her admission stand, but they'll pull the scholarship. That's what I really think will happen."

Mrs. Stevens pulled a tissue from her purse and blew her nose. "This is awful. It couldn't get much worse."

Numb, Amber still said nothing. What could she say?

"It could be worse. Mrs. Stevens. We could have found out about this the hard way—it would be much different for Amber if that had happened. But even worse—we might have never found out. That would have meant Amber was capable of letting her best friend take the blame and suffer all that Amber deserves to suffer herself."

That sounded familiar to Amber. *Jesus.* The name echoed through her mind. *Jesus. He paid my penalty, He suffered my consequences, and I've totally blown Him off.*

Chapter 11

LOVE, AMBER

Now what? Amber kicked the stones and twigs out of her way as she trudged up the hill behind her house. She cast a backward glance at her home—it had once been a happy place. Even with the worn-out tile and cracked countertops, even with the ten-year-old carpet and the beat-up car in the garage, it had been a haven for a happy family. Why had she worried so much about things that didn't matter and hurt her family in the process?

She slid to the ground, then leaned her back against her favorite tree and peered up into its boughs. Remembering hours upon hours of climbing and swinging from those branches, Amber smiled before she could help herself. Oh, for those easy days of no responsibility, no choices, no disappointments. She pulled her knees up to her chest and buried her face in the crook of her arm. She let the tears fall onto the dirt between her feet.

After a few minutes, she heard footsteps coming up the path. Before lifting her head, she used her sleeve to wipe the tears but couldn't do a thing about her puffy eyes. Good enough.

She peeked up to see who approached. Mom. Having not spoken much since the principal's office the day before, Amber didn't know what to say. *Don't cry.* But she couldn't help it. Her eyes welled up again, and the tears continued to stream down her face.

Mom rushed to her side, gathered her daughter in her arms, and rocked her. For a moment, Amber felt like the little girl who had once climbed in the tree above them.

When she'd cried her last tear, Amber lifted her head to look at her mom. "I'm so sorry," she whispered. "So sorry."

"I know you are." Mom lightly scratched her forearm like she used to do long ago. "I'm sorry, too, Amber."

Amber eyes widened and she sat up straight. "You're sorry? What on earth are you sorry for?"

"Your dad and I, well, we realize we failed

as your spiritual guardians. In all of our effort to be 'cool' and to let you find your own way, we let you veer so far off the path that you lost your way completely." Mom shook her head. "And what's worse, we knew you were trying to come back. If only we'd reached out more. Maybe if we'd found a church where we could all be happy, then none of this would have happened."

"Mom, you can't blame yourself. No matter how confused I got about faith, I never doubted what I was doing was wrong. Cheating is wrong in every situation."

"Well then, why? Why did you do it?"

Amber hung her head. "I wanted to do my part. I wanted to help. We needed the car. Now we have nothing. I even lost my scholarship, which I already had before I cheated. We're worse off now than we ever were before."

"Sweetie, you need to stop this. Our car, our finances—they aren't your concern. God has always taken care of us, and He always will." Mom stood up and brushed off her running pants. "You know, there's a reason God made adults the parents. You're too young to carry that burden. At your age, you can't possibly understand the right way to deal with the pressures of life. You're learning, though—

the hard way, unfortunately."

"I really messed up, big-time. Didn't I?"

Mom chuckled. "Yeah, you sure did." She crouched down to make eye contact. "But wait a second. I don't want you to lose sight of the fact that when it came down to it, you did the right thing. That had to be a very difficult thing to do."

"Yes, it was. But nowhere near as hard as watching Brittany go through what she did."

She slugged Amber in the arm. "See, there's hope for you, yet." Mom winked. "Now, come on. Enough moping around. Let's go for a nice long run."

"Ugh, Mom!" Amber groaned and then smiled as a thought came to her. "I'm grounded, right?"

"Nice try. Come on, you'll love it once you get into it—you always do."

❀

Amber's rubbery legs climbed the stairs to her room. The three-mile run had felt good. The fresh air helped clear her head. She knew just what to do now.

Sitting at her desk, she reached into the drawer and grabbed a few sheets of paper. A real letter—Amber couldn't remember when, if ever, she'd made the effort to write a handwritten letter. But this occasion demanded the personal touch—e-mail simply wouldn't do.

Dear Brittany,

I'm sorry. I wish I could go back and change everything—especially the way I felt about the contest. I was so wrong. I let those feelings lead me down a path and make a decision that caused you and other people I love a lot of hurt. I hope you can forgive me and let me try to repair what I've done. I'm sure you won't be able to trust me right away, but with your forgiveness, I'll be able to work on the trust part over time.

I wish I'd tried harder to be involved in your church. I was starting to find my way back to God, and then I cut Him off by doing something so wrong. I'm sure even He wants nothing to do with me. Maybe in time, when things have healed a little bit, you can help me find my way to Him—if He'll have me.

I hope you're enjoying your new car— you truly deserve it. I love you, Britt. You're the most honest, loyal, and kind person I know. I let you down, I know that. I have a long way to go to grow into being even half the person you are. I don't deserve you

for a friend, but I miss you so much. This is
a difficult time for me—I hope you can find
it in your heart to forgive me and let me try
to rebuild what I destroyed. I'll do whatever
it takes.

Love,
Amber

With her letter folded into a square, Amber hurried down the stairs as fast as her wobbling legs could carry her. "Dad, I need to use the car to take this letter to Brittany. It's really important. Is it okay?"

He looked up from his magazine and pulled off his reading glasses. "Yes. It is. But first your mom and I want to talk to you. We have some news we want to share with you."

He put his magazine on the floor and grabbed Amber's hand, pulling her to the couch beside him. "First, I want you to know your mom told me everything you two talked about—I'm so sad this happened, but I'm proud of the way you're handling it. It's a rough learning experience, but we all make mistakes in life. Your mom and I are going to figure things out so we can all find the kind of relationship with God you described to me. No more facts and doctrine—we're going to find His heart—together."

"I'd like that, Dad."

He smiled warmly. "Now. I have some news, and we've made some decisions." He glanced at Mom and smiled.

She winked and nodded.

"I got a job—a good one. I got the call today."

"Dad! That's wonderful! Congratulations." Amber beamed.

"Thank you. It's very exciting. The thing is—" he glanced at Mom and then back at Amber—"we're going to have to move. Believe me, it's worth it. They are paying for the move, and we'll be able to get this old house and all of its headaches off our back. Your mom and I need to downsize our lives a bit, anyway. A smaller, one-level ranch house is all the three of us need."

Where? When? Amber waited. His hesitancy assured her he had more to say.

"We'll leave right after summer school is over. We're moving only about forty minutes away from UW. My job is at the community college there." He rushed his words. "Since I'll be working at the college, you'll get free tuition. Because of all that's gone on, and since you'll likely lose your scholarship, your mom and I want you to attend the community college for at least one year. And. . .you'll have to live at home with us."

Amber's shoulders dropped. She and Brittany had had such big plans. *I blew it.* She sighed. "I don't blame you guys. I mean, we can't even be sure they'll let me go to UW next year anyway. And if we're getting free tuition, it's only logical. Don't mind me." She wiped the tears from her eyes. "I'm sorry I'm crying. It's just. . .I had such big dreams—going away to school, being on a big college campus, driving my new car. It's no one's fault except mine, though."

Mom and Dad waited and let her cry.

Dad rubbed her shoulder. "We know, sweetie. It has to be difficult for you. Sadly, the price for poor decisions can be really high sometimes. But, hey, we'll be in a new house, you'll get to go to college, you'll meet new people. . .who knows, maybe this is all part of God's plan for you."

"Actually, I'm quite sure it is." Mom nodded. "We need more time together. It's not the right time for us to be pulled apart—too much has happened. We have to find a way to fix things before life tears us apart forever. One more year should do it." She smiled.

One more year. "That's a good way to look at it, Mom." She turned toward her dad. "I'm so happy for you, Dad. I'm going to have to come to terms with my own stuff a little later. It's going to be okay, though. I can feel it." She picked up the keys and dangled them. "Is it okay if I head over to Brittany's for a few minutes? I have something I really need to take care of."

"Sure. We'll be praying for both of you, Amber."

On the drive to Britt's house, Amber considered the move. At least there would be a fresh start, and she'd be close to Brittany. She could get a job, save money for college, maybe buy a used car. She hadn't planned for this, but it wasn't the end of the world. *It could have turned out a lot worse.*

The car puttered up the driveway and stopped with a hiss. One more hurdle to jump. Note in hand, Amber approached the doorway. It opened before her finger reached the doorbell.

"Hi." Brittany held the door open with one foot but didn't invite her in.

"Britt. Would you read this? I'd like you to

do it while I'm here. But if you don't want to, that's okay, too."

"I'm sorry, Amber. I'll read it. But not in front of you." Brittany took the note and shut the door.

Amber's shoulders slumped as she walked to the car and got into the driver's seat. The final hurdle proved to be the most difficult. She gripped the steering wheel with one hand and reached for the ignition with the other. *Might as well go home.* The faithful car sputtered to life. Amber checked her rearview mirror and put the car in reverse. Just as she started to lift her foot off the brake, she heard a knock on the window.

Brittany's tearful face peered into the car.

Trying not to get too hopeful, Amber unlocked the door and motioned for Brittany to get in. While she settled into the passenger's seat Amber tried to think of something to say.

Brittany beat her to it. "I read your letter."

"Well, I—"

"Hold on. Let me say this." Brittany took a deep breath. "Some of this problem came up because I didn't accept your apology the first time. I didn't let you change your mind about what you said on the ski lift. I held it over your head, and it caused you to have to stew over it and think about

137

it when you wanted to let it go. . ."

"This isn't your fault, Britt."

"Oh, I know. I'm just saying, you apologized to me, and I believe you meant it then and now. I accept your apology. For real this time. I'd forgotten that being a Christian requires me to forgive others like I've been forgiven. So, it's done."

"Really? It's that easy?"

"It's not easy. I'll be honest. I feel so betrayed by you. But then again, I have to realize how much you gave up to come clean when you saw me hurting. That definitely counts for a lot."

"I'm so sorry. I wish there was something more I could say." Amber clenched the steering wheel. *Please let it be that easy. Please help her forgive me.*

"I know you're sorry, we're past that. I also know you love me like a sister. I know that for sure. Somewhere along the way, you lost faith in everything, though." Brittany looked out the window and shook her head. "Life became too heavy for you, and you trusted in yourself way too much. I, as your best friend, need to help you figure out a better way." Brittany looked in Amber's eyes, the concern evident on her face. "So. . .what happens to you now?"

Amber chuckled. "Want to go for a little drive? This could take a while."

"Yeah." Brittany smiled. "Hey, I could seriously use some ice cream."

"Me, too. Boy, could I use some ice cream."

Chapter 12

A FRESH START

"Be careful with that. It's fragile." Amber directed the movers to place her mom's favorite antique curio cabinet in the sunny dining room near the huge wall of windows. She'd never seen a house with as many windows or surrounded by so many mountains in the distance. Light filled the whole house all day long.

She heaved a heavy box of books into her arms and tried to carry it to her room at the end of the long hallway. About halfway down the hall, she lost her grip and the box started to slip. Squatting down, she let the box slide to the floor and pulled it the rest of the way to her room. Weird not having stairs, but at times like this it sure came in handy. The cardboard slid easily on the hardwood floors her mom had always wanted.

Once she made it to her room, Amber opened the box and began to arrange her books and photo albums on the built-in bookcases. A large, hardcover photography book slipped from her hands. *Whap!*—the loud sound made her jump. Not having carpet would take some getting used to.

Thirsty, Amber wandered down the hallway from her bedroom, past the French doors that led to her parents' master suite. She glanced in and saw them in the bathroom, looking at the whirlpool tub, in deep conversation with the Realtor. She moved through the huge great room with its vaulted ceilings and room-dividing fireplace that reminded her of a ski lodge—and into the bright, green and white kitchen with its granite countertops and ceramic-tile floor. This house was quite a bit smaller than their old house. But what it lost it size, it sure made up for in character. Mom's dream house in every way. She deserved it—in fact, moving into her dream house was a great way to spend her birthday.

With a lump in her throat, Amber thought of her mom—faithful, giving, patient. She worked hard at making their house a home and showing love to her family. Mom had done without for so many years, just so Amber could have the best possible stuff. Amber couldn't remember a time when she'd had to do without. Ever. She thought of the surprise package she had stowed away in her room—couldn't wait to give it to her mom later over a special dinner Amber planned to prepare for her. This would be Mom's best birthday ever.

Amber glanced at her can of Coke—the days of generic cola were apparently over. She took a long drink and gazed out the window at the mountains. On the way to the new house, Amber had been surprised that the five-hour drive only took them as far as the other side of the same mountain range she'd admired her whole life.

Same mountain, whole new perspective.

Same Amber, whole new perspective.

She shook her head and chuckled. Since when had she become a philosopher? Time to unpack some clothes. She grabbed her Coke and headed to her room, tempted to take a running start and slide across the floors. Before she had a chance to do it, the doorbell rang. Who could it be? They didn't know anyone in town yet.

Rounding the corner toward the small foyer

off the dining room, she could see an arm in the smoky-glass window that ran the length of the door. The visitor shifted, and Amber could make out a bit more of the arm and a bit of leg. Then, even more. *Brittany!* She threw the door open and hugged her. "What are you doing here? I didn't think I'd see you for two weeks."

"Oh, I came a little early. We need time to explore, silly! My parents are going to drive up with my stuff in ten days."

"You mean we have ten days just to hang out before school starts?"

"Yep, I have to be at UW for registration on the nineteenth. Until then, we can do whatever. Your parents were in on it, too. Surprise!"

"This is exactly what I needed! I tried to be brave, but I definitely felt a little sad." She threw her arms around Brittany again. "I'm so glad you're here, Britt. What are we going to do first?"

"Well, from the looks of things around here, unpack." Brittany looked in exaggerated horror at the boxes and piles of things to be put away.

"I do have a lot to do here, and it's Mom's birthday. I was going to make her dinner." Amber shrugged her shoulders. "Sorry. I know it's probably not what you had in mind. But we can hit the town tomorrow. Okay?"

"That's perfect. Now, show me around so we can get started." Brittany headed into the house. She whistled when she saw the great room. "This is awesome. Wow." She stepped back and looked up at the vaulted ceiling with the skylights. "This is so different from the old house."

"I know. I'm never going to want to leave here." Amber grinned. "Really, though, I'm just so happy for my mom and dad. They deserve this."

At that moment, Amber's parents came into the room and rushed to hug Brittany. "We're so glad you could come and stay with us for a little while. It helps the transition for Amber, I'm sure."

"I'm glad to be here. I can't imagine why this"—she gestured around the room—"would be a difficult transition, though."

"Change always has its challenges. Even good change." Dad flipped the switch to turn on the gas at the fireplace. "Actually, I can't stand gas fires. They don't come close to the sound of crackling wood and the smell of the real thing. I have wood being delivered tomorrow that we'll burn during the colder months. For now, though. . ." He pushed a button and the fire roared to life.

Amber glanced at her mom. She seemed

happier than she'd ever been. *Hmm. She'd been right all along.* God had met their needs in perfect timing—more than their needs. She looked beyond the fireplace to the setting sun beyond the mountains. *Wait. Setting sun? Dinner!* "Britt, I'd better start dinner if we have any hope of eating it before midnight."

"Great. I'll help."

In the kitchen, both girls washed their hands.

"What's on the menu?" Brittany asked.

"It's all her favorites. Grilled lamb chops, double-baked potatoes, grilled asparagus, and fresh salad with homemade dressing."

"Wow. You can cook all of that?"

"Sure. I have the chops marinating, and the salad is ready to be tossed right before dinner's ready. I've baked the potatoes once. Now we need to scoop the potato out of the skins and mix in the good stuff, then re-bake them." Amber reached into the stainless steel refrigerator and handed Brittany the sour cream, butter, cheese, and green onions. "The asparagus will go on the grill at about the same time as the chops do. All that's left is to make the dressing."

"I had no idea you could cook like this."

"Yeah, there's a lot about me no one. . .well, what I mean is. . .I think I've been pretty selfish.

I never bothered to do much for other people." She started scooping out the potatoes into a large mixing bowl, careful to leave the skins intact. "That's changing."

"I can see that." Brittany grabbed the sour cream. "Here, let me help. How much of this goes in there?"

"Oh, let's not count calories tonight. Pour the whole thing in here."

"You read my mind." Brittany scooped every last drop of sour cream into the bowl along with the shredded cheese, onion, and butter.

Once they mixed it all together, then salted and peppered it, Amber scooped huge mounds of the potato mixture into the skins that lay waiting on a tray. They sprinkled bacon, a few more green onion pieces, and some paprika on top. A piece of aluminum foil covered the tray, which got set aside until a bit later.

"I cannot wait to eat those potatoes!"

"Wait until you taste the lamb."

❀

"I want to unbutton my pants. . .how gluttonous is that?" Amber's mom laughed. "That is the best meal I've had in a long time. Thank you so much, sweetie."

"Oh my. I agree. You girls did an amazing job."

"Don't thank me." Brittany shook her head. "Amber pretty much had it all done before I even got here. It was all her."

"Well, I'm glad you liked it. Don't go anywhere, though. There's still dessert—strawberry shortcake." Amber stood up to get the cake.

"Oh no." Mom laughed. "That's going to have to wait until later, I'm afraid."

"That's fine. But I want to give you your birthday present now. Okay?" She couldn't wait any longer.

"Sure. But this dinner was present enough for me. What else could there be?"

Amber scurried to her bedroom, socks slipping on the floor as she went. She dived to the floor and dug under her bed for the wrapped package she'd hidden there. As she left her bedroom, she reached up to switch off the light. *No sense wasting money.* She smiled to herself—amazing how things had changed.

Back in the dining room, she handed her mom the box. "Before you open this, Mom, I want to say thank you."

"You're giving me a present, but you're thanking me? I don't get it."

"I want you to know how much I appreciate

147

all you've sacrificed for me over these past years. I think back and realize I've acted like a spoiled brat. You gave up the most—you wore old clothes, you never bought new furniture or cars, you never got to go out to nice places, you didn't even have a cell phone—but I did." She gestured around the room. "I'm so glad to see you getting the chance to have some things that you've wanted."

"Amber, all I've ever wanted has been to see you and your dad happy. I don't really care about those things you mentioned. I'd rather have time with you guys than a new car. I'd rather sit down to a dinner like this, lovingly prepared by my daughter, than go to the fanciest of restaurants." She dabbed her eyes with a napkin. "I've lived my dream. This house is just icing on the cake. I'd have been fine, forever, without it."

"That's exactly what makes you so wonderful." Dad spoke up and reached across the table to pat her hand. "I'm dying to see what's in the box, though."

"Yeah, open it," Brittany urged. "I think I know what it is."

Amber winked at her.

Mom pulled off the pink bow and tore off the floral wrapping paper. She turned the box

148

over and read the words on the cover: *Donna Karan.* "Really?"

"Yeah. Whenever we watched those designer shows or flipped through magazines, she's the only designer you really seemed to like."

"Wow. I had no idea you noticed that." She started to open the box. "It's not that I didn't like the other designers—I just felt Donna Karan designed the clothes I'd want to wear if I could—classic, yet stylish. Upscale, but not too flashy. A lot of her stuff, you could wear during the day or at night—if you're the type of person who goes anywhere." Mom laughed.

"Yeah, yeah, yeah. Would you open it already?" Dad sounded impatient with all the talk of designers and fashion.

Mom pulled the top off the box and parted the layers of tissue paper, savoring the moment. She gasped when she saw the crisp white blouse layered under the emerald green pin-tucked blazer, lying on top of the perfect pair of black pants. "Oh, Amber. This is beautiful. How on earth did you ever afford this?"

"Oh, I returned a pair of jeans," she winked at Brittany, "saved up some money, did some odd jobs—nothing major. Do you like it?"

"Sweetheart, I absolutely love it." Mom

wiped her eyes. "I. . .well. . .you know. . .this stuff isn't important to me. But it sure does make me feel special—like a lady." She looked at her husband. "Don't get me wrong. I don't want many things this expensive. But one or two classic pieces like this that will last forever—that can't be bad, can it?"

"Babe, I wish I could have done this for you years ago." He shook his head. "You've sacrificed too much."

"No. It was just right. Without the waiting, none of this"—she gestured to the present on her lap and the house all around her—"would have been special at all."

"You know what, Mom?" Amber piped up. "I totally get what you're saying. If I hadn't gone through—scratch that—if I hadn't done what I did, I'd never have learned about what I had become. Now, the contrast is so glaring that it makes me appreciate the change so much more."

They sat in silence, taking in the words. Amber soaked up the love around the table and felt bathed in warmth and love from her heavenly Father.

Mom stood up from the table. "You girls go on now, your dad and I will clean up." She started to collect the dishes. "Go explore, see a movie, do something fun. Thank you so much for. . .well. . .for all of this—the dinner, the present, the love."

"Okay. Thanks, Mom. Thanks, Dad." Amber hugged them both. "I love you both."

"Bye, Mr. and Mrs. Stevens. We'll be back before too long."

They turned to leave the kitchen, but Amber stopped short. "Hey, you guys. Would it be okay if we tried out a church together on Sunday?"

"Oh, Amber. And I thought my birthday couldn't get any better."

Dad smiled and nodded. "I'm pretty sure that can be arranged."

❀

The next three chapters tell the story of what happened to Amber when she decided not to admit to cheating and clear Brittany's name.

Chapter 10

TOO LATE

No way. As much as her insides screamed at her to put a stop to the whole thing, Amber sat still, frozen to her seat. What could she do? Walk right into the principal's office and hand over her car keys, turn in her college scholarship, and disappoint everyone? People wouldn't really expect that of her, would they?

Amber looked around the room. Lucy and Kara sat in the corner applying makeup. Pete had his nose in a book, as usual. Chet stuck a gooey wad of gum to the bottom of his desk. *Eww.* She'd gone to school with most of the students since kindergarten. She knew them well. Not a chance any one of them would turn themselves in—not if they stood to lose what she did. *Never.*

Her stomach churned as she watched through the window. Mr. Kim turned toward the backseat where Brittany sat.

Brittany nodded, wiped her face with her sleeve, put her head back, and closed her eyes.

Mr. Kim gave a slight smile and one small nod to his grief-stricken wife, then started the car. It roared to life, the lights blinked on for a brief moment, and then he eased the car into reverse.

Why did he drive so slowly? Almost as though he were waiting for something. Someone? Amber's thoughts swirled and bounced out of control. She exhaled the breath she'd been holding and unclenched her stiff fists.

The second hand on the clock over the chalkboard ticked by, each minute feeling like an hour. The teacher's voice droned on and on, but Amber barely heard a word she said. Twenty seconds until the bell, then escape. Only two more days until graduation. Would Brittany even be there? What would happen to her? Amber made a snap decision to go to Britt's house right after school. After all, it wouldn't be natural not to reach out to her best friend at such a troubled time—someone might suspect something if she went home and hid.

Finally, the bell clanged, signaling the end of the school day. Amber scooped up her belongings and hurried from the classroom. She wanted to get out of there and over to Brittany's house to find out if she had any idea of the truth. She couldn't. Could she?

Amber rushed down the long hall, avoiding eye contact with everyone, and stepped out into the fresh, springtime air. *Ah*. She took a deep breath, filled her lungs, and then released it in a cleansing flood. When she stood a few yards away from her car, she pressed the little button on her key chain to release the door locks. *Beep-beep*. The lights flickered as the alarm shut off. She opened the car door and got inside just in time to hear someone call her name.

Kyle. She forced herself not to glance in his direction, closed the door, and started the engine, pretending not to hear him. He approached the car just as she finished backing up and got the car pointed around toward the exit. She looked in the other direction.

Glancing up to the rearview mirror, Amber saw Kyle standing alone in the parking lot, looking rather upset and pale. *Hmm*. Not like him at all. Maybe he'd wanted a ride. Oh well, he could take the bus like any other day. She had other, much more important business to attend to. With Brittany on her mind, Amber turned left and headed away from the school.

During the short drive to Britt's house, the new-car smell brought on waves of nausea—too sweet, too clean—something. She put the window down to get some fresh air before she vomited. When that didn't help, she opened the moon roof to let in even more air. She gulped deep breaths and exhaled, trying to calm her churning stomach—her nerves.

The drive took forever—everything dragged on in slow motion. She wanted to make it past the next few days, get to the other side of all the drama and confusion, with her friendships and her future intact so she could sit back and enjoy it all. But one day at a time. One hour at a time. One minute at a time. That's how it had to be—whether she liked it or not.

Standing on the Kims' front porch, waiting for someone to open the door, Amber wiped her sweaty palms on her pants. She'd know in an instant if Brittany suspected her. A few seconds later, the door flew open and a blubbering heap threw herself onto Amber's shoulder. Britt clung to Amber and sobbed. . .and sobbed.

"I. . .didn't. . .do it. . ." Brittany gulped and

took a ragged breath. "I. . .promise. . .I didn't cheat."

Amber brushed the hair off Brittany's forehead and helped her into the house, away from the prying eyes of the neighbors. "I know. I never thought for a second you did." She deposited Brittany into a kitchen chair and filled a glass of water from the kitchen sink. Not too cold—just the way her friend liked it.

Brittany blew her nose and then added to the mounds of tissues already piled high on the kitchen table.

Walking across the room to give Brittany her water, Amber noticed the trash can overflowed with wads of used tissues. She could remember two times—maybe three—that Brittany had cried over something. This reached far beyond that. Amber had never seen Britt so upset. Of course, she couldn't exactly blame her.

"Britt, tell me what happened." She settled into the chair across the dinette and held one of Brittany's hands between both of hers.

"They said I. . .I. . .cheated on my tests. They aren't going to. . .to let me. . .gr–graduate." Her words started a fresh round of sobbing. "I l–l–lost everything today. College. The scholarship. Everything." Brittany pounded her fist on the table. "But I didn't do it!"

Oh God. "You're just going to have to tell them that, Britt. They'll have to believe you. If you didn't do it, they can't have hard proof that you did. Right?" *She has to get out of this. She has to.*

Brittany snorted. "You'd think. But no. They have proof that I had signed into one of the computers in the computer room with my library password—who else would know my password? And while still supposedly signed in, I hacked into the teacher's files and printed out three final exams. What's worse, I printed ten copies of each. . .supposedly."

"Why does it matter how many they think you printed?" It took all of Amber's strength not to run away, but instead, she pulled her chair closer to Brittany and leaned forward, resting her forearms on the table.

"It matters because they're pressuring me to tell them who else I gave those copies to—or they'll expel me, and I won't even be able to make up the courses in summer school. I have to come up with ten names. Problem is, I didn't do it, so I'd be lying if I gave them names." Brittany's watery eyes looked deeply into Amber's. "Basically, it comes down to this: They said if I tell them, I'll have the chance to make up my classes in the summer. If I don't, I'm expelled."

Expelled. Things grew more serious as the moments drew on. Amber could never come clean, now. *No way.* "You know I love you no matter what. So, you can tell me if you had anything to do with this." That kind of talk should convince Brittany that Amber had nothing to do with it.

"I'm only going to say this to you one more time. I didn't do it. Period. I had nothing to do with it." She buried her head in her arms. "You of all people should know that."

"You're right. I'm as confused by this as you are." Amber stood up, the legs of her chair screeching as she pushed it back across the tile. "Okay then, who could have done it?" Amber tapped on her chin as she paced the floor. "Have you ever shared your password with anyone?"

"I've been racking my brain trying to think of who it could be. But I've never even given my password to you, why would I tell it to anyone else?" She shook her head and released a fresh stream of tears.

"Yeah, that's true. You've never told it to me." *Phew.* "Hey. Where are your mom and dad?" Amber realized she hadn't seen either of them since she'd arrived.

"They're pretty stressed over this. They're hiding out in their room. Probably praying." Brittany's eyes glazed as she watched the rotating blades of the ceiling fan. "You know, I think I'm going to try to sleep. I can't think about this anymore, and I'm all prayed out."

"Okay. One more question, and then I'll go so you can rest." Amber maneuvered her head into Brittany's line of sight, forcing eye contact. "Do your parents believe you?"

Brittany didn't hesitate for a second—didn't even blink. "One hundred percent."

"Okay then, with them by your side and with me in your corner, we'll get you through this. It's totally not fair, but it will pass. I promise." She walked to the front door.

"I hope you're right, Amber." Brittany fell into Amber's outstretched arms for a final hug.

When the door clicked shut behind her, Amber leaned against it for a moment, her heart racing. *What have I done?* She'd destroyed her best friend's life. Now, she alone had the power to stop it from going any further. Amber weighed her options and then the cost. No. There was simply no way she could say anything now. *It's too late.*

She looked toward heaven, then squeezed her eyes shut. *Lord, please don't let anyone find out the truth.*

Wait a minute. What did she say? Did she actually pray that God would help her get away with cheating? *What nerve.* Shaking her head, she hurried to her car, the solitude of her bedroom her only goal.

❀

Parking her car in the garage where they used to park the old one, which now sat on the street in front of the house, didn't have the same excitement it had the day before. Amber hurried into the house, hoping to make it up to her bedroom without having to talk to her parents.

"Amber, honey? Is that you?" Mom's cheerful voice called from the family room.

Amber's stomach flipped. She had to pass through the family room to get to the stairs leading up to her bedroom. There'd be no way to avoid a little chat. "Just getting a Coke."

"Okay. I need to talk to you for just a sec."

"I'll be right there, Mom." Amber reached into the fridge. Oh, right, cola. Oh well, the caffeine would still do its thing. She popped the tab and took a long swig. When she'd stalled long enough, she squared her shoulders and went to face her mom.

"Hey, Mom. What's up?" Amber asked as she casually walked into the family room.

"What's up? Are you serious? Did you see today's paper?"

Amber's heart sank. The newspapers had already reported about Brittany? But Mom looked excited, so that couldn't be it. "What's it about?"

"Let's see. . ." Mom ran her finger down the page as she scanned the paper, probably for the best spot to start reading. "Oh, here it is. 'Local student, Amber Stevens, wowed the school and the community with a record-breaking high-school career. She maintained straight A's throughout all four years of her schooling as well as a perfect attendance record. In a crazy twist. . .' And then it goes on to tell about the contest between you and Brittany and the car you won." Mom beamed. "You're a celebrity, sweetie."

"I don't feel much like a celebrity." While Mom had been reading, Amber realized she should fill her mom in on the details about Brittany, or Mom would wonder why she hadn't. Under normal circumstances, she sure wouldn't be excited about a newspaper with what Brittany was going through. "Did you hear what happened today?"

Concern immediately lined her face. "No. . . What happened?"

"It's Brittany. They caught her cheating. Well, I should say they're accusing her of cheating. She promises that she didn't do it."

"Well, then, I believe her. She's not the type to cheat." Mom stood up and paced across the room. "They're going to have to clear her name." She went the window and then turned to face Amber again. "You aren't suggesting that you think she did it, are you?"

"No, of course not. But. . .well. . .they do have strong evidence." Amber tried to sound logical. "But that doesn't always mean anything."

"Oh, the poor girl. How is she?"

"She's in agony. I mean, think about it. She lost everything today." Amber went to the window and looked out. "Her record, her scholarship, her admission to college, and probably even graduation."

"Oh Lord, help her. Give her peace. Let the truth come out."

Her mom's spontaneous prayer took Amber by surprise. Would she have prayed that if she knew the truth? "I'm not sure even He can help her now, Mom."

"You'd be surprised at what He can do."
Mom stepped over and put her arm around
Amber's shoulder and joined her looking out
the window. "Maybe this situation will be the
faith builder you need, sweetie."

"Maybe." *Maybe not.*

"Before I forget, Kyle called for you. He said
to call him right away."

❁

"You phoned?" Amber didn't bother to hide her
irritation when she returned Kyle's call.

"Stay put. I'm coming over." The phone
went dead.

A feeling of dread washed over Amber.
Suddenly it all came crystal clear to her. Kyle
waiting for her after school with that perplexed
look on his face, phoning her house, coming over
without an explanation. Something happened.
Something had gone wrong, very wrong.

What options did she have? If they were
going to get caught for sure, maybe she should
call someone and confess in a hurry before it
became too late. They would go much easier on
her if she came forward. No, she was getting
ahead of herself. She'd wait to hear what Kyle
had to say.

Amber paced the short distance back and

forth across her room until Kyle arrived.

A knock at her door pulled her from her thoughts. "Come in."

The door swung open and Kyle stood there—a very sad-looking, pale Kyle. "I'm so sorry."

"For what?" Amber voice sounded flat. She figured she knew the answer, but still needed to hear it.

"We're being turned in." Kyle sat down and shook his head. "I never saw this coming. One of the other people I gave the tests to had an attack of conscience and confessed. Now they're making him tell who else cheated."

"There were others? Besides, how would he know, anyway?" Amber already knew. Kyle had a big mouth and liked to brag. He told.

"I told him. Ten people actually used the test, plus me, of course, who accessed and printed them." He shuffled over to the bed and fell back onto it, staring at the ceiling.

Amber didn't care much about anyone else involved. All that mattered now was that she let Brittany take the fall, and now Britt would know the truth. "Is there any chance he hasn't told yet? Is it possible I can still confess?"

"If you'd have stopped to talk to me after school, maybe. But by now, it's too late."

Too late.

Chapter 11

CAUGHT

Zombie-like, Amber made her way from class to class. She'd considered staying home from school that day, after hearing Kyle's news the afternoon before, but what would that have solved? It would have just prolonged the agony. With Brittany not there to see the truth come out, Amber figured it would be best to stare it right in the face.

It didn't take long. Halfway into third period, the loudspeaker clicked on. "Amber Stevens, please come to the office."

It was time. She shuffled out to the hall with her books in her arms. A quick glance at the front doors—she could make a run for it. Her car had a full tank of gas. *My car. . .not for long.* The walk to the office ended all too soon. She stared at the closed door, unable to open it, not wanting to go in.

She heard fumbling with the handle, someone trying to open the door from the inside. Two angry-looking parents finally spilled out into the hallway dragging a student behind them by the sleeves of his jacket. He had his head hung low as they appeared to head for the front entrance.

"Amber?" Principal Warner leaned forward at his desk and looked out through the waiting area to the door that Amber still hadn't walked through.

Time to face the consequences. She somehow made it into the office and then slumped into a chair, but had yet to say a word.

"I take it you know why you're here?"

Amber nodded, tears burning her eyes.

"Why, Amber? Why would you do something so stupid?" Principal Warner shook his head. "In all my years as principal here, I can honestly say this is the biggest shock to me—the biggest waste." He blinked back tears. "I would do anything to erase this—as I'm sure you would, too. But alas, here we are—faced with the harshest reality."

Head down, Amber lifted only her eyes,

begging, pleading for him to do something. What? She had no idea—just something to fix the mess she was in. Anything.

"I'll be calling the other involved students in as a group. But your situation is quite different." He rubbed his forehead. "Your parents are on the way. We'll talk about consequences when they get here. In the meantime, there are some other people who need to see you." He sighed and went to open his door.

Brittany and her parents came through the door. No more tears—only fire.

"How could you?" Brittany roared.

Mrs. Kim grabbed onto her daughter's forearm, but Brittany shook her off.

"This is the absolute worst thing you could have done. You completely betrayed me. It's not the car. It's not the contest. It's not even the cheating. It's that you sat there with me, watching me agonize over being wrongly accused. . .and you did nothing, said nothing." Brittany put her hands on a chair back and looked into Amber's eyes. "What kind of friend—what kind of *person* could do that? You're evil. I never, ever want to see you again."

Amber felt like the breath had been sucked out of her with each word. She slumped in her chair, defeated, deflated. *Brittany's right. I am evil.*

"Brittany, I understand you're hurting. But I think that's enough." Principal Warner stood up at his desk.

Amber glanced at Mr. and Mrs. Kim. "I'm so sorry."

They nodded curtly, but had nothing to say.

"Amber?" The principal held out his hand.

Amber knew what he wanted. She placed the car key into his outstretched palm.

"I'll have the secretary walk out with the Kims and retrieve your belongings from the car."

Amber's ears buzzed—she didn't hear another word. Until her parents arrived.

They blustered into the office. Mom's cheeks were pink like they got when she was angry or nervous. Dad, pale and somber, looked exactly like he had at Aunt Barb's funeral last year.

"Mr. Warner," Dad began, "there has to be some mistake here."

Mom held Amber's gaze, pleading with her eyes. "There is. Right?"

Amber broke eye contact and gave a slight—almost imperceptible—shake to her head. No mistake.

Mom sank into the chair beside Amber and

exhaled like she'd been punched. She reached up a hand for her husband who moved to stand behind her.

He grabbed her hand and squeezed.

"What happened? What happens now? What do we do?" Mom rattled off her questions, not waiting for answers. Then she got to the question she must have most wanted answered. "Why?" She faced her daughter and waited.

Amber shrugged.

Dad stepped forward. "You're going to have to do much better than that, young lady."

Amber winced. It had been years since she'd given them any reason to use that term. "I don't know why. . .well. . .I guess I do know why. I was scared. Scared for me—for my future—and scared for you guys."

"So you think this is the way to solve our family problems? Which, by the way, we repeatedly asked you to leave in God's hands." Mom shook her head in disbelief.

"I *tried* to leave them in His hands—look what happened."

"This isn't God's work, young lady. This is your own doing." Dad's forehead furrowed, causing his bushy black eyebrows to rise to a point over dark, glaring eyes.

"Mom, Dad. I wanted out, but it was too late. I'd already done it and there was no going back. I regretted it almost instantly."

"Hold on a second." Mom stood up, the light dawning. "Brittany wasn't involved in any of this. Was she?" She looked at the principal.

"No. She wasn't."

She looked at her husband, mouth wide open, obviously shocked, and then she turned on Amber. "You mean you let her take the blame for what you did? How could you do that?"

Amber shook her head and started to cry.

"Okay, this isn't going anywhere, and we don't need to put Principal Warner through any more of our family drama. So, let's wrap this up and deal with things at home." Dad turned to the principal. "What now?"

"I'll send all of the details to you in a letter once I meet with the school board. Basically, Amber is dropped from all three classes that she cheated in. She is suspended from school until after graduation and will not graduate with her class. She might be able to make up some of the classes in summer school, but I'm going to have to check on that. She relinquished the car to Brittany already."

"What about college?" Mom whispered, her head in her hands.

"I can't speak for the university, but I can give you my opinion. There's a chance they'll still let her attend after she makes up those classes, but I can't guarantee it. They'll definitely pull her scholarship funds, though."

Amber's stomach churned and threatened revolt. She searched for the trash can in case she needed to throw up. She'd blown it. Ruined everything she'd worked so hard for. Why?

Because I have no faith. That's why.

❀

"I can't believe you!" Mom raged as they entered the kitchen after a silent drive home from the school. "It's like we've never even met you. I'd have never thought you were capable of something like this."

"Sweetheart, calm down." Dad massaged her shoulders.

"Stop it." She turned to him. "Don't you see? It's not the cheating that bothers me so much— well it does, but everyone makes mistakes, and I could get past that. It's the coldhearted way she let her best friend take the blame. What kind of person have we raised here?" She put her hands on the kitchen counter and rocked back and forth.

"I know! I know!" Amber shouted. "I hate myself enough already. I got trapped in my own dumb choices and couldn't find a way out. I made a huge mistake—many huge mistakes. I. . ." Throwing her hands up, she ran from the room without finishing her sentence and stomped up the stairs to her room. She threw herself on the bed and sobbed. *What a mess.*

Some time later, Amber heard a soft knock on the door.

"Can we come in?" Mom's voice called through the door.

"Yeah, I guess so." She pulled herself up and let her legs hang over the edge of the bed. Her head pounded out a drumbeat. Without looking, she heard the door open and soft footsteps pad across the carpet.

"Amber." Mom spoke gently. "Can we start over? I didn't handle myself very well downstairs, and I'm sorry for that." She sat down on the edge of the bed. "But we do need to talk. Okay?"

"Sure. I guess." Amber hung her head and bit her fingernail.

Dad cleared his throat. "First of all, your mom and I are disappointed on so many levels. We really don't know what to do or what to think."

"Did you even think about Kyle"—Mom

started with the frustration evident in her tone, and then took a breath. With more control, she continued—"and the trouble he'd get into, before you let him cheat for you?"

"He was going to cheat anyway. He's the one who offered." Amber knew she shouldn't try to defend herself, but she didn't feel bad for Kyle, of all people.

"I wouldn't be so sure about that. You know how he's always looked up to you and wanted you two to be friends." Mom waved her hand and shook her head. "But that's not the point here. I want to know what went through your mind to convince you to do this. Why, Amber? Make me understand."

Amber stood up, exasperated. "Mom. You'll never understand, because I don't get it, either. I felt compelled to win that contest. Originally, I wanted the recognition because I hoped it would help me get into college. I wanted to have a career one day that would help you guys out." She threw her hands in the air as she paced the room. "Then, when I got the scholarship, all I cared about was getting that car—we needed that car. I don't know. . .it was such a mistake." She sat down on the floor and leaned against the bed, drawing her knees up to her chest and putting her head in her hands in one motion. "I wish I could take it all back."

"Well, sadly, that's not possible." Dad reached down a hand and stroked her hair. "Amber, it pains me to realize how much of the burden for this family you carried on your shoulders. Why couldn't you trust us a little more? Trust God, even?"

"I don't know," Amber mumbled. "What's going to happen to me?"

"A lot of this is going to take time to figure out." Dad shook his head. "Summer school is a sure thing."

"And UW is out." Mom sighed.

"Out?" Amber squeaked. "Why out? Principal Warner said they might still let me go."

"They might—although I doubt it. It's a competitive entrance process. There are lots of students eager and willing to take your place. But even if they let you attend. . ." Mom shrugged her shoulders.

"What, even if. . .what?"

"We can't pay that tuition. You know that." Mom looked away. "Without the scholarship. . ."

Dad cleared his throat again. "You'll have to go to community college."

Ah. There it is. The final death knell to her

dreams had sounded. Amber knew she had no one to blame but herself. "Yeah. I guess you're right." She nodded and tried not to cry.

"Amber, your dad and I love you very much. We're so sad this happened, and we're both trying hard to figure out how we can all pull out of it. You need to give us some time."

"I understand that, Mom. My problem is that I can't figure out how to make people believe how sorry I am. Not just because I got caught—I'm really truly sorry." Amber wiped her eyes. "You know, a lot of people have mentioned my lack of faith. It's been a real problem, and it's something I want to fix. You may or may not realize, but I was starting to try to find my way to God—a real relationship with God. I just dragged my feet a little too long, I think."

She shook her head. *If only.* "I hope. . .well. . . I hope you'll let me do that and accept my apology. I don't want this to define me, but I'm so afraid it already has." She put her face into her hands, her shoulders shaking with the sobs.

"Amber, that's what I've been waiting to hear. Something real that tells us how you feel." Mom slid to the floor beside her and pulled her close.

"Have we ever kept you from growing?" Dad sounded perplexed.

"No."

"Well, don't think for a moment we're going to start now. We'll figure this out, and we will not let this define you," Dad promised. "Now, not to change the subject, although I'm sure we'll be talking about this for days, weeks—who knows, probably months." Dad chuckled. "But we have some news that we need to share with you—even if the timing's all wrong. You want to give her the bullet points? I'm spent." Dad sat in the desk chair and waited for Mom to speak.

"Yeah, sure." She sighed. "Your dad was offered a job today. It's at the community college about forty minutes away from UW. He starts in August. So, right after you're done with summer school, we'll be moving. You'll go to school there because you'll get free tuition since your dad's going to be a teacher there."

"Wow. That's great. Congratulations on the job, Dad." Amber knew she should be more excited for her family. A fresh start. But she felt too drained to care that much. "I'm sure it'll sink in after I get some rest. I'll have questions then, okay?"

"Sure, we'll talk more tomorrow." Dad rose to leave the room. "Are you going to eat some dinner?"

"I'm too tired." Amber climbed between her sheets. "I'll eat tomor–"

The next thing she knew, the room was pitch black save for the red glow of the digital numbers on the clock beside the bed. She rolled over, stretched, and opened one eye to peer at the clock. 4:13.

Ugh. If she didn't get back to sleep, she would have a horrible day at school. *Oh, wait. No school for me.* No way she'd be able to fall back to sleep after ten straight hours, so she decided to get up. Time to deal with a few things.

Amber went to her desk and took out a few sheets of paper and a pen. E-mail just didn't seem appropriate. Certain circumstances demanded the special effort of a handwritten note.

> *Dear Brittany,*
>
> *Where do I start? How can I ever come up with words that will make you understand what happened—why I did what I did? I'm afraid I'll never be able to. My biggest fear is that you'll never speak to me again and never truly understand how sorry I am and how much I love you.*
>
> *You are my sister, my soul.*
>
> *I know, you're thinking, "How could*

she do that to someone she claims to love so much?" I wish I had a good answer. The whole thing started as a way for me to win the car and help my parents. Things haven't been good around my house, financially—but you know that already, and it's no excuse for cheating. But it is why I did what I did . . .initially. Then, when Kyle told me you were going to be framed for it, I felt trapped. I agonized over coming forward with the truth, but I couldn't bring myself to do it. In a weird way, I convinced myself that you wouldn't want me to, that you'd want to me hang on to the "prize," so to speak.

I can't believe I thought that! I know now that I was rationalizing. It's all so stupid—I was so wrong. Please, please, please forgive me. Please, Brittany.

My dad got a job today. We're going to be moving in August. I'll be living about forty minutes from the UW campus. I'll even get to go to the community college there. I've lost a lot, but one thing I'm going to gain is my family back and the start of a real search for faith and God. I hope you'll help me with that search. Is there any way, Britt? Please?

With all my love,
Amber

Chapter 12

FORGIVEN, WITH A PRICE

"Summer school's not that bad." Amber told her mom while they washed dishes together. Being grounded brought on a lot of family togetherness. "It could be a lot worse." She had nothing to do, and no one to do it with, anyway.

"Yeah, poor Kyle has it a lot worse."

"I had no idea he'd been in trouble before. I hope he gets things figured out. He's getting his GED, right?"

"Yeah, he's working on it. His future isn't very bright right now, though." Mom shook her head. "It's so sad."

"Yeah. I'm thankful that I've got three weeks down. Only three more to go." Amber counted down the days until their move. She couldn't wait for the fresh start. Go to a new school. Make some new friends. Find a church. It had been a lonely few weeks.

"Hellooooo?" Mom waved her hand in front of Amber's glazed eyes. "Are you going to wash those dishes or just stand there?" Her eyes twinkled.

"Sorry. Daydreaming." Amber started scrubbing again.

"Obviously." Mom stacked some plates in the dishwasher. "Hey, what do you say we get up early and go for a run? It might be our last one together before the move. Things are going to get busy around here."

"Okay. I'm good with that. Just. . .Mom. . ." Amber hesitated.

"What is it?"

"It's just. . .can we please not run like we're out to prove something? A couple of miles at a nice steady pace—like when I run by myself. That's enjoyable, invigorating even. I don't want to have to crawl into bed after we're done."

Mom laughed and flicked water into Amber's face. "Wimp."

"Hey, I've been called worse. I can take it."

"After dishes, want to find your dad and play Risk?"

"No, I think I'm going to go to my room, work on some homework, maybe even read something that isn't homework." Too much togetherness.

"Okay, Dad and I can play Yahtzee or something. Join us if you change your mind."

Not likely. Amber smiled to herself as she headed for her room. Mom and Dad were great parents—she wouldn't trade them for the world. But they were still Mom and Dad. *Sigh.* A college-bound eighteen-year-old shouldn't have to get all of her entertainment from her own parents, no matter how wonderful. *Things are bound to change once we move—they have to.*

Mom knocked on the door before she opened it a crack to whisper, "Six a.m. We'll run the track at the high school since we'll be on a time limit."

At least she knocked. "Okay, Mom. I'll be up." Amber forced a smile. "Would you mind shutting the door?"

"Sure, sweetie. 'Night."

❀

The chirping of birds followed Amber's lone figure up the mountain pass. The last time she'd run this particular path, it had been snowing and she'd been with her mom and Brittany.

This time, she ran alone. While she was still in summer school, she'd taken to running after class—it brought her healing, time to think.

Time—it moved so fast. . . . Thank God for that. Amber tried to put the past few months behind her with each step she took. She looked around the familiar terrain. In all likelihood, it would be the last time she'd ever be in this spot. Tomorrow was the big move, and she couldn't see getting back to Gwinett any time soon. Sometimes a fresh start meant never looking back. Would she be able to do that?

Good-bye. Good-bye. Good-bye. She recited the mantra in her head with each footfall. Good-bye to the home and the town where she'd lived all her life. Good-bye to her school. Good-bye to her mountain. *Good-bye, Brittany? No.* Amber shook her head, not willing to let go of her, yet. Unfinished business made it so difficult to let go.

Amber ran longer than she usually did. It felt so good, she didn't want it to end. *Where are You, Lord?* She searched; her soul cried out. . . but she found silence. Was she looking in the wrong place? Her body tired, she sank into the car after an almost four-mile run. She hadn't made it all the way to the top, to the waterfall, but she got close enough to hear it, close enough to feel it. Good enough—wasn't it?

On the drive down the mountain toward home, Amber decided she couldn't leave without giving it one last try. She'd see if Brittany would come to the door today. Turning right instead of left at the bottom of the mountain, she drove the short distance to Brittany's house.

Parked in the driveway a few minutes later, Amber's legs felt like rubber. From the run or from nerves? Probably both. Lights shone in the house, but that didn't necessarily mean they were home. Then, one of the bedroom lights shut off as someone must have left the room.

Amber blew all of the air out of her lungs— still not fully recovered from her run—and inhaled deeply. What would she say to Brittany if she came to the door? What would she do if she didn't?

Please, God. Ah, He hadn't gotten in the habit of answering her prayers yet, so what made her think He'd start now?

She climbed from the car and shut the door with a soft click, not wanting the sound of the car to alert anyone to her presence. Stepping onto the porch stoop, Amber reached up and pressed the doorbell. She moved in with her ear against the door so she could make sure it actually rang. Last time she had to ring twice because, when no one came to the door, she thought it possible she hadn't pressed hard enough. Not this time, though. It resounded through the house.

Amber waited. Maybe they were in the bathroom. And waited. Maybe only one person was home and in the bathroom when she rang. Should she ring again. . .just in case no one heard it? She pressed the button a second time. And waited. No one came. Should she try knocking in case the bell was broken? But no, she'd heard it ring. Twice. Time for Amber to face facts. Brittany knew she was there but wouldn't talk to her.

Amber turned away and shuffled to her car, hoping someone would have a quick change of heart and come running after her. She listened for the sound of fumbling with the door locks, someone shouting, "Wait!" from an upstairs window. Something. But nothing happened, so she got into her car and drove away.

She thought it should hurt more, and it did hurt. . .but not nearly as much as it had at first. *Not nearly as much as Brittany hurt, I'm sure.*

❋

"Careful with that one!" Amber called to one of the super-sized movers who had a box of her mom's prized antique dishes balancing on his shoulder as he jogged up the brick porch steps to the dining room. Better not to look. Amber shook her head and checked her watch. Ten thirty. Mom and Dad thought they'd be back with the paint samples by then. She couldn't wait to get back to unpacking and setting up her new room, but someone had to babysit the gorillas.

As they went for another load of boxes, Amber's thoughts returned to the day before. It had taken them almost five hours to drive out to their old house, just on the other side of the mountains.

When she toured their new house for the first time, Amber had been shocked at the bright, fresh feeling of the new construction. The walls were white, but Mom planned to remedy that as soon as possible, thus the trip to the paint store for swatches. Wood floors gleamed in every room of the house. Mom had always wanted a house with no carpet— supposed to be good for allergies. The huge windows—floor to ceiling in some places—let in tons of bright light, and the vaulted ceilings in the great room lent a cavernous feel to the place. *Awesome.*

Amber's favorite part of the whole house was the enormous fireplace that divided the dining room and family room—people on both sides could enjoy the fire and even see through to the other room. The weather had already started to turn toward fall, and it would get lots of use.

Speaking of lots of use. . . Amber chuckled to herself, *the whirlpool tub.* She smiled at the thought of the endless hours her mom would soak in the warm water with the jets pummeling her sore muscles after a long run—she deserved every minute of it. Mom had been so excited at the prospect of having her own whirlpool tub in her very own bathroom that she'd gone shopping for special scented powders that she could use without clogging up the jets.

Crash!

"Wha–" Amber jerked from her thoughts and ran into the dining room. No one there. *Phew.* The crash had been something other than the china. . .but what?

She hurried from the dining room through the bright kitchen and out to the garage.

"What's going on out here?" With her hands on her hips, she stared down four of the beefiest men she'd ever seen.

One smirked. "Simmer down, cupcake."

"Hey!" *They can't talk to me like that.*

Another one, probably the boss, shot him a dirty look. "Miss, everything's fine. That crash you heard was one of our dollies falling from the truck. No harm done."

"Oh. Okay." She suddenly became aware of her stance and relaxed. "Sorry I overreacted. I just want this day to be perfect for my mom. It's her birthday, you know."

"I didn't know that. We'll have to make sure it's a special one." He turned to his men. "Back to work, boys."

Satisfied, Amber turned to leave the garage. For what seemed like the hundredth time that day, she glanced each way down the street before walking into the house. What was she looking for? It felt uneasy, as though something was about to. . .or should.. . .happen. They weren't expecting visitors, but something was missing. Amber watched the street for signs of life, or a sign of something anyway. No cars headed her way, no one moved about on the streets. Who did she expect to see anyway?

187

Brittany. That's what was missing. Brittany should be there sharing the change with her, helping her make this new house a home, exploring the town. But no. She wouldn't be coming. Nothing had been the same since she cut Amber out of her life. Britt had never replied to the letter, never answered her phone, wouldn't come to her door—she had washed her hands of her best friend. How could someone do that?

Amber snorted—amazed at her own thoughts. She'd been the bad friend—not Brittany. She couldn't blame Brittany for being so mad and hurt, but she sure did miss her.

What if she never forgives me? Amber couldn't shake that thought as she turned back toward the house. *What if?*

"I FORGIVE YOU."

Amber reeled back, stopped in her tracks by a powerful force. The thought—the words—hit Amber's gut, pierced her heart like an arrow shot from a bow. She knew those words were intended for her, and somehow she knew they had come from God.

She grabbed hold. Waves of peace washed over her. She stood and reveled in the feeling, engulfed by complete acceptance. Amber felt loved. The warmth, the presence, surrounded her—she didn't feel alone anymore, never would. She'd found what she'd been looking for all this time. It had been right there, she needed to reach out for it, to grab on and claim it for herself.

Amber made her way to the front porch where she sank into the swing and took in the scenery. No more looking back. No more looking side to side, up and down the street. No more waiting. Amber looked up to the hills—to the mountains. There she found her hope.

My Decision

I, *(include your name here)*, have read the story of Amber Stevens and have learned from the choices she made and the consequences she faced in both her education and her relationships.

So:

- I will avoid cheating in any form: sharing homework, cheating on tests, plagiarism, etc.
- I will be honest in all things, even when it means I might face hardships.
- I will guard my friendships and uphold my sense of loyalty, treating my friends as I would want to be treated.

Please pray the following prayer:

Father God, please let the lessons I learned as I read about Amber imprint onto my heart, that I might remember to uphold these standards I've committed to. Help me to be an honest person in all things, placing honor and godliness above personal gain, recognition, success or anything else the world might dangle before me. I know You have everything under control, so I submit to Your will. Amen.

Congratulations on your decision! Please sign this contract signifying your commitment. Have someone you trust, like a parent or a pastor, witness your choice.

_____

Signed

_____

Witnessed by

ESSENCE OF LILLY

DEDICATION

Wil, when I think about true love and God's design for marriage, I'm so grateful He led me to you. Your sense of humor and your patience have taught me so much—you bring music to our home. I wrote this book—which deals with one of life's touchiest subjects—with the desire to help our daughters prepare for their future. You are a wonderful father, and I pray our girls demand nothing less in a husband. I love you.

—Nicole

Chapter 1

IN A CORNER

Lilly LeMure pressed the pillow over her ears, trying to drown out the shouting. *You can't hear them. Nothing's happening. You're safe in your room.*

No use. The voices coming from down the hall grew louder.

"You need to get a real job. You're getting fat and dumb sitting behind a desk all day, fetching coffee for middle managers." Stan's voice held an edge, taunting Mom to fight back—which she usually did.

"That's not what I do, and you know it. How can you even say that?" Mom's voice rose with each word. "I make more money than you. You're just lazy."

Didn't they care that Lilly could hear everything they said? She squeezed the pillow harder. Fights between Mom and Stan headed downhill fast—faster each time. She pondered the few moments of peace that had peppered the past few years. Those times used to be more frequent but were a rarity lately.

Still covering her ears, Lilly strained to hear sounds of the fight. Silence. She slowly let go of one side of the pillow and waited a few more seconds—no yelling. Releasing the other side, she sat up on her bed, letting the pillow fall to the floor, then leaned toward the door to listen.

Lilly's West Highland terrier jumped up on the bed, nails plucking at the crocheted afghan, and started licking her hand. "Not now, Paisley. Shh." She moved the fluffy little dog to the floor and leaned even closer to the door.

A thick blanket of blond hair hung over her eye. She brushed the hair away and tucked it behind her ear, but it fell right back. Irritated, Lilly pulled the hair tie from around her wrist and gathered all of her thick, straight hair into her hands, twisted it into a bun, and slipped the band around the whole thing, securing it behind her head, out of her way.

There it was. *Sigh.* Muffled crying. The familiar sound of Mom's soft sobs. Lilly looked up at the ceiling and shook her head. Why did

Mom always let it come to this? What kind of person allowed herself to get pushed and worked up to the point of tears so often? What a way to live.

She waited a few minutes to make sure the fight didn't start up again. It rarely did after Mom dissolved, but Lily could never be sure. No loud bangs, no yelling, no dangerous crashes. All she heard was the sound of her mom crying.

Unwilling to let Mom suffer alone, Lilly stood up. She tugged her sweater down to cover her midriff and stepped over her pillow on the way to the door. One hand on the knob, she took a deep breath. Blowing the air from her lungs, Lilly opened the door swiftly to keep the hinges from squealing, then stepped out into the hallway.

She crept toward her mom's bedroom, trying to step over the floorboards that creaked—no sense alerting Stan to her presence. Peering around the corner and through the doorway, Lilly's breath caught at the scene. Mom sat on the floor, her back against the wall with her knees drawn to her chest and poking out through the slit in her once-pink fuzzy bathrobe. A faded pink slipper covered one foot, but the other was bare. Lilly's eyes located the missing shoe on the floor across the room where it had most likely been thrown.

Why, Mom? Didn't she believe she was worth more than this? Paisley snuck into the room, went right to Mom, and started licking the pink toenail polish on her naked foot.

No light shone from the bathroom, and except for the sobs, the room stood silent. Stan must have left the house. Had the garage door gone up? Lilly couldn't remember hearing it, but it was possible she just hadn't noticed. What should she do? If Stan was in there, she sure didn't want to draw any attention to herself. Go to Mom? Wait?

The door to Stan's walk-in closet flew open and banged against the wall. He barged out with his coat on and keys in his hand, then stormed across the room and blustered through the doorway Lilly leaned against. Stan didn't say a word—didn't even glance at her. Invisible—which she preferred at times like this.

Lilly heard the garage door go up. She waited. A few seconds later, it went down. Mom used to beg him not to drive when he got like this—now she just let him leave.

With Stan finally gone for sure, Lilly hurried

across the room, stepping over a lamp and several books strewn across the floor. Crouching beside her mom on the floor, Lilly put her arms around her. "Are you hurt anywhere?"

Mom shrugged her shoulders and shook Lilly's hands off her arms. "I'm fine. We only had a little argument." She wiped her nose with her sleeve. "He didn't mean anything by all of this. Stan's been working two part-time jobs, and now he's feeling pressure to get another one. He'll be okay."

Sigh. Same old excuses. *Stan's under pressure. Stan didn't mean it. Stan means well.* It had been four years. When would it end? When would Mom get some self-respect? She still seemed to hope Lilly would grow to like, even love, Stan. Not a chance.

Lord, please help her. "Okay, Mom. You want to be alone?"

Mom ran her fingers through her mop of curly hair—dyed to her original honey blond, which matched her daughter's—then blew her red, puffy nose into a crumpled tissue. "Yeah. I'll pull myself together and be downstairs in a few minutes."

Lilly knew what came next—it always happened the same way. She'd leave, and Mom would start bawling again—might even turn on the tub faucet to drown out the sounds of her sobs. Eventually, she'd take a shower, trying to wash away the tears. After about an hour, Mom would emerge from her bedroom with makeup on, fresh clothes, perfume trailing behind her—the works. All in an effort to prove she had it together. The next day, Stan and Mom would be all lovey-dovey. They'd spend the day together and pretend they were newlyweds. Then, on Sunday, they'd sit beside each other at church, hold hands, smile, and nod along with the sermon. Monday? It would start all over.

Lilly walked from the room and pulled the door toward her. Right before it closed, she tilted her head and waited. On cue, the faucet came on in a loud gush, but not before the crying resumed. Unable to listen any longer, she hurried to her room and shut the door. Ridiculous. She'd never let a man treat her like that. Shouldn't a husband love and protect his wife? Not badger and belittle her, that's for sure. Not that Mom acted like a perfect wife, but still.

Lilly reached for her phone. Talking to Jason always made her feel better. Holding down the number two button until the speed dial kicked in, she waited for it to connect. Oh fun. He'd changed his caller tune. As she waited for him to pick up, she listened to a few bars of a love song they'd heard on the radio the other day.

"Hey, cutie." Jason answered his phone with his customary greeting.

"Hey." Lilly smiled. "I like the new caller tune. Sweet of you to remember."

"Ah, I'm like that—nice, ya know."

"Yeah. I'm the only one who can hear it, though. Right?"

"'Course. You think I want my buddies hearing me be all romantic like that?"

"Ha-ha. I'm going to tell them." Memories of the past hour flew from her mind; stress rolled off her shoulders.

"You go right ahead. They'll never believe old manly me is sappy."

"You're probably right." Lilly wished she could see him. His clear blue eyes always had a calming effect on her. "What are you doing right now?"

"I'm hanging out in Dad's garage. We're changing the oil in his car and replacing the filter so we can tuck 'er in for winter."

Lilly could picture Jason in his greasy work jeans and a white T-shirt with oily handprints, bent over the tricked-out hood of his dad's vintage silver Jaguar. They babied that car, treated her like a pretty lady should be treated. She wondered if he'd shoved his thick, wavy hair into a cap as he sometimes did when he worked. His brown curls never stayed tucked under there for long.

"Sounds like fun." Lilly put a carefree lilt in her voice, not wanting to distract him with her worries. "I won't keep you then. Just checking in."

"'S'okay. Your voice sounds like you're lying down, which usually means you're frustrated. Which always means there was a fight."

How did he know that? He could see into her soul—knew better than anyone it seemed. "Yeah. No biggie, though. Don't even worry about it."

"We'll talk about it, cutie. Later tonight, okay?"

"I'll be looking forward to it." Lilly smiled. "Call me when you're free." She pressed the OFF button on her phone and slipped it into the front pocket of her jeans. She rested her hands under her head and stared at the ceiling. Stan and Jason. Different as night and day. Her stepfather could really take some sensitivity lessons from her boyfriend. Poor Mom. She deserved someone like Jason—not like the jerk she married.

202

Enough. Lilly stood up, adjusted her sweater again, and resolved to put the misery behind her and grab something worthwhile out of the afternoon. She looked out the window. There were tons of leaves all over the yard. Maybe if she raked them up, Jason—or maybe even Stan—would burn them; the smell of burning leaves would put everyone in a good mood. Plus, it would sure feel good to get outside in the fresh air.

While Lilly dug in the hall closet for something warm to wear, she finally heard the shower stop. She pictured her mom toweling off, looking at her puffy face and red eyes in the mirror, wondering how she could possibly hide the evidence of the afternoon. She'd be awhile.

Pulling on boots and a green puffy vest, Lilly hurried out of the house, letting the aluminum screen door snap shut with a slam. If Stan were home, he'd bellow from his recliner, "Don't slam the door." Lilly realized long ago that Stan much preferred to pretend she didn't exist than to hear her or, worst of all, see her. Fighting the urge to go slam the door again, Lilly went to the garage for a rake.

The leaves were wet and heavy from the damp Chicago weather. She inhaled deeply, replacing the stale air of the depressing house. The leaves gathered easily at first. *Pull. Drag. Pull.* Lilly's muscles ached, but she kept going— she felt alive. The burn started in her shoulders; then her elbows started to scream. After a bit, blisters formed on her hands. No matter—she felt in control, invigorated.

Two hours later, spent but revived, Lilly looked at the green grass. Leaves that had once blanketed the grass now stood heaped—one pile on each side of the house, two in the front yard and three in the back. It would take a wheelbarrow to get them all to one big burn pile in the backyard.

Trudging up the sloped backyard with a wheelbarrow full of sopping wet leaves proved harder than Lilly had imagined. Two more loads about did her in. Facing the burn pile, she wondered what would happen if she burned the rest of the piles right on the lawn where they sat. *Nah.* Stan would consider that justifiable cause for homicide. Maybe he'd be right. Lilly shook her head at her own crazy thoughts and turned around to grab the wooden handles of the wheelbarrow with her blistered fingers. To her surprise, a familiar blue Toyota pulled to a stop in her driveway.

Jason!

She released her grip, ran over to the car, and leaned down to look in the window.

Jason, dressed exactly as Lilly had imagined he would be, reached over to turn down the music. He flashed his movie-star teeth in a grin.

Lilly opened the door and stood aside so he could climb out. "What are you doing here? I thought you were helping your dad."

"I was. I did." Jason pulled her close in a playful hug. "But you needed me more."

"Thanks. I'm so glad you're here." Relieved, Lilly watched as he surveyed the yard.

"You do all this by yourself?"

"Yeah, and I have the blisters to prove it." She held up her raw, peeling hands.

"Oh man. That must hurt." Jason got some leather work gloves from his trunk and pulled them on. He walked over to the wheelbarrow. "What's left? Just those few piles?"

"They need to go in back onto the big one. You'll see it when you get back there." Lilly breathed a sigh of relief as Jason dug in with a rake, putting his strong shoulders to use.

Jason would make everything all right.

Chapter 2

MY LILLY

"Want to go out and get something to eat?" Jason looked hopeful. "All that raking made me hungry."

"What, and leave this haven of bliss even for a moment?" Lilly gestured around her dark house from the dining room table where they sat talking. Stan had returned from pouting and taken his throne in front of the television where he'd likely remain all evening, even through dinner. Mom puttered in the kitchen making bologna sandwiches—those and a bag of ruffled potato chips to rest on his belly, and Stan would be in heaven. Lilly rolled her eyes at the thought.

"Right." Jason smirked and shook his head. "As much as I'd love to, you know as well as

I do, he isn't going to let me." Lilly shrugged and jerked her head toward the family room. "He doesn't let you in my room. I'm not allowed out after dark, even on the weekends. No way he'll let me go out to dinner on a school night unless it's for a school or church activity."

"Why don't you ask your mom? Why even ask Stan?"

Lilly dropped her voice to a whisper. "Because my mom doesn't have an opinion about things these days—you know that. She isn't given a say in what goes on." She looked toward the kitchen entrance. "Watch. I'll show you."

Sliding her chair back, Lilly walked into the kitchen and stepped up behind her mom, who stood at the counter spreading Miracle Whip on white bread. Mom preferred real mayonnaise, but Stan hated it. So, no more real mayo. "Mom?"

She whipped around with a stunned expression—must not have heard Lilly approach. "Ooh. You scared me." She laughed while she fanned her face and patted her chest. "What is it, Lill?"

"Calm down. . .it's just me." Lilly laughed, relieved at the lightened mood. *Must act casual.* "I wanted to ask if Jason and I could go for a quick burger."

Mom's eyes darted toward the family room.

"You'll have to ask Stan about that." She returned her focus to the sandwiches, slapping even more Miracle Whip onto the bread.

Gross. Lilly grimaced and shook her head. "Mom. Can't you make the call? You parented me alone after Dad left until I turned twelve. If I remember correctly, you did a pretty good job of it those six years. You make the decision for once."

She gripped the counter and leaned her head down, almost between her elbows. "Don't put me in that position, Lill. Not today."

Enough's enough. "If not today, when, Mom? Don't you think this is all going too far?"

"What's going too far?" Stan spoke from the doorway.

Mom's arms stiffened and her shoulders tensed, but she didn't turn around at the sound of Stan's voice. "We were talking about how Lilly and Jason want to go out to grab a burger right now."

Stan snorted. "Yeah, like that's going to happen." He grabbed a handful of chocolate chip cookies from the cookie jar and left the room, leaving a trail of crumbs behind him.

Lilly waited, but her mom never turned around or commented. "Whatever." Shaking her head in disgust, Lilly stormed out of the kitchen and into the dining room where Jason sat. She tilted her head toward the front door. "Outside."

They stepped out onto the porch and sat down on the brick stoop, legs touching. Lilly hadn't put on a coat, and the night air felt chilly, but she didn't care. After being in the stifling house, the cold felt good.

"I'm sorry things are so rough for you." Jason stuck his hands in the pockets of his leather jacket.

Lilly shivered and nodded. "It'll be okay. I just get fed up sometimes. I wish my mom could be stronger."

Jason tugged his coat off his arms and slipped it around her trembling shoulders. He pulled her close. "Yeah. I'm sure you do. She probably wishes the same thing."

"But she *is* strong sometimes—in a weird way. He pushes her buttons and she gets really mad. *Crazy* mad. Then he does something stupid like throwing a lamp or knocking over a chair." Lilly shook her head. "Why get married if you can't respect each other? I'll never stand for that. . .never."

"I guess they probably rushed into things

and didn't know how it would be. Now they're kind of stuck. And," Jason shrugged, "maybe in a weird way they even love each other."

"They need serious help. . . . We all do, I guess."

Lilly and Jason sat silently on the cold bricks, staring at the starry sky. Jason reached over and took her blistered hand from her lap. He held it between both of his and looked deeply into her eyes. "It's going to be okay."

She tried to believe him. "I know." Lilly forced a smile and nodded. "You know what else? I wish Mom had stuck to her promise that I could date when I turned sixteen. I mean, how long are you going to put up with having to hang out with me at home all the time? You're seventeen, after all. Plus, you have normal parents."

"Oh, that doesn't matter much to me. I'm not going anywhere." Jason winked and smiled. "You're my Lilly."

Comforted, Lilly leaned back against his chest and shoulder. She felt at peace, safe, loved. How long had she known Jason? Ten. . .no, twelve years. They'd shared a neighborhood, a church, and a school for almost her whole life— all she could remember anyway. He became her best friend. Her future. Her soul mate.

At first it had seemed weird to think of Jason like that. Lilly smiled at the memory and nuzzled in a little closer. Until about the time she turned twelve, he'd just been *Jason*. But then something clicked—Jason turned cute. Over the past four years, they'd grown closer and closer. "My rock," she whispered.

"Huh? Did you say something?"

Did she say that out loud? "No, no. Just mumbling. . . . Nothing important."

❀

"Ugh. It's so good to get out of there, Grams." Lilly sank into the passenger seat of her grandma's Saab Turbo. "Where're we going?"

"Two girls, out on the town with no parental fuddy-duddies? Why, shopping, my dear, of course." Grams flipped down her visor, checked her lipstick, and adjusted her short, spiky wig.

Lilly smiled at her. No one would ever guess Grams to be sixty-five. She looked younger, but more than that, she had the spirit of youth. Even a bout with breast cancer hadn't slowed her down more than a day or two at a time. Lilly remembered the day, the moment, a few months ago when she found out her beloved Grams's cancer had gone into remission. She had been so scared—what would she ever do without her Grams? She shuddered, grateful she didn't have to find out.

The bass thundered through the car—*boom, boom, boom*—as the Christian rock music thundered from the car speakers. Grams bounced and danced in her seat as the little rocket sped along the highway toward the mall.

"Grams, do you ever drive the speed limit?" Lilly laughed as the needle on the speedometer hit eighty miles per hour.

"Nah. I've got places to go and things to do. When you get to be my age, a speed limit feels like a waste of good precious time." She flipped the satellite station when a slow song came on.

"What if you get a ticket?"

"I guess I'd have to pay it. I can afford it." Grams winked. "Oh, unless I can flirt my way out of it. Show a little leg, you know?" She lifted the leg of her jeans just enough to show Lilly a veiny ankle.

Lilly grinned and shook her head. "You're crazy."

"Nah. I'm not crazy." Grams looked in her side mirror and changed lanes to go around a Honda.

"Certifiable." Lilly winked. "But I wouldn't

have it any other way."

Grams turned the car into a parking lot and pulled into a space right in front of Lilly's favorite restaurant, Olive Garden.

"Can I interest you in some lunch?" Grams gave a little bow toward the door.

"Oh cool! Really?" Lilly scampered out of the car. In such a hurry to get out of the house that morning, she'd skipped breakfast. She'd eaten half a bologna sandwich the night before and nothing since. "I'm absolutely starving."

They got seated right away, and Lilly picked up a menu, but Grams left hers on the table. "Why don't you order for us both, Lill. Whatever you want."

"Great! I know just the thing." Lilly looked at the waitress. "We'll each have a cup of the chicken gnocchi soup. We'd also like an order of bruschetta. As an entrée, I'll have the chicken alfredo. She'll have the ravioli." Lilly paused and looked at Grams. "We'll share them both."

"That sounds perfect."

"Okay, then, anything else I can get you?" The waitress waited, her pen poised on her order pad.

"Oh, an iced tea—unsweetened—and a Coke. That should do it." Lilly closed her menu

213

and handed it to the waitress.

"So, Lill." Grams folded her hands on the table in front of her and leaned forward. "Talk to me. What on earth is happening at home?"

Lilly sighed and shook her head. "It's bad. Really bad." She waited while the server sat their drinks in front of them, then filled Grams in on all the details, leaving nothing out.

Grams didn't say a word while Lilly talked.

The bruschetta and soup came to the table at the same time. Famished, Lilly picked up her soupspoon and started to tear right into hers.

Grams covered her hand and squeezed gently. "Let's give the Lord His due first." She bowed her head, still holding Lilly's hand. "My heavenly Father, I thank You for the decadent food You provide for us to sustain our bodies in such a pleasurable way. I also thank You for the rich food You feed to our souls. Guide us through this time of uncertainty and need. Show Your presence among us and our loved ones. Amen."

"Amen." Lilly smiled. Grams always had a way with words. Really knew how to get to the heart of a matter. Lilly picked up her spoon and scooped up a gnocchi, blew the steam away, and then took a bite. *Oh. So good.*

Grams swallowed a bit of soup but quickly put down her spoon. "Listen, doll. I heard everything you said. I want to give you a wise piece of advice that will change everything for you, but, sadly, I don't have any." She picked up her spoon and started to take a bite but returned it to her bowl. "The thing is, words can't change this. Only God's divine intervention can accomplish His will. What you need to do, Lilly, is join me on a prayer campaign. We need to pray every day—for your mom, for Stan—"

"But—"

"Yes. You need to pray for Stan. He might not be acting like someone worthy of your effort, but God still loves him. He can work a miracle—even in Stan. But you have to ask Him to." Grams took a bite and chewed slowly, obviously deep in thought. "The other thing, Lilly, is that you need to get things on the right footing between you and God even in the midst of all that's going on. Even when you think your mom and Stan are hypocrites, even when you don't see or feel much love at home. Turn to Jesus for approval and love."

"I get what you're saying. But it's so hard." Lilly fought the urge to scrape the bottom of her bowl and grabbed a piece of bruschetta instead.

"I know. I fear for you right now, Lill."
Grams shook her head and looked down at her
soup. "This is such a touchy age for you. You're
on the edge. You'll slip off to one side or the
other as you choose your path. I want you to
choose the path that leads to life, joy, happiness,
peace. Not to chase after the happiness that
the world promises, which only leads to
destruction."

"I hear you, Grams. Really." Lilly wanted the
heavy stuff to be over. She'd had enough of that
lately.

Probably sensing her need, Gram's face
brightened. "Okay then, that's all I wanted to
hear. Now, look behind you."

Lilly turned to see the waitress with two
steaming plates of Italian pasta—her favorite. She
set the plate of chicken alfredo in front of Lilly.
Another waiter stepped forward and offered her
fresh Parmesan cheese and a pepper mill.

"Lots, please." Lilly leaned back to give him
access to her plate.

"Mmm. This is delicious." Grams wiped the
corners of her mouth. "Food, then shopping.
We're on the hunt for the perfect pair of jeans."

"I'm not sure I need jeans. I need tops more
than jeans. Oh, and shoes—totally need some

shoes." She picked up her drink and took a long sip.

Grams waved her hand dismissively. "Oh, I wasn't talking about you, silly. The perfect jeans are for me. Grams's tushie is getting a little droopy. There has to be a denim remedy for that."

Lilly snorted, almost choking on her soda. "Grams!"

"What? I'm serious." She looked completely innocent.

"Let's just eat lunch, okay?" Lilly laughed and coughed, still choking a bit. The thought of her Grams's droopy anything. . . . *Nope. Don't go there.*

Chapter 3

DISAPPEARING ACT

"They're at it again." Lilly gripped her phone and cringed at the sound of a loud bang—like someone slammed a kitchen cabinet door shut. A week had passed since the last fight, so this one would probably be outrageous.

"Let's talk about something else. Let's see. . ." Jason got quiet for a second. "I'm trying to think of a distraction, but I can hear them fighting even over the phone. Wow. Where are you in the house?"

"I'm in my room, sitting in my papasan chair. But I'm tempted to climb out my window and disappear for a while." Lilly turned on her stereo—not too loud.

"If you do, I'll come pick you up." Jason sounded animated, almost excited.

"Yeah, right. Like I would do that." She laughed. "Do you have any idea what would happen to me if I left this house through my window?"

"Yeah, it's probably not a good idea. But we've got to figure something out so we can spend more time together. I. . .I. . .want to be there for you. You need me." As the exclamation to his point, a glass shattered in the kitchen.

Oh God, please don't let anyone be hurt—especially Mom. Lilly couldn't pray for Stan no matter how much Grams wanted her to. She closed her eyes, trying not to focus on the fighting. She did need Jason—he brought sanity and happiness to her life. "I want that, too, Jase, more than you can know. I can't come up with a way, though."

"I was thinking. . . . You mentioned the other day that you weren't allowed out except for church activities or school events. Right?" He paused.

"Yeah. Why do you ask? I mean, isn't the fact that I can't get out of here the point of this whole conversation?" Lilly took a deep breath. It wasn't Jason's fault. No need to take it out on him.

"Right. So, why don't we do more of those things?"

"You mean like go to church more than we do?" Lilly sat up a little straighter. Why hadn't she thought of that? "You might really be on to something with that. Keep talking."

"Sure. We go to church, sit together—starting tomorrow. Go to youth group and events—whatever's going on at church, we're there. Same thing with school."

"That's brilliant. How could anyone find fault with us getting more involved in *responsible* things?" Lilly walked over to her window.

"Exactly." Jason sounded proud of himself. "So, what's our first—"

Slam!

Lilly saw Stan storm from the house, get in his car, and tear out of the driveway, tires squealing. "Jase, gotta go. Stan left. I need to check on Mom." She hung up the phone without waiting for a good-bye.

Creeping down the hallway, Lilly feared she'd find the worst. She didn't really think Stan would severely hurt her mom on purpose, but what if he pushed too hard? What if she slipped and hit her head? What if she hurt herself on purpose? No! She'd never do that. Would she?

Lily tiptoed to the kitchen entrance and peeked around the corner. At first, she didn't see any sign of her mom in the disheveled kitchen. A cabinet door swung loose, hanging on one hinge, the silverware drawer had been overturned, forks, knives, and spoons strewn everywhere. And—*oh gross*—sopping wet coffee grounds had been flung across the kitchen. They were spread the entire length of the island and reached all the way to the patio door behind the dinette. But where was Mom?

Panic rising in her throat, Lilly stepped into the kitchen. "Mom? Are you in here?"

Nothing.

"Mom?" A little louder and more insistent.

Silence.

Wait. Soft sobs came from behind the island. Lilly stepped over the soup ladle and around the soppy coffee grounds to find her mom, in her faded pink bathrobe, crumpled on the floor like a discarded blanket.

"Mom?" Lilly crouched down and touched her arm.

She flinched. "It's no big deal. Just a little fight." She sat up and dried her eyes with the soaking wet sleeve of her robe.

"A little fight? Seriously, this can't continue."

"Stan got some bad news today."

Cancer? Lilly hoped. Not likely, though.

"What news?"

"He lost one of his part-time jobs."

"Let me guess. Problem controlling his temper at the workplace?" Fed up, Lilly didn't even try to hide the sarcasm.

"Try to understand. Stan's under a lot of—"

"—pressure. I know, Mom. I know." Lilly shook her head. No use trying to talk self-worth into Mom. They'd been down this road to nowhere so many times. "What do you want me to do? Can I make you a cup of tea?"

"No, really, I'd rather go soak in a bath. I'll be out in a little bit." She pulled herself to her feet then looked around the kitchen and grimaced. "What a mess." She shook her head.

"Go take a hot bath. I'll take care of this."

Mom left the kitchen looking ten years older than she had earlier that day. Each fight, each week, each day seemed to take more and more of a toll on her. Lilly sighed and grabbed a broom. Her mom had once been so bright, so beautiful—the life of the party, everyone's best friend. Now she hardly went anywhere but work and church. She had no girlfriends, she never dressed up. Only a shell of the woman she'd once been.

Lilly swept up the mess and filled the

dishwasher with the silverware from the floor. As soon as she finished and flipped off the kitchen light, the phone rang. The caller ID said CALLER UNKNOWN. Hmm. A blocked call? "Hello?"

"Lilly. Don't hang up."

She stiffened at the sound of Stan's voice. "What is it? I'm busy cleaning up the kitchen."

"Listen, I'm sorry about that."

Sorry? Lilly waited for more. Nothing came. "What do you want me to say? That it's okay? Well, it's not."

"You're right. I—I— Well, let's go to church tomorrow, and then we'll go out for lunch—as a family. We'll try to get things back to a happy place, okay?"

Too little, too late. "Yeah, whatever you say."

❀

"Where are we going?" Lilly sat forward to look out the front window when Stan took the I-355 North exit toward Chicago instead of the south exit toward their church in Naperville.

"We're playing hooky today." Stan gave her a nervous smile in the rearview mirror. "Your mom and I thought we could all use some family fun."

Oh no. What about Jason? He'd be waiting

223

for her at church. "Mom? Don't you think we should go to church?"

"It's going to be fun. We're going downtown—we'll visit the Museum of Science and Industry, have lunch, and then go to the Shedd Aquarium." Mom grinned.

Lilly had to admit, all of that sounded much more fun than church—and, wanting to be a marine biologist one day, she loved the aquarium. But what could she do about Jason? And why did Stan have to be with them? "Jason's going to wonder where I am. He thought I would be at church today—I guess I'd better call him." On second thought, she'd text him so her mom and Stan wouldn't listen in.

J—Mom & Stan made plans for a day in Chi. No church 4 me. B home later. Come over?

She closed her phone and leaned her head against the seat and watched the cars and trucks stream by them toward the towering skyscrapers in the distance. Within seconds, her phone beeped.

No prob. There's a game/movie night here at church on Friday. Should I sign us up? & yes, I'll come over later.

Lilly pecked out her reply. YES! Sign us up.

His sign-off came within a few seconds. K. TURNING OFF FOR CHURCH NOW. LUV U.

Her eyes grew huge when she read the message. *Luv u.* What did that mean? Was it as serious as "I love you"? Not quite. . .was it? Almost? Should she reply or play it cool?

Lilly closed her eyes. *Love.* Did he love her? Her head swam with the possibilities. They were so young. But, then again, they'd known each other for so long. Maybe they were just meant to be. *Love.* Is this what it felt like to be in love? Her rock, her support, her shoulder to lean on and cry on. She felt accepted, protected, and yes, loved with Jason by her side.

She slid her phone open and closed a few times, considering her response. If she texted him a reply, he might think she took it too seriously—and what if he regretted saying it? But if she didn't, he might never say it again. What to do? Finally, she slipped her phone into her pocket. She'd wait and see what happened. If he said it again, she'd address it, but she didn't want to make it a big deal if he hadn't meant anything by it. She closed her eyes. He did mean something by it—didn't he?

Shock coursed through Lilly's system as she awoke, startled. Approximately thirty minutes had passed, judging by their location. Skyscrapers, in the far-off distance when Lilly drifted off, now towered right outside her window. Downtown Chicago always excited her. Maybe her favorite place to be—people milling about, tall buildings, cars, taxicabs.

Lilly buzzed her window down a few inches so she could hear the sounds. Impatient taxicab drivers honked their horns, policemen blew their whistles, and buses squealed to a stop at almost every corner. Then, while Stan waited at a red light, Lilly heard the telltale *cl–clomp, cl–clomp, cl–clomp* along the passenger side of the car. She opened her window all the way, just in time to see a horse-drawn carriage pull up to the entrance of the Palmer House.

The tuxedoed carriage driver set down his reins and climbed down from his perch. He lowered the steps from the side of the carriage and reached up to assist the most beautiful bride Lilly had ever seen. She wore a pure white dress with a sweetheart neckline. It hugged her hips and then gently cascaded into folds of rich silk with lace appliqués and rhinestones. A dream dress. Her hair had been swept into an elegant updo, secured at her crown with the wispiest of veils. A princess.

Stan started to inch forward, so Lilly had to crane her neck to see more. The bride, on the sidewalk in front of the ritzy Palmer House, looked into her groom's eyes. Lilly thought for sure they'd kiss. About to lose sight of the couple, she turned completely backward in her seat to watch out the rear window. There—the kiss. What must it feel like to be united with someone else? No more loneliness, nothing to be afraid of. *Love.*

How can I have that kind of love? Do I have it already? Could Jason be her future groom? Lilly pulled her cell phone from the pocket of her jeans and scrolled to the last message he sent her. *Luv u.* Maybe he wanted to see if she'd move things along from there, and if she didn't, it would be like telling him she didn't love him. She didn't want that.

She typed Luv u 2 and stared at it for a moment, afraid to touch Send. There would be no going back after saying something like that. Once she put it out there. . . Lilly glanced out the rear window, the bride nothing but a puffy white dot on the landscape behind her as they drove farther and farther from that dream. That's it. Lilly shook her head, decision made.

Send.

Chapter 4

THE GREAT ESCAPE

Almost ready to go, Lilly stood in front of the full-length mirror in the hallway. Was she too dressed up for a youth group game night? Probably, but did she care? She wore a shimmery silver shirt that hugged her slim figure in all the right places. Her favorite dark jeans, fresh out of the dryer, fit like they'd been poured over her body and left to dry into a second layer of skin. Large silver hoop earrings peeked out from the drapes of her long blond hair. Some eyeliner and rosy lip gloss finished off the look. How about the backside? She pirouetted, turning first to the side and then all the way around, peering over her shoulder. She had to admit, she looked good. Surely Jason would think so, too. No one else mattered.

Wanting to head over to the church, Lilly poked her head into the kitchen looking for Mom—her ride. Not there. "Mom?" she called up the stairs. No answer. She looked out the window into the backyard—no one. Where could Mom be? Stan hadn't come home yet. Had he? A quick check in the garage revealed two cars—Mom's red Windstar and Stan's black Accord. So they were both home, but where were they?

Lilly jogged up the stairs to their bedroom. Empty. Their bathroom door was shut, but no light shone from under the door, and she didn't hear any water running. Still, she knocked softly. "Mom?" No answer. Growing slightly nervous since she had no idea what kind of mood Stan had been in when he got home, Lilly rushed out to the hallway and looked in both directions. Where were they?

"Mom?" Lilly hurried down the stairs, calling out every few seconds. "Mom?"

Crash!

She turned toward the loud sound and noticed the basement door cracked open with the lights peeking through. What could they be doing downstairs besides laundry? Lilly went to the doorway and listened.

"Well, if you didn't eat like such a pig, your shirts wouldn't be stained." Mom sounded as if she spoke through gritted teeth.

"That's what laundry detergent is for. . .if you were smart enough to know how to use it, anyway. You ruined my shirts, just like you ruin everything."

"No, Stan." Her voice maintained an even tone. "I didn't ruin your shirts. Grease ruined your shirts."

"Oh boy. Here we go. Miss Smarty-pants. You really think you're clever, don't you?" Stan begged for a fight. Even worse, Mom took the bait—as usual.

That's it. If they wanted to act like that, they'd have to do it without an audience. Lilly decided to leave. How to do it with some damage control, though? She could drive, but even though she had her driver's license, taking the car was a sure ticket to major trouble. Call Jason to pick her up? No way. That would be much worse. What about her bike? No, a little too cold to have the wind whipping her face on a bicycle. Looked like she would walk the mile and a half to the church. She didn't mind; the walk would do her good.

Lilly pulled a notepad and pen from the

drawer by the refrigerator and wrote:

> *Mom, I didn't want to interrupt to ask*
> *for a ride, so I went ahead and walked to*
> *church. I have my cell phone if you need me.*
> *I'll call for a ride home. Have a nice night.*
> *Love,*
> *Lilly*

Lilly put the note under the apple-shaped magnet on the refrigerator that Mom once used to display Lilly's art projects. She picked up her shoulder bag and grabbed her coat on the way out. She slipped her arms into the sleeves as the front door closed behind her. Freedom. It might cost her, but for the moment, it was worth it.

Lilly's breath came out in little white puffs as she hurried along the sidewalk on the dark autumn evening. She felt exhilarated to be powering along, each step taking her farther from the chaos at home. How long would it take for them to notice she left? Would they come after her?

Ahh. She breathed the air deep into her lungs.

Would Mom be okay? Her steps slowed, and she looked back toward her house, which had faded too far in the distance to see. What if Stan hurt her? Lilly couldn't do anything to stop it anyway. She could call the police again like she did last year, but Mom would just deny any problems. Should she call Grams? No. Lilly shook her head and cleared her mind of the worries. She needed to leave it behind her and go be with Jason. She couldn't fight the battle herself. If her mom wanted to keep at it, Lilly couldn't do a thing about it.

Lilly stepped through the trees that lined the parking lot of the church. Not quite Thanksgiving yet, she was surprised to see colored, blinking Christmas lights through the garden window as she approached and peered in. Teens milled about the basement youth room, hanging decorations, stringing popcorn, signing Christmas cards. It looked like a scene right out of a movie. Her spirits suddenly buoyed, Lilly hurried inside.

"Hey! What's going on here?" Lilly dropped her purse on a metal folding chair. Christmas music boomed through the sound system. Lights were strung over anything that stood still. Mulled cider gave off a tangy-sweet aroma from the slow cooker on the countertop.

"Hi, Lilly." Heather, the youth pastor's bubbly wife, popped up from the other side of the counter, her brown curls bouncing. "Zach and I decided to go festive tonight. Everyone seemed in the holiday spirit." She went to the sink, set down a pitcher, and started to fill it with water. "Grab an ornament and jump in." She grinned, revealing her deep dimples.

"I sure will." Lilly looked around the room. "Have you seen Jason Peters yet?"

"Nope. Not yet." Heather grinned. "You two getting serious?"

"Yeah. I think so." Lilly sighed. "If my parents would lighten up and let me out of the house, it'd be a lot better."

"Lilly, I don't want to overstep my boundaries. . . ." She paused as though considering her words. "Just. . .just be careful. Don't rush things. You're still young."

"I know. I'm being careful, re—" Lilly gasped and squeezed Heather's forearm. "He's here. I'll talk to you later." She hurried to the door where Jason stood unzipping his jacket and looking around the room.

"Wow." Jason whistled. "You look great." He reached around and gave her a discreet side hug and then added an extra squeeze before he released her. "I was afraid you wouldn't be able to come for some reason."

"That sure looked like a possibility. The *parentals* were fighting, as usual." Lilly tried to look nonchalant. "So I left." She reached up and picked a string off Jason's shirt, then gestured toward the snack table. "Thirsty?"

"Hold it." Jason opened his eyes wide. "You left?"

Lilly nodded. "Yep. Left."

"You didn't take the car. Tell me you didn't." Jason shook his head.

"No. I'm not that stupid. I needed to get out of there and wasn't about to jump into the fray by asking for a ride." Lilly walked toward the snacks with Jason at her heels. "They'd already given me permission, so I don't see what the big deal is."

At that moment, her cell phone vibrated in her pocket. She pulled it out and looked at the touch screen. *Mom.* Lilly glanced up at Jason, suddenly doubting the wisdom of her decision. She bit her lip and pressed the green button. "Hi, Mom. What's up?" She forced her voice to sound natural.

"Lilly? You walked all the way to church?" Mom's tight voice sounded fearful.

Lilly took a calming breath. "It's not that far. It felt good to get some fresh air."

Jason grabbed her hand.

"But. . .I told you I'd drive you." Mom sounded defensive.

"I know. I didn't want to interrupt." *Don't make a big deal out of it.* "Where's Stan? Is everything okay?"

"I'm fine." Mom hesitated. "Are you okay? Do I need to come pick you up now?"

"No, I'm good, really. But where's Stan?"

"I don't know. He took off in his car."

Could he be on his way to the church? Lilly looked at the door in panic as she imagined Stan storming in there and yanking her out by the sleeve of her shirt. "Did he see my note?"

"No. He came right up the basement stairs and left." Mom sighed. "He doesn't know you left the house, and I'm not telling him. But you can't do this again, Lill. Okay?"

Phew. "Okay, Mom. I promise." She paused a moment. "Do you want me to come home?"

Jason squeezed her hand and shook his head.

"No. You stay. Might as well have some fun. I'm going to take a shower, and then I'll pick you up at ten o'clock like we'd planned."

Lilly looked at her silent phone and then up at Jason. "She hung up on me. She didn't exactly sound mad—more like. . .um. . .defeated."

Should she call back and try to talk her? Maybe she should go home. Lilly looked at Jason, unsure of what to do next. No, she decided after a moment. Mom only wanted her space now. She probably had the shower running already.

Jason rubbed the top of her hand with his thumb and shrugged.

Heather walked over and smiled. "Hi, Jason. Good to see you." Her face darkened a bit as she searched their eyes. "Is everything okay?"

"Yeah. We're fine. Just had to take a phone call from my mom." Lilly pulled her hand from Jason's grasp. "We're ready to help. Where do you want us?"

Chapter 5

TOO LITTLE TOO LATE

Lilly shivered when she walked into the cold kitchen after school on Monday. She went to the thermostat on the wall and adjusted it a touch—too much and she'd have to listen to Stan bellyache about the gas bill. She turned to the refrigerator and found a piece of paper under the magnet on the door.

Lill, we'll be home with dinner around 5:30. We're having a family meeting tonight. The meeting might take a while, so try to get your homework done before we get back.

Love,
Mom and Stan

Great, what could that mean? A family meeting? Maybe Mom and Stan were separating. It would be for the best. Sure, things would be difficult financially, but Lilly could get a job. She'd do that to help out. Plus, she'd probably be allowed to date Jason and have more freedom—only Stan stood in the way of that. The best part would be that Mom would get some of herself back; she'd finally have peace. No. Lilly shook her head. Letting her thoughts run away like that never did her any good. She'd just have to wait and see what the meeting was about.

A couple of hours later, Lilly slammed her Spanish book shut. Paisley, asleep on top of Lilly's feet, jumped at the loud noise. "Sorry, Paise." Over four years of studying Spanish and Lilly only knew enough to order food, find a bathroom, and inquire about a person's day. But what did it matter in real life if she could conjugate the verb *to drink* or count to a thousand?

Now what? She looked at the clock on the microwave. 5:11. She had a history test on Friday, but it would be a waste of time to study now—she wouldn't be able to concentrate. Instead, she pushed her chair back and stood up, stretching her arms far above her head as she yawned. She'd set the table. Maybe if the house was nice and neat, things would go well.

5:14. Lilly wiped off the table and put the fruit basket back in the center. Her fuzzy sock stuck to a sticky patch of dried orange juice on the floor, so she wiped it up. Lilly stepped over Paisley, who had moved to the heat vent, to get the place mats from the buffet drawer in the dining room. That little dog sure could snore.

5:25. Table set—even place mats. Glasses filled—water for Mom and Stan, Coke for herself. Paisley's food and water bowls topped off. Nothing left to do but wait. Lilly sat down in a kitchen chair where she could watch the driveway. *Wait.* Should she have set the dining room table for dinner instead of the kitchenette? They hardly ever ate together, and she didn't know what they were eating, so it was a tough call. Probably didn't matter. Either way, Stan would find something to complain about.

The garage door roared to life, and Lilly's stomach flip-flopped. Why was she so nervous? After a minute, Stan came through the kitchen door first, laughing. He held it open for Mom and took the grease-stained Portillos package she held in her hand.

239

"Thanks, dear." Mom smiled sweetly at Stan who put the bag on the counter.

Dear? It sure didn't look like this would be the big divorce announcement she'd been expecting. "What's going on?" Lilly tried to act normal even though her insides were churning.

Mom started to unpack the food. "Nothing, Lill. How was your day?" She playfully swatted Stan's hand away as he tried to steal a fry. "Hold your horses, mister."

Hold your horses, mister? Was she serious? Lilly grew more nauseated as she watched their sickening display. The smell of grease didn't help matters either. "So what's this family meeting about?" She studied them as they got everything out for dinner.

Stan put the ketchup on the table and smiled. "Let's get settled, and we'll talk over dinner, okay?"

Uh-oh. The calm before the storm? Lilly didn't say another word until everyone sat at the table. They all had a thick, juicy Italian beef sandwich with plenty of sweet peppers, a big pile of french fries, and a puddle of ketchup. Lilly salted and peppered her ketchup—just the way she liked it—then added more pepper to her fries. Comfort food. She sure didn't *feel* very comfortable.

Each of them took a bite in silence. What were they going to talk about? How long would she have to wait to find out? "Mom? Stan? What's going on? What's this meeting about?"

Mom wiped the corners of her mouth with a napkin and looked at Stan. "Honey?"

Honey? Lilly's eyes twitched as she forced them to stay in place even though they wanted to roll to the back of her head. Disgusting.

Stan cleared his throat. "Lilly. . . I'm sorry."

She choked on a mouthful of soda. "Sorry? For what?" She still had the straw in her mouth.

"I'm sorry for the way I've treated you and your mom. And I'm sorry for the way I've made your home an unhappy one."

Seriously? He didn't actually think he could apologize and then everything would be fine, did he? She glanced at her mom who sat still, looking down at her hands.

"I don't expect this to fix everything. I know it's going to take a lot of work. But I started seeing a counselor. I'm willing to do whatever it takes."

Could it be a start? Could he ever change? Lilly doubted it.

Stan cleared his throat again. "In fact, I want all three of us to see this counselor. We need to be put back together as a family."

241

Whoa. You can't put something *back* together that never existed. Lilly stared at Stan and thought about her next words while she chewed on her straw. She pried her eyes away from Stan without a word and turned toward her mom. "Mom? What do you think about all this?"

Mom's shoulders raised and lowered as she heaved a heavy sigh. "Lill, I know you doubt Stan's sincerity. Right?" She still didn't look up.

"Why wouldn't I?" Lilly spoke softly, trying not to anger Stan. But, really, it might be a good test.

"I suppose it's natural. I hope you'll give it a chance." Mom finally glanced up at Lilly.

"Give 'it' a chance? What's the *it*? Stan? Counseling? Peace? You?"

Mom sighed again. "Yes. All of it."

Lilly twisted her hands in her lap. "That's a pretty big request, Mom," she whispered.

Stan cleared his throat. "I understand how you probably feel, Lilly. I hope you'll work with us to put this family back together."

Again with the *back* together. "Why Stan? Why now?"

Mom and Stan looked at each other; then Mom gazed up at the ceiling and exhaled a ragged breath.

"What's going on, you guys? What's this all about?" More games. When would it end?

"She's going to find out sooner or later, Stan." Mom spoke in a whisper.

Lilly's eyes darted from Mom to Stan and back to Mom. "I'm starting to freak out a little. What is it?"

"Well, Lilly, your mom and I—we're going to have a baby." Stan sat back in his chair with a big grin on his face.

Lilly stared at him with her mouth wide open. She closed her mouth, opened it again. No words would come. She could imagine nothing worse. A baby? Mom and Stan? Together? "How? What are you going to. . . ? When? Are you crazy? Did you plan for this to happen?" Lilly fired off her questions, not really expecting an answer to any of them.

"I'm already fourteen weeks." Mom's shoulders slumped, and she started to cry. "I'm sorry, Lilly. Really. It wasn't planned. These things happen sometimes."

"Why would you be sorry?" Stan turned to Mom and covered her tiny hand with his beefy paw. "It's not like you're doing this to spite her. A baby is a good thing."

"Stan, things haven't exactly been great

around here for Lilly. I'm sure she's worried about the way things will change and the kind of home this baby will have, too." Mom pulled her hand away and rubbed her temples.

"Time will prove everything is going to change. I'm giving it—I've given myself—to God. You'll see. It's going to be okay—more than okay."

A baby? She'd always wanted to be a big sister, but this meant Stan and Mom were glued together. Mom, pregnant? What would this mean? It didn't matter much. Lilly would leave for college in a year and a half. She'd pick one far away. But what if the baby needed her? Not really her problem. But. . .still.

She ate a french fry then shoved her plate away and stood up. She turned to her mom. "I love you, Mom. I hope you're going to be okay. . . . I just. . .I can't. . ." She shook her head and left the kitchen, hurrying away before they saw her tears.

Lilly couldn't see very well past the flood that rose in her eyes. She made her way to her bedroom, grabbed her puffy down comforter, and climbed into her papasan chair. Cocooned in her favorite blanket, she curled up in a ball and let the tears come. If she'd felt like a third wheel *before*, she'd seen nothing yet. Lilly's family was growing, but she'd never felt as alone as she did at that moment. Could she leave, move out, go to college, run away—anything?

Sniffling, she pulled a tissue out of the box on the floor by the chair and blew her nose. She wiped her eyes and tried to compose herself. Her phone vibrated in her pocket. *Please be Jason.* Lilly pulled her phone out and looked at the display. *Oh, thank God.*

"Hi Jase." Lilly tried to sound normal.

"Hey. . .what's wrong?"

"You can tell?"

"You sound like you've been crying. What's happening?"

"I don't know how to tell you this." Lilly shivered and pulled the cover up around her chin. "Mom's pregnant."

"What?" he practically shouted. "Are you kidding me?"

Lilly started with a fresh round of sobs. "I wish."

"Oh, Lill. I don't know what to say."

"I mean—it's not the baby's fault. But now Mom is stuck with Stan. And if he mistreats Mom, what will he do to a baby? A kid shouldn't have to grow up in a house with so much fighting."

"I know. What do they say about it?" Jason

seemed at a loss for words.

"Mom and Stan? Well, Stan apologized for the way he's been acting. . . . Oh, and he wants us all to go to counseling together."

"Hey, that's something. At least he's aware that there's a problem."

"I'll do it. But I'm afraid it's too little too late."

❁

A sterile family room—that was the best way Lilly could describe the counselor's office. Stan and Mom sat on the plush love seat facing the roaring fireplace. Mom held one of the many multicolored throw pillows in her lap, pressed against her belly. Lilly wandered the room, looking at the diploma on the wall and the books on the shelves.

Hmm. Why was *What Every Counselor Should Know* such a thin book but *Putting Families Together God's Way* the size of an encyclopedia?

The door opened, and a woman with curly black hair, beautiful ebony skin, and a kind face entered, her high heels clipping against the tile floor. The door closed behind her, blocking out the sounds of the medical center. She stretched out her hand as she crossed the room with long strides. "Mr. and Mrs. Sanders?" She pumped their hands. "I'm Dr. Shepherd."

"I'm Stan, and this is Peggy." Stan nodded across the room at Lilly. "That's Lilly."

"Lilly LeMure." *Not to be mistaken with Sanders, thank you very much.* She crossed the room and shook the doctor's outstretched hand. "It's nice to meet you," Lilly murmured as she sank into an overstuffed chair next to the fireplace.

Dr. Shepherd sat on a leather office chair, placed a few files and a clipboard on her lap, and clicked open a pen. "You gave your permission," she said, turning to Stan, "for Dr. Johnson to share with me what you two have been talking about in your sessions over the past month. It's at his recommendation that we're coming together for family therapy. Is that right?"

Mom and Stan nodded.

"From his notes, I have a general idea about how you feel about things, Stan. So if you don't mind, I'd like to hear from the ladies first."

"Fine by me." Stan smiled.

Lilly rolled her eyes.

"Lilly, would you care to start? I noticed a reaction to Stan. Can you help me understand what caused that? Feel free to speak openly." Dr. Shepherd waited.

How much could she share? But what did she have to lose, really? Things couldn't get any worse. So. . .if she wanted open, Lilly would give her open. "What caused what reaction? That I rolled my eyes? It's him. He is acting all happy lately. Smiling, trying to have conversations, being nice. But I don't trust him. As soon as I let down my guard, he'll change back."

Stan stared at the fire.

"Change back to what?"

Lilly shook her head.

Dr. Shepherd turned to Mom. "What are your thoughts on what Lilly had to say?"

Mom picked at her fingernails. "I can understand why she'd feel that way." She spoke in almost a whisper. "Things have been. . .well, they've been pretty bad around our house these past few years. We need help getting them back to what they once were."

Lilly glared at her mom. "How can you say that? What they once were? Things have always been the same." How could she not see that?

"No, Lill. You forget the good times. It's not your fault, though. You were young when things changed." Mom stared into the fire.

"Can you pinpoint the reason? What do you think caused the change?" Dr. Shepherd looked at Stan.

"I have no idea." Stan shook his head.

Mom smiled softly at Stan. "I know the reason." She took a deep breath. "When you lost your job at Ameripro and I got my promotion in the same week, everything changed, and I think you became depressed. You took it out on me and Lilly. It started all kinds of battles and power struggles. I know I didn't help matters." She wrung her hands in her lap. "I often thought about recommending counseling. But I was afraid to set you off."

Stan wiped his teary eyes. "I've been a real jerk." He looked at the counselor. "I know I can change. I'm doing it—me and God. But I don't know how to help my family trust me. Suddenly, with the new baby on the way, it *has* to work. It just *has* to."

Ah. Lilly sighed as she watched the passing cars through the window. So, the new baby was the reason for all this? *What about me?* Why hadn't she been enough of a reason before now?

Dr. Shepherd turned to Lilly. "What do you think of what Stan said?"

"We'll see." Lilly shook her head. "I'm sorry, but I've seen too much. I'll try. I promise. . . . But it's going to take time." What did they expect of her? It wasn't as if she could all of a sudden open

249

up about her feelings or trust a word Stan said. Fat chance he'd ever change for real.

"That's all we can ask of you." The counselor looked at each of them. "Are you ready for my recommendations?"

Mom and Stan nodded expectantly.

Lilly crossed her arms and waited.

"Okay. Stan, I'd like you to continue seeing your counselor individually—weekly would be best. I'd like to see all three of you together weekly, and I want to see Lilly alone each week, too—at least for a while."

"That sounds like a great plan." Mom smiled and nodded. "Don't you think, Lilly?"

"It's fine." Maybe something would come of it. It couldn't hurt anyway.

Chapter 6

INVISIBLE

The disco ball made the whole roller rink look like the inside of Lilly's head. Thoughts swirled, bright highlights glittered in the darkness, and sparkles of excitement were driven by the music of hope. There was always hope. She took Jason's hand as the DJ announced a couples' skate.

Jason squeezed her hand and pulled her close.

They fell into an easy rhythm of long strokes as they circled the rink. Lilly wished the song would never end. She smiled up at him and laughed at his white teeth that glowed neon blue in the funky lighting. She'd never been happier.

The song ended way too soon. The calm, snuggly mood disappeared as shocking bright lights flooded the rink. Lilly squinted against the glare. With Jason still holding her hand and guiding her forearm, they barely made their way off the rink in time for the mass of younger kids and die-hard skaters to flood onto the floor in preparation for the races.

"Let's go get a drink." Jason tipped his head toward the snack bar and led the way.

With a soda and a plate of nachos to share, they headed for a table in the rear, far away from the crowds. Starving, Lilly took a bite right away.

Jason grinned, his eyes twinkling, as he reached his hand out and wiped away a dollop of melted cheese from Lilly's chin. He licked it off his finger.

Lilly blushed at the intimate gesture and smiled at him.

He took her hand and squeezed it.

She felt so protected, secure, wanting nothing more than to be enveloped by his arms and stowed away there forever.

"I love you, Lilly."

"I love you, too, Jase." There. She'd said it. It rolled off her tongue like the most natural thing in the world. Just as it should be. Love shouldn't be forced. It shouldn't need counselors. Right? It should just *be*.

They smiled at each other, neither one saying anything to break the special moment.

Heather and Zach skated by from around the corner. Heather grabbed on to the table to stop herself, her feet almost rolling out from under her. Zach grabbed her arm and helped her steady herself.

"Hey, you two. We're taking a head count and making sure the youth group is all present and accounted for. You're all tucked away in the dark. Come on out into the light." Heather did a shaky turn on her skates. She could barely stand straight without help—her turn was even worse.

They all laughed.

"Oh, we're just chatting and having a little snack." Jason winked at Lilly. "Skating made us hungry."

"Everything makes Zach hungry." Heather patted her husband's belly. "Isn't that right, babe?"

"Yep. I'm daydreaming about last night's leftovers right now. Lasagna, garlic bread, some salad. . . It's a perfect midnight snack."

"Oh man, that would give me nightmares." Lilly shuddered.

"Me, too." Heather grimaced. "But, hey, we wanted to tell you that the bus pulls out in forty-five minutes. We'll take a head count, but be sure you're out there. We need to leave right on time."

"Sounds good. We'll be there."

"How 'bout coming and joining the fun for now, though?" Zach motioned toward the rink. His mouth smiled, but his eyes didn't.

Oops. That sounded like more than a friendly invitation. Seemed they were making the youth pastor uncomfortable by hiding out in the corner alone. They'd have to tone down the affectionate displays for the rest of the evening. Didn't want to raise any red flags.

❦

"How does that make you feel, Lilly?" Dr. Shepherd held her pen poised over her notepad, apparently expecting some brilliant revelation from her.

Sorry to disappoint you. "Um. I dunno. Pretty invisible, I guess."

"Invisible?" The doc scribbled on her pad without tearing her piercing gaze away from Lilly for even a second. "Explain."

"Well. Stan has always preferred not to see or hear me or any evidence of my existence."

"How do you know this?" Dr. Shepherd tilted her head toward Lilly.

"He does nothing but bark at me. He doesn't want me to have anything lying around anywhere, and he always wants my door shut, music turned down, talking kept to a minimum. It's just how he is. I can't really explain it."

Dr. Shepherd waited.

"And now, all of a sudden with the baby coming, he had a reason to change. I guess the baby is worth the effort—me, not so much."

The doctor wrote another note to herself.

Not going to deny it, huh? "Maybe the baby will be okay because Stan's the real dad. But I already feel sorry for it." Lilly offered a wry smile. "I know you probably think I'm jealous of the baby. I'm not. Really. The poor thing barely stands a chance. I wish you could hear one of their fights." Lilly held up a finger. "Hey, I know. You want me to tape them the next time they fight?"

Dr. Shepherd laughed. "No. As interesting as I'm sure that would be, it won't be necessary." She turned back a few pages in her notes. "Tell me, Lilly. When's the last time they had a big fight?"

"I can tell you the exact night, because we had a youth night at church." Lilly pulled out her calendar. "Let's see. Today's Monday. . .so. . .six weeks ago this past Saturday." She looked at Dr. Shepherd in surprise. "Hmm. That's probably the longest they've ever gone without fighting."

"What do you think is the reason?"

Not me, that's for sure. "I'd say it's because of the baby—and probably the holidays. They're both trying really hard. But will it last?"

"One can never know these things for sure. But if each of you tries your hardest to do your part toward fixing things, there's always a chance." She made a note on her paper. "And, baby or not, wasn't it about six weeks ago Stan committed to this change?"

Lilly nodded and stared into the fire.

Dr. Shepherd cleared her throat. "Tell me, Lilly—I know about your boyfriend, but do you have any really good girlfriends?"

"I used to." Lilly looked down at her hands. "I don't see them much anymore." *Ever.*

"Why is that?" Dr. Shepherd put her pen on the clipboard resting on her lap.

"Why? Because I never knew what would be happening at my house, so I didn't invite them over. When they were never invited, they started to take it personally. They thought I was a snob." Lilly shrugged it off.

"What would have happened if you'd been honest with them about your reasons?"

"They'd probably have felt sorry for me or

thought I wanted their sympathy—which I didn't." She shrugged again.

Dr. Shepherd made a note. "How did you overcome those obstacles when you let Jason into your life?"

"Well, Jason's always been there. And at some point, he just slipped into the role he's in now. I never had to hide anything from him because he knew it all already."

"Have you and Jason been intimate with each other?"

Lilly's mouth dropped open. Was she serious? "If you're meaning what I think you are, the answer is *no*. But isn't that kind of personal?"

"It helps me know where things stand with you. It's okay. Nothing you tell me goes beyond this conversation. So. . .you're still a virgin?"

Lilly nodded, her face hot as the flush rose up her neck. Her cheeks must have been flaming red.

"We're almost done here for the day, but I have two things I'd like to say if I could have your permission." Dr. Shepherd put her clipboard under her chair and leaned forward with her elbows on her nylon-clad knees.

Lilly shrugged.

"First of all, I'm so glad to hear you've been

protecting your purity even though you and Jason are serious about each other. He's very good to you and good *for* you right now. He's helping you with your self-esteem and helping you keep your head on straight." The doctor sat back and crossed her legs. "On the other hand, those things could cause you to fall so hard into his arms that you do something you'll regret one day. So, please, think twice before you take things any further physically. Call me at any time if you're considering something and want to talk." Dr. Shepherd slipped Lilly a business card. "My personal cell phone number is on the back. You can use it anytime. Just keep it to yourself, okay?"

"Thanks." Lilly averted her eyes in embarrassment and tucked the card into her purse.

"The other thing is a request, really. We'll call it a homework assignment." The doctor winked. "I'd like for you to contact and visit with an old friend before the end of the month. Tell her why you let your friendship lapse, ask her to forgive you, and set up a date to get together for something fun—just the girls."

Lilly shook her head. *How embarrassing!*

"I know that sounds difficult, but it will be so freeing. I promise." Dr. Shepherd gathered her papers. "Do you think you can do that?"

258

"Well, I can try."

"Even a marathon starts with one step." Dr. Shepherd smiled. "I'll look forward to hearing the results next week." She stood up to see Lilly to the door. "Remember, you call me if you get into a tricky spot, okay?"

"Jason's not like that. But I appreciate the concern." Lilly smiled and opened the door to the waiting room where her mom sat.

"Ready?" Mom stood up from the couch and collected her purse and jacket.

Lilly held open the door for her as they walked outside. Stan had pulled the car up to the entrance to wait for them. As they got in, he said, "Chinese or Mexican?"

Mom grinned at Lilly. "Mexican!" they both shouted.

Stan's eyes twinkled. "Chinese it is." He turned the car toward their favorite Mexican restaurant.

Could he be changing for real? If he was, he'd already admitted it was for the baby, not Lilly. Still, any change for any reason had to be better than nothing.

They pulled into the parking lot of Chevy's—Lilly loved their salsa—and parked next to a familiar Saab Turbo. "Grams? Is she meeting us here?"

259

"Yep. Someone else is, too." Stan pointed across the parking lot.

Jason, dressed up in a sleek black knit shirt and a pair of khaki pants, smiled and waved.

"Jason!" Lilly squealed and ran to hug him. She fought the urge to give him a quick kiss, because her parents—er, Mom and Stan—were watching.

"Come on, you two lovebirds." Mom laughed. "Let's get inside. I'm sure Grams has a table for us."

Conversation over their pleasant dinner was free and easy. Grams kept them all laughing with tales of the blind dates she'd been on lately. She'd been meeting men online and going out to fancy dinners and plays. "Time of my life," she kept saying.

After dinner, while they waited for dessert to arrive, Mom cleared her throat. "We have a few things to say." She glanced at Stan.

"Yeah." Stan cleared his throat. "First of all, we're so glad you're all here. It's been a great six weeks, as far as I'm concerned, and I look forward to many, many more."

Mom jumped in. "I agree. I couldn't have asked for more." She smiled sweetly at Stan.

Lilly still had to fight the urge to gag, but it

wasn't as strong as it had been a few weeks prior.

"We have several announcements to make."

Grams's eyes opened wide. "Don't tell me it's twins."

"Oh no." Mom laughed. "This first part is about Lilly. Stan, you tell her."

"Okay, Lilly, your mom and I feel like you're ready for some freedom. You've been such a good girl—you always have—and now you deserve to be trusted, set free a little bit, so to speak."

"What does that mean?" Lilly's eyes darted between Mom and Stan.

Stan continued. "For one thing, you're sixteen. Your mom always promised you could date at sixteen. So we're going to allow that to happen. The rules are, you have to be home by ten o'clock, and we want to know where you are at all times. If anyone other than Jason is driving, we want to know about it first. And you can only go out one weekend night for now. How does that sound?"

"Are you serious?" Lilly bounced in her seat and grinned at Jason. "Thank you! Thank you! Did you hear that, Grams?"

"I heard. Congratulations, dear." Grams smiled and nodded toward Stan.

Was there more? Lilly waited.

"One more thing, Lilly. Layoffs are over. Ameripro hired me back full-time."

So he hadn't been fired? "That's great. Congratulations. I'm sure the extra money will come in handy with the baby coming." *Not sure what it has to do with me, though.*

"So. . ." Stan dangled a key in front of her face.

"What's this?"

"I got a new company car—well, actually, I pick it up tomorrow. So I'm giving you the Accord."

"Really? Wow! Thanks so much, you guys. I can't believe it!" Lilly grinned at her mom and then turned to Jason who winked at her. He reached under the table and squeezed her hand.

"We have one more announcement." Mom beamed at Stan. She pulled a little piece of paper out of her purse. It looked like a piece of black-and-white film. "We had an ultrasound today. The baby looks perfect—here's a picture. There are the little feet. Here's a little hand." She pointed at the picture with the tine of her fork.

Wow. Lilly stared at the human being inside her mother—her baby brother or sister. She couldn't take her eyes off the picture.

Grams asked, "Hey, do you know the sex?"

Lilly dropped the photo and waited. Was that even possible?

Mom grinned at Stan. "You tell them."

His eyes welled up with tears, and he puffed up with pride. "It's a boy. I'm finally going to have a son."

Lilly deflated like a soccer ball that had been kicked hard too many times. She let herself imagine that love was developing, that they were going to be a real family. But this whole thing—the dating, the car—was just another way, a seemingly happy way, for Stan to get her out of the house and away from his perfect little family with his new son. Why hadn't she seen it sooner? She'd fallen for it because she'd hoped for it.

Her eyes pleaded with Jason.

He nodded and winked at her—assuring her that he'd stay right by her side. What did it matter anyway? All she'd really wanted was to spend more time with Jason—looked like she got her wish. No way she'd rock the boat by confronting Stan's true motives.

She'd do what she did best—make herself invisible.

Chapter 7

DATE NIGHT

Lilly stared at her blank cell phone screen.
What was the worst that could happen?
Rejection? Mocking, humiliating laughter?
Would it be worse to return to Dr. Shepherd
having failed to do her homework assignment?
She was supposed to do it before the end of
January but was quickly running out of time.
Expecting both reactions, Lilly picked up the
phone and reached out a finger for the buttons.

No! She dropped her phone, covered it with
a pillow as though it might bite, and jumped
off her bed. She paced the length of her room,
twisting a lock of her hair around her fingers.
This was getting her nowhere. She had to make
the call—dragging it out just made it worse.

Reaching her hand under the pillow, Lilly

picked up the phone and punched in the numbers before she could change her mind.

A familiar voice answered. "Hello?"

Samantha Pruitt. It had been at least a year since they'd spoken on the phone. Lilly saw her in the halls at school from time to time, but they seldom spoke anymore.

"Hello?" Samantha's insistent voice snapped Lilly from her thoughts.

"Um. . .hello? Sam?" Not off to the best start.

"Yes, this is she. Who's this?"

"It's Lilly." She waited.

Silence buzzed through the phone lines. "What do you want?" Sam sounded aloof, uninterested.

Lilly cleared her throat. "Um, I. . .well. . . here's the thing. . . . Things have changed a little bit for me, and I need to tell you the truth about some stuff. I feel bad for how things are with us, and I wanted to tell you I'm sorry and explain myself."

"Okaaaay?" Sam sounded doubtful but willing to listen—maybe.

Lilly forced herself to open up. "Listen, it's my fault I never let you see the truth about my home life, but things were pretty awful. I didn't want you to come over and have to see or hear

265

my mom and Stan fighting—which they did all the time. So I never invited you here. I'm sure it made you feel bad that I hardly ever had you over or even let you come in. Eventually, I got so sick of trying to come up with excuses and worrying about it that I pulled away completely."

"Is that the truth?" Sam sounded hopeful. "I mean, I don't want that to be the truth, because that would be awful, but at least it would mean that I. . ."

"That you didn't do anything wrong." Lilly sighed. "Yes, it's the truth, and no, you didn't do a thing wrong. I'm really sorry."

"Why are you telling me this now, though? What happened?"

Lilly thought about that for a moment. "Umm. . .things have kind of changed around here. There've been no fights for a couple of months. We're going for counseling, and Mom's going to have a baby in a few months. I guess I feel ready to try to bring someone else in." Lilly hesitated. "I want that someone to be you."

"Wow. I'm really glad. I missed you a lot. I never could understand what I did to push you away. I thought maybe it was because of Jason, but that didn't seem likely since the three of us had always been friends. Although, he. . . Oh, never mind."

Hmm. What was she about to say about Jason? *No, don't ask.* Back to the point of the call. "Hey, want to continue this conversation over a pizza and movie over here?" Lilly's voice rose with hope.

"Really?" Samantha's voice lifted, too. "I'd love to. What time?"

"Whenever you can make it. I'll be here."

"Give me about twenty minutes." Sam's words rushed out; then the line went dead.

Lilly smiled and turned off the display on her phone. Surveying her room in a panic, she threw some laundry into the hamper and scurried to fold the bedcovers. *Good enough.* She lay back on her bed and took a deep breath. A few seconds later, she felt her cell phone vibrate. Had to be Jason.

"Hey, Jase, what's up?"

"Hi cutie. What are you doing?"

"You'll never believe it. I just got off the phone with Samantha Pruitt. I called her because. . .well, to apologize." Lilly stumbled over her words.

He listened silently until she finished. "Well, I guess it's okay as long as you don't expect to give her our date night."

"What do you mean?" He *guessed* it was okay?

"You get one night out each weekend, right? I hope you're not going to want to go out with Sam now."

"I don't get why you're saying that. And it's not that I only get one night out—I get *one date night*. There's a big difference." Why was he acting like that? She'd never seen this possessive side before.

"Oh, that's true." Jason's voice perked up. "So maybe you could get out an extra night if you tell them you're going out with Sam. Now *that's* a good plan."

"That's not what I. . .oh, whatever. It'll be fine." Lilly didn't want to argue with Jason of all people.

"So we're still on for tomorrow night?"

Lilly breathed a sigh of relief that his mood had returned to his normal teasing. "Of course, silly. I can't wait." She thought she saw headlights in the driveway and walked to her window to see. Yep. Sam had arrived. "I gotta go, Jase. Sam's here."

"Okay. Have fun. Think about me. Talk about me—good stuff only."

"Always."

"Love you, Lilly."

"Love you, too."

Lilly had bounded halfway down the stairs when the doorbell rang. She rushed to answer it before Stan could get to it. She threw it open to see her old friend on the other side. With a big grin, Lilly reached out and hugged her. They clung to each other for a few moments. "I missed you!" they said at the same time, then laughed.

"Okay. Time to move on. Let bygones be bygones and all that." Sam peered over Lilly's shoulder into the house. "Show me around."

❀

"Bye, Mom." Lilly gave her mom a quick kiss and reached for the door handle but didn't turn it. She scrunched her eyes together and squared her shoulders with resolve. "Bye, Stan." Dr. Shepherd would have been proud that she included Stan. Lilly hurried through the door, skipped down the porch steps, and slid into Jason's car.

"Hey, cutie. You look great." Jason's eyes roved up and down her body. "C'mere." He pulled her close for a kiss.

Lilly gave him a quick peck then pulled

away and darted a nervous glance at the upstairs windows. "So, where're we going?" She pressed herself against the door, crossed her legs, and played with the frayed edges of her denim skirt.

"Well, since we haven't gotten out alone in forever, I thought we'd go to dinner and talk. Then maybe go for a drive. Sound okay?" Jason turned to look over his shoulder as he reversed out of the driveway. Could he be nervous, too?

"Sounds great. Romantic." Lilly touched the back of her hand to her flaming cheek. She knew her face must be turning pink. They rode in silence until they got out into traffic near the restaurants. Her stomach churned. Why did she feel so jittery? She wiped her clammy hands on her skirt and exhaled deeply, leaving a smoky white cloud on the cold window.

Jason flipped the turn signal on and turned into Olive Garden.

"Oh goody! I hoped we'd go here." Lilly beamed at him and relaxed her shoulders. It promised to be a nice night.

After dinner Jason held her hand as they walked through the parking lot toward the car. He pulled her to a stop at the passenger door, reached around her, and pulled the door open. As Lilly lifted her foot to step in, Jason grabbed her hand a little tighter and pulled her close. He leaned forward and softly kissed her lips as the snow fell around them.

A few flakes fell onto Lilly's cheek, but she didn't move to brush them off. Jason must have seen them, because he leaned his head to the side and kissed her cheek right where they had landed. Lilly giggled, but Jason silenced her with another kiss—this one more insistent. For a second, she pulled back a tiny bit as warning bells about Jason's intentions rang in her mind; but tired of listening to them, she pushed them away and relaxed in Jason's embrace. It felt like home.

After a few minutes of standing in the snowy parking lot, they both started to shiver. Jason pulled away and gazed into Lilly's eyes. "Why don't we get in the car, drive for a few minutes to warm up, and then find a place to. . .um. . .talk?"

Lilly didn't trust herself to speak. She climbed into the car in silent agreement. Her thoughts went wild. What did Jason want from her? Should she stop him? Did she even want to? She'd never been that close to a boy, but she knew all too well that Jason had had other girlfriends. Did that mean he'd kissed them like that before? *Ewww*. Lilly didn't want to have a string of boyfriends in her past. But Jason, being a boy, probably didn't feel that way. That was normal, right? Plus, they were in love—so his past shouldn't matter. Should it?

After the car had been running for a few minutes, Jason flipped the heater to full blast. It blew out freezing cold air for a few seconds but quickly warmed up. "How about we pull over here?" Jason turned into the parking lot of a deserted playground, right behind the row of tennis courts. "We'll leave the car running." He reached over and switched the car to defrost, then pulled off his gloves and laid them on the dashboard.

Lilly stared out the window at the falling snow, afraid to move. What should she do—let him take the lead or reach out for him? Should she demand he take her home or relax and enjoy the moment? Already startled by her own physical reaction to Jason's touch, she decided to wait and see what else he had in mind.

Jason took one of her hands and carefully pulled the glove off, then reached for the other one. "Your fingers are still cold." He kissed each of her fingertips, sending electric shocks through her entire body. Pulling her closer to him, he tucked her hands into the warmth of his jacket.

She snuggled close and murmured a comfortable sigh. So strange how she could be so nervous one minute and then cozy right up to him the next.

They sat still for a few minutes, not moving. Lilly could feel the beating of Jason's heart beneath her hand. The beating got faster like a crescendo before a cymbal crash. He clutched her shoulder and leaned across the console for a long kiss. Lilly's stomach flip-flopped, and her own heart started pounding out of her chest. His kisses grew more intense. He moved his body so that more of them touched—the console between them jabbed her in the ribs.

"Why don't we move to the backseat where we can be more comfortable?" Jason's breath came out in short pants.

Lilly glanced outside the steamy windows. "What if someone comes?" What if things got too heated? Would she be able to control him? Herself?

"It's not illegal to be in the backseat. Come on." He climbed over the seats and reached up to help her.

Lilly took a deep breath and put one hand

on each of the front seats as she tried to make the transition in her denim skirt. "Um, could you look away for a second? I don't think I can do this and keep my dignity if you're watching."

Jason covered his eyes with his hand but separated his fingers to look through them.

Lilly laughed. "Come on, Jase. I'm serious."

"Okay. Okay." Jason turned his body and faced out the side window while Lilly got herself situated in the backseat beside him.

"There. I'm all set." Whatever that meant. Lilly's heart beat wildly, and her mind raced. What would happen next?

Jason turned around to face her and didn't waste a second. He scooted over and leaned forward so half of his body lay on top of her. His weight pressed her against the door. The handle jabbed her in the back of the head, her neck bent at an odd angle.

She felt his warm breath on her cheek as he leaned in to kiss her. His lips pressed tightly against hers, and she sensed him trying to part her lips.

No. Too much. "Jason." She struggled to speak but couldn't move her head back any farther against the window. She put her hands on his shoulders and gently pushed him up and away.

274

"Jason. That's enough for me tonight. I think I should go home."

His breath puffed in short gasps, and he looked perplexed. "What? What did I do?" He frowned and ran his hand through his mussed-up hair.

"Oh, you didn't do anything wrong. This"—she gestured at the car and the steamy windows—"is all new to me. I need to take things slow."

"Okay. I didn't mean to push you." He sat up and adjusted his sweater. He opened the door and climbed out into the cold air where he stood for a few moments longer than Lilly thought necessary. Probably needed some fresh air to clear his head.

While he stood outside the car, Lilly took the opportunity to climb into the front seat in privacy. Once she settled in her seat, since Jason hadn't gotten back into the car, she leaned over and put the driver's window down. "You okay?"

"Yeah, sure. Just getting some air. I'll be right there."

Lilly put the window up, sure she'd upset him. Had she acted like a child? Maybe she should have gone on with things for a little longer. Physical stuff was kind of inevitable between them—probably sooner rather than later. Did it have to be, though? What if she never felt comfortable with what Jason seemed to want? Would she lose him? Visions of a future without Jason in it assailed her thoughts and made her shudder. She couldn't let that happen.

No matter what.

Chapter 8

DIVERSIONS

Heart beating wildly, flames sizzling on her cheeks, Lilly jumped up, knocking Jason to the concrete floor. Things on the couch here in his basement were getting a little too heated— much as they had in the car last week.

"I'll be right back." She scurried to the nearby bathroom. A quick glance backward revealed a bewildered-looking Jason picking himself up off the floor.

Lilly pulled the bathroom door closed behind her and locked it as quietly as she could. She hurried to the far wall and flipped the window lock. As soon as she started to crank the window open, she found relief. The cold air rushed in and enveloped her still burning cheeks with as much intensity as the heat had consumed her. Lilly breathed deeply, hoping the fresh air would help her regain her composure.

What had happened back there on the couch? What were those feelings that coursed through her bloodstream? It was like an out-of-body experience. Lilly had felt completely out of control—almost like watching a film of two unknown people. She didn't like that feeling one bit—yet she did. It scared her. . .but was Jason *the one*? If so, that changed everything—didn't it?

Still a bit trembly, she took one more deep breath and closed the window. She needed to get a handle on herself fast. Splashing her face with cool water, she tried to hum a silly song to take her mind off what had just happened. Feeling better, she turned and flushed the toilet so Jason wouldn't wonder what she'd been doing in there. After a quick shake of her hair and a last glance in the mirror, she pasted on a carefree grin—at least she hoped it looked carefree. Deep breath. She only needed to stay in control. That should be easy enough.

Lilly returned to the rec room where Jason had turned the television on. "Whatcha watchin'?" She plopped down on the sofa, crossing her legs under her body, and leaned against the armrest, as far from Jason's end of the couch as she could get.

"C'mere, silly." Jason grabbed her hand and pulled her over to him.

She slid over and rested her cheek against Jason's chest and pulled her feet up on the couch next to her. Lily promised herself she wouldn't let things get heated again—his parents were due home soon anyway. He laid his heavy arm across her shoulder and down the length of her body. He grabbed her hand and squeezed softly. Now that she could handle. Sighing, she snuggled in and closed her eyes, breathing in the musky scent of his cologne mingled with the fresh soapy smell of his clothes. *Ahhh.*

Could Jason be as nervous as she? It sure didn't seem like it. Maybe he had more experience with this sort of thing than she knew. *Nah.* She already knew about all of his girlfriends, and he told her she was his first true love. He sure seemed confident, though.

"Ha! Did you see that?" Jason pointed at the television.

Lilly jerked herself out of her thoughts and tried to focus on the program they were watching. "Um. . .no. . .I guess I missed it. Sorry."

"Missed it?" Jason laughed. "We're both sitting here watching together. How could you miss it?"

"Oh, just lost in thought. You know." Lilly smiled up at him.

Jason's eyes twinkled, and he leaned over to kiss her. "Ah. I can't stop thinking about it either."

That's not what I meant. Lilly kissed him back then tried to pull away.

He kissed her harder.

"Okay." Lilly stood up. "Time for a diversion. Um. . .let's go build a snowman." She didn't wait for his reply and started to pull her coat on.

"A snowman? You want to build a snowman?" Jason narrowed his eyes. "We can't wait to have time alone, and then as soon as we do, you want to go outside and play in the snow?"

"That's still time alone. In fact, it's closer to what I had in mind than all this." She gestured at the couch. "I mean, it's all good, but I think we need a break before we get carried away." Or, any *more* carried away. "Come on." She gave his sleeve a playful tug.

Grudgingly shrugging his arms into his coat, Jason sighed. "Okay. Okay." He chuckled, shaking his head. "This is not at all what I had planned for this evening."

"Way to be flexible, Jase." Lilly grinned and put her hands up in the air in a mock cheer.

They pulled on their snow boots and clomped out to the backyard. The wind hit Lilly's face, so she tightened her scarf. "How about we start over there? There's a big drift that will make it easy to make the big snowball for the bottom."

"You're the boss." He set off toward the snowdrift. "I can't believe I'm doing this," he muttered.

Lilly pushed a small snowball toward him. "Here, let's roll this around for a while to get it bigger."

After a few minutes of rolling the ball, Jason stepped back to survey the results. "Don't you think that's big enough?"

"No way! Keep rolling." Lilly laughed. She tugged, rolled, and grunted. Finally, with Jason's help, she had a ball for the base of the snowman that would make even a champion snowman builder proud. "There. That'll do just fine. Where should we put it?"

Jason grinned. "How about over there by the corner of the patio so we can see him out the kitchen window?"

"Oh? It's a him? I don't think so." Lilly winked. They rolled the ball into place and started on the middle one right away.

With all three balls in place, they stood back to look at their snowwoman. "Okay, she needs a face and some accessories." Lilly surveyed the yard, looking for possibilities.

They dug in a pile of brush, and Jason found two perfect branches to use as arms. Cleverly, he turned them so it looked as if she had one hand on her head and the other on her hip.

Lilly squealed. "Oooh! That's so cute!"

"Hold on a sec. I need to go ask my mom for a couple of things. I'll be right back." Jason ran off toward the house and stomped his boots when he reached the back door.

While he was gone, Lilly used evergreen boughs to give her snowwoman long hair and tiny twigs to make long eyelashes. Just as she finished sticking the last eyelash in the snow, the back door opened and Jason came out with his arms full.

He hurried over. "Check this stuff out."

Someone seemed to be having fun after all, hmm? "Oh cool!" Lilly held up a feather boa and a sequined scarf. She draped them both loosely around. . .um. . . "Beatrice. We'll call her Beatrice."

"Beatrice it is." Jason held up some plastic fruit. "What can we do with these?"

"Ooh, let me see the grapes. She'll have green eyes. And the strawberries will be her mouth. Here, look." Lilly positioned the strawberries sideways in a half circle like a smile but turned the center two vertically. "See, it looks like those peaks we have on our lips. What are those called, anyway?"

"How am I supposed to know?" Jason laughed.

"Okay. I think we're about done." Lilly nodded, happy with the results. "Hey. Do you have your cell phone on you?"

Jason nodded and reached in his pocket.

"Cool. Take a picture of me and Beatrice. Okay?" She put her arm around the snow-woman and grinned for the picture. "Now one like this." Lilly put one hand on her head and one on her hip, mimicking Beatrice's stance. When the picture had been snapped, Lilly jogged over to see the display. "Great!"

Jason slipped the phone into his pocket, and Lilly turned her back to secure Beatrice's scarf so it wouldn't blow away.

Whomp! Lilly instantly knew what hit her in the back, but she was afraid to turn around. She surveyed the area in front of her. She could hide behind Beatrice, but she didn't want the poor snowwoman to suffer the pummeling Lilly knew was coming. The patio table! With a burst of speed, Lilly dove headfirst under the patio table, but not before she got walloped in the side of the head. *He's going to get it!* She gathered up some snow and packed it together into a hard ball. As soon as she had a clear shot, she took it. Right in his face. *Oops.*

"That's it. You're in trouble now." Jason brushed the snow off his cheeks while he lumbered through the mounds to reach Lilly's hideout under the table. Rather than stoop down and pull her out, he simply moved the table, leaving her exposed. "Now I've got you right where I want you." He clapped his hands together and laughed wickedly as he stood above her with an arm full of snow—enough to fill a bucket. He stooped down to a crouch and held the snow inches above her face.

Lilly couldn't watch anymore. She scrunched her eyes shut and waited for the cold snow to land on her face. Then it happened—the tiniest, softest flutter on her nose. He kissed her. The electric shocks coursed through her body again. How could he have that effect on her time after time? She slowly opened her eyes, expecting to find Jason with his eyes closed. Nope. He stared back at her and leaned down to kiss her on the lips with an intensity that scared her. They should stop. *But I don't want to.*

Bundled in their puffy winter gear, they lay in the snow on Jason's back porch for about thirty more minutes. They watched the stars twinkle and kissed softly every few minutes. It was the most romantic night Lilly could have imagined.

"I love you, Lill."

"I love you, too, Jase."

Jason pulled back his glove and looked at his watch. "I really hate to say this, but I think it's time I take you home. We sure don't want to be late."

Not that anyone at home would notice since they had severe baby-on-the-brain. "Yeah, you're right. I could stay like this all night, though."

"Oh, that time will come." Jason winked.

What did he mean by that? Scary thought. Or was it?

❁

Pastor Michaels had dyed his hair a shocking jet black. Jason kept nudging Lilly and trying to get her to look, but whenever she glanced up at the pastor, she'd start giggling. The fake tan, the ultrawhite teeth, the jet black hair—midlife crisis, perhaps? Instead of looking at him, Lilly read her Bible while she tried to listen to the pre-service announcements.

"...Women's League has a bake sale in the gymnasium from twelve to two on Saturday. Hopefully the youth group will be cleaned up and cleared out after their all-night lock-in on Friday night."

Jason squeezed her hand and motioned for her to pay close attention.

Pastor Michaels cleared his throat. "Did you hear that? Teens, make sure you attend the lock-in this Friday night. Be here by 7:00 p.m. There will be pizza, snacks, pop, games—video and otherwise, I'm told. You need to be picked up by ten o'clock on Saturday morning. If you have any questions, you can see Zach or Heather. Now, if we could all stand for the reading of God's Word. . . ."

Jason leaned over to whisper in Lilly's ear. "We need to go to that."

Lilly nodded, keeping her eyes on the Bible reading displayed on the screen.

"No, I mean *goooo* to that." Jason winked. "Rather, *not* go to that."

Huh? Did he want to go or not? "We'll

talk about it later." What did he mean? *Hmm.*
Lilly supposed he had trouble making on his
mind. But she couldn't ignore that twinkle in
his eye like he got whenever he had something
up his sleeve. Wait! Did he mean he wanted
them to pretend to go and then not go? To
an overnighter? No way she could do that.
Could she?

What if she got caught? Besides, what
would they do all night? Surely Jason could
come up with something. *Sigh.*

The service couldn't end quickly enough.
As they walked out to the parking lot to meet
up with Mom and Stan, Lilly turned to Jason.
"What were you trying to whisper to me back
there?"

"Don't you get it? There's an all-night lock-
in. Your parents heard it right from Pastor
Michael's mouth. If we say we're going, we'd
have the whole night to be together."

Just what she feared. Or just what she
wanted? Lilly had never been so confused. "Oh
man. I could get into so much trouble."

"We won't get caught. They're not going to
call to see if you're there."

Lilly nodded. Jason was right about that. All
they could think about lately was the baby. As

long as Lilly kept quiet, they left her alone. "But what would we do? I mean, we can't sit in a car all night."

"Ah. This is the great part. My parents are going out of town next weekend—for their anniversary on March 25th. We'd have the house to ourselves." He wiggled his eyebrows.

Excitement tickled Lilly's tummy. The chance to be alone with Jason for a whole night? It would feel so grown-up—like they had their own house. She could even make him dinner. But what would Jason expect from her? "Jase. . .I. . .um. . .I'm a little afraid that I might not be ready for whatever you might have in mind."

"I hear you, Lill. It's okay. We'll take things slowly. Nothing you're not ready for." Jason nodded over her head. "But, shh. Here comes your mom."

"Hey, Mom. Hey, Stan. How's it going?"

Stan waved at a church member across the parking lot and then turned to Lilly. "Church was great today. Hey, did you hear about the overnighter on Friday?"

Perfect opportunity. "Yep. I think I'd like to go if that's okay."

Mom smiled. "Of course it's okay. You know

your dad. . .er. . .Stan and I love for you to be involved in church."

"Uh-huh." Guilt and fear congealed into a lump in her stomach. What if she got caught? They'd never trust her again. But she wouldn't get caught.

Would she?

Chapter 9

OVERNIGHTER

Grams! Lilly pulled her car into the driveway, right behind her grandma's car, after school on Friday. She threw the car into park, grabbed the keys, and ran into the house.

"Grams?" She let her book bag slide to the living room floor and bent down to kiss her grandmother, who turned up her cheek and kissed the air.

"Fresh lipstick." Grams puckered her lips.

Lilly laughed and sat down beside her. "What do you have? A hot date or something?"

"Yeah, something like that. But I'll never tell." Grams winked. "What's new with you? I feel like I haven't seen you in months."

Lilly shrugged. "I'm good. Nothing new."

"You enjoying that car of yours?"

"Oh yeah. It's been great. I think it helps Mom that I have wheels, too." Lilly nodded toward the kitchen where her mom banged things around, probably making tea. "How's she feeling today?"

"As good as can be expected. There are definitely reasons why it's usually young people having the babies. She's feeling her forty years, I think. But she'll make it another month." Grams cast a quick glance toward the kitchen. "Before she comes back, Lill, tell me how things are *really* going."

Lilly knew exactly what she wanted to know. "There have been no fights at all since we started counseling. Actually, since Stan started going on his own. Things are good." She turned her hands up. "No telling if it will last after the baby comes. But it seems possible. Makes me feel pretty good about going away to college. I won't have to worry so much about either of them—Mom or the baby."

"Good." Grams nodded. "How about you and Jason? You two keeping things pure?"

Grams always knew how to get to the heart of the matter, didn't she? Lilly laughed. "Grams! That's kind of personal, isn't it?"

"It's only personal if you have an answer I

won't like. If your answer is the right one, then you should be proud to say it." Grams raised her eyebrows and waited for a reply.

"Well, you don't have to worry." Lilly smiled confidently. "In fact, we're going to a youth group function tonight instead of going out alone." Why did she lie to Grams? She could have left that last part off.

"Hey now, that's what I like to hear. If that ever starts to change, you come talk to me first, promise?"

"I promise." If she only knew.

Mom walked into the room and stooped down to sit on the edge of the sofa.

Lilly grabbed a throw pillow to put behind her mom's back. "I'm going to get ready for tonight. I'll be down in a minute."

What to bring? Lilly stood staring at the contents of her closet. She went to her dresser drawers and pulled them open. Pajamas? No. That would be weird. She pulled out a pair of green Victoria's Secret sweatpants that said PINK across the bottom and a pink hoodie and put them into her bag. They should work for movie watching and still not give Jason the wrong idea. Was she kidding herself? Of course Jason had expectations for the night. Could she stop him? Did she even want to?

No use. She couldn't figure it out ahead of time. She'd have to take things as they happened and make her decisions along the way. At least she knew Jason respected her enough not to push her. She hoped.

Sigh. Lilly shook her head to clear her thoughts. What was next on the list? Dinner. She planned to stop at the store on the way to Jason's house to buy stuff to make spaghetti. Maybe some candles. She grew more excited but was still so nervous. She should probably take a shower and change into something nice. Not too nice, or someone would get suspicious.

Thirty minutes later, freshly showered and dressed, Lilly shouldered her overnight bag and put her pillow under her arm—if she were spending the night at the church, she'd want her pillow. Where would she sleep at Jason's? The couch? The floor in his room? In his bed while he slept on the couch? No way she'd sleep in his parents' room, and their guest room had workout stuff and a computer desk—no bed for her to use. Did Jason plan for them to sleep together? Probably.

She flipped off the light in her room and skipped down the stairs.

Grams slipped her jacket over her arms. "Oh good. I'm on my way out, and you're parked behind me. Now we can leave together."

"Great. Bye, Mom." Lilly gave her a quick kiss. "I have my phone, and I'll be home before noon tomorrow."

"Sounds good. Call me when you get there." Mom slipped her a twenty-dollar bill. "Just in case."

Standing in the driveway, Lilly hugged Grams and kissed her cheek. "Have fun tonight, Grams—but not too much fun."

"You, too, Lill." Grams swatted her behind and slipped her another twenty-dollar bill. "Just in case."

"Mom gave me some money. You don't have to." Lilly tried to hand it back to her.

Grams already sat in her Saab with the engine running. "Put it in your purse. You never know when you might need it."

"Thanks!" Lilly sighed as she backed out of the driveway. Grams would be so disappointed if she knew what Lilly had planned. All the more reason to make sure no one found out.

After a quick stop at the grocery store for ground beef, noodles, sauce, garlic bread, a pre-mixed salad, and frosted brownies for dessert,

Lilly turned down Jason's street. She could still go to the church and skip this crazy plan. What was she thinking? Jason—she really loved him. Time with him meant more than anything. God had brought them together, right? No one would find out.

She pulled into Jason's driveway, turned off the car, and quickly sent a prepared text to her mom: I'M HERE.

The front door opened, and Jason came bounding down the steps over to the driver's side. He took Lilly's hand to help her out. She handed him her groceries and grabbed her bag from the backseat.

"Ready?" He looked like a little boy on Christmas.

Lilly took a shaky breath. "R–ready."

They went straight to the kitchen where they put the groceries on the butcher-block island. "We'll get to that stuff in a minute. Let's go put your other things away." He led her down the hallway and stopped outside his room. "After you, madam." He gestured with a flourish and bowed as she walked into the room.

"Where are you going to sleep?" Lilly had a feeling she knew the answer.

"Huh? Well. . .with you, of course." Jason

looked bewildered. "Isn't that okay?"

Lilly eyed the twin-sized bed and shrugged. "I don't know, Jase."

"Look, I told you that nothing would happen you weren't comfortable with. But wouldn't it be nice to sleep next to each other all night, even if nothing else happens?"

Divine. But could it stop at that? "I'd love that. As long as we're careful. I'm not ready for certain things, Jason. I don't think premarital sex is right." Had Jason already done it? Lilly didn't think she wanted to know the answer.

"I'm not talking about tonight, but if two people love each other, you still think it's wrong?" Jason sat down on the bed.

"Yes. I mean, the Bible says it's wrong. My mom, Grams, my Sunday school teachers— everyone says it's wrong. Plus, don't you want to have that special thing to look forward to for your wedding day?" Granted, that was a long way off.

"What if I wanted to marry *you*?"

Really? Could what he was saying be true? Was he her Prince Charming? They could get married after high school and help each other through college. They could do it together. "Well, if that were the case, I don't know about right or wrong. Still, sex before marriage takes away from the wedding day, don't you think?"

Jason shrugged.

"Well, we don't have to solve this today. We've got dinner to cook." She grinned and threw her hair over her shoulder as she bounced from the room.

In the kitchen, she pulled out a big pot from under the stove and filled it with water. While that heated, she browned the ground beef then added the sauce to the meat and the pasta to the boiling water. While they simmered, Lilly put the garlic bread on a cookie sheet and slid it into the oven. "Why don't you light the candles, Jase? Oh, and can you fix us a Coke or something?"

Jason slid off the stool where he'd been perched and set to work.

The candles he lit cast a warm, romantic flicker over the adjoining dining room. Lilly wished she could take pictures—but evidence of this night would not be wise. She heaped a serving bowl with steaming pasta, poured meat sauce over it, piled the garlic bread on a serving tray, and carried it all to the dining room. She sat in the chair Jason held out for her and reached for her napkin to put in her lap.

Right next to her napkin stood a wine glass full of a bubbly pink liquid. "Jason? Is this wine? Where'd you get it?"

"Oh, I have more than a few tricks up my sleeve." Jason winked. "We can't have a romantic night like this without champagne."

"You know what? I think I'll pass. I hope you don't mind. But I've never had a drop of alcohol, and I'm not going to start tonight." *Not when I need to keep my head on straight.*

"Okay, well how about just a sip for a toast and then I'll get you a Coke." He held up his glass.

A toast couldn't hurt anything. "Okay." Lilly held up her glass and waited.

"To the love of my life and our night together." He clinked her glass and took a drink.

Lilly lifted the glass to her lips and sipped. The bubbles tickled her nose, but it tasted sweeter than she expected—kind of like a fruity 7UP. One sip, no more. Lilly put the glass down and slid it as far away as she could reach.

The clinking of the silverware was the only noise in the room for a little while. Neither of them knew what to say. Jason sipped on his champagne—he even got Lilly to take a few more sips. When they were finished eating,

Lilly headed out of the dining room with a load of dishes, but Jason stopped her. He took the plates from her, grabbed both of her hands, and pulled her around so she faced him. "Lilly, I need to ask you something. Am I pushing you?"

Lilly sat down beside him. "I don't know. This is all so much to take in. I mean, at sixteen, I know most of our friends have had sex already. I know you, at seventeen, might have—but I hope not." She held up her hand when he opened his mouth. "I don't want to know—not now." She rolled her napkin between her fingers. "But I haven't—not even close—and I truly plan to wait until marriage. Not that I ever planned to get married—until you. . . Oh, I don't know, Jase. I'm confused." Lilly felt her eyes welling up with tears.

"Okay, listen. I'm really sorry. I'll back off. I don't want to push you. Let's get things cleaned up and go watch a movie. We'll just hold hands. I won't kiss you again tonight. If you want to kiss me, you can—anytime. Fair?" He waited expectantly.

Phew. "That's fair. But if I do kiss you and then want to stop. . . ?"

"We stop. And I'll sleep wherever you want me to. Okay?"

"Okay. I feel so much better now."

They cleared the table and cleaned up the kitchen—laughing, joking, teasing. Lilly felt so comfortable she even swigged down the rest of her champagne and giggled at the feel of the sparkly bubbles on her upper lip.

A few minutes later, after changing into her comfy sweats, Lilly went to the family room where Jason had a fire roaring in the fireplace and a movie ready to play on the big-screen television. Boy, he moved fast.

He patted the seat next to him, so Lilly sat down close and he covered them both with a fleece blanket. A bowl of popcorn sat in front of them, and to each side of the bowl stood a freshly filled glass of champagne.

Lilly chuckled and shook her head. She could no longer say she'd never had any alcohol before. Her first taste had already happened, and she didn't have to drive until morning—so why not? She lifted her glass and tipped it toward Jason, then took a teeny sip. She settled back in his arms, and he started the movie.

True to his word, Jason didn't touch her in any way except for holding her hand. With the pressure off, Lilly felt like she could really relax. She barely paid attention to the movie as she thought back over her relationship with Jason. He'd been a part of her life forever. She'd loved him since they were little. He suffered with her when her dad left them. Then suffered equally when her mom married Stan. Jason showed her how a woman should be treated. He was so gorgeous, and his kisses. . .oh, his kisses.

Hmm. Could she steal a kiss now and not have it unleash a firestorm she couldn't put out? She snuck a quick glance at Jason.

He smiled down at her.

Losing her nerve, Lilly leaned forward and took a sip of her drink.

Do it, Lilly. She raised her eyes to Jason and then pulled him toward her in a kiss. This time she didn't let go. It went on for minutes until finally, she pulled away, breathless.

"I need some air." Lilly headed for the bathroom.

"Me, too."

Midnight came and went. One o'clock chimed on the clock. Finally, out of movies, conversation, and champagne, she had to make a decision.

"Well, Lilly, what's it going to be? You sleeping with me, or are you banishing me to the couch?" Jason's voice teased but also held an edge—a hint of a challenge.

Lilly knew what would happen, though. She knew that if they got into that bed and cuddled up, one thing would lead to another and everything would change. She knew the alcohol, the sleepy, heady feeling she had, the way she felt about Jason, and the intimacy of being in the bed together would be too much for her. She should say no. She should sleep on the couch—or let him.

But she didn't want to do that. She wanted to sleep with Jason in the bed. That *was* what she came over here for, right? To be a grown-up? Jason was her love, her hero. But wasn't God her ultimate hero? Memories of how she used to feel about God flooded her mind and tried to drown out her thoughts of Jason.

No! She pushed those thoughts away. She didn't want that right now. Or did she? What if she told Jason no and then he thought she was too immature for him? What if he dumped her? But if he dumped her, then she didn't want him anyway, did she?

Yes, I do.

What to do?

→ IT'S DECISION TIME

The time has come to make a decision. Think long and hard about what you would do if you were in Lilly's situation. It's easy to assume you'd make the right choice. But are you sure you'd risk losing your boyfriend, especially one you thought you loved and might marry one day? Are you sure you could withstand your own temptations and desires?

Once you make your decision, turn to the corresponding page to see how it turns out for Lilly—and for you.

Turn to page 304 if Lilly chooses to say no to Jason.

Turn to page 337 if Lilly decides to give in to Jason's desires—and her own.

❁

The next three chapters tell the story of what happened to Lilly when she rejected Jason's advances.

Chapter 10

JUST SAY NO

What was she thinking? Reality washed over Lilly like a bucket of ice water poured on her head. Mouth hanging open, she stared at Jason—shocked at what she'd considered doing. But how could she tell him? "Jason, I. . .I. . ." *Lord, give me the strength to do what's right.* "I can't. This is all wrong."

"What's *all* wrong?" Jason stood with his arms crossed on his chest.

Lilly gestured around the room and at the two of them. "This. Us being here like this. *That.*" She pointed at the bedroom. Clarity rushed at Lilly. What if she had. . . ? She shook her head to clear her thoughts, squared her shoulders, and faced Jason. "I'm going home."

Jason stared at her.

Lilly held his stare without blinking.

"Now? You're going home *now?*" Jason peeked at his watch and then laughed. "No way you're driving. First of all, you've had a few drinks, and you can't take a chance like that. Second, if you think you can leave and then we'll be fine like nothing ever happened. . ."

"Never mind. You're right. I forgot about the drinks. Of course I'm not going to drive." Lilly went to the kitchen. She could hear Jason's footsteps right behind her.

"Well good. At least you're being sensible." Jason put his hand on her shoulder. She shuddered at the smell of his musky cologne—a scent that *used* to make her swoon.

Lilly shrugged his hand off while she pressed and held the speed dial number for her home phone. She lifted her cell phone to her ear and looked out the window while she waited for someone to answer.

"Wait. What are you doing?" Jason tried to grab the phone. "Who are you calling?"

She held up her hand to quiet him. "Stan? Could someone come pick me up?"

"Are you okay?" Stan actually sounded concerned.

"Physically, I'm fine. But I'm not going to be

fine after you guys find out what's been going on." Lilly sighed heavily. Had it been a mistake to call? She turned toward Jason only to find him glaring at her. Nope. Calling home was not the mistake.

"Okay. I'll be right there. Your mom isn't feeling well tonight, so I'm going to let her sleep."

"Thanks, Stan. Only"—Lilly hesitated; the moment of truth—"you're going to need to come get me from Jason's house, not the church."

Lilly gripped the phone during a several-second pause, then heard a heavy sigh from the other end of the phone line.

"Okay. I can see there's going to be a discussion about things. So I'll wait until we get you home where you belong before I ask my questions. Give me five minutes." Stan disconnected the call.

Shivering, Lilly slipped her jacket on and pocketed her phone. Jason eyed her like a sideshow knife thrower. Feeling exposed under his gaze, she zipped her coat all the way to her chin. What could she say to make things better? "Jason, I—"

"No. Don't talk to me. There's nothing you could say that I want to hear. You're just a baby, and it's good you're going home to Mommy and Daddy." He stormed off to his room and slammed the door. The lock clicked.

Who's the baby?

Lilly gritted her teeth and fought the urge to pound on the door and defend herself. What would be the use? Even through her anger, she couldn't stop the tears leaving streaks down her cheeks. Why was she even crying? She knew why. Lost dreams. The dose of reality. The trouble she faced. Sadness over what she thought might be and now never would. All of the above and more. She gathered her belongings and went to the front door to wait for Stan.

Moments later, headlights appeared in the foyer window. Deep breath. Everything would be okay. Anything would be better than how she felt at that moment. She pulled the door open and bent for her things but jumped back when she found Stan already on the porch with smoke billowing from his ears. His face was enflamed and his nostrils flared. *Uh-oh.*

"I've got this." Lilly tried to step past him with her things. He wouldn't hit her, would he?

"Go ahead and wait in the car if you want to. I have a few words to say to Jason." Stan stormed into the house.

Oh no! Lilly ran to keep up.

A bewildered-looking Jason stood in the hallway—must have thought they'd left. He shrank against the wall when he saw Stan. "You c–c–can't be in here." He sidestepped toward his bedroom.

Coward.

"I'm not going to touch you, boy. But you are going to listen to me, whether you like it or not." Stan's hand snaked past Jason and gripped the door handle.

"Y–yes, sir." The defiant tilt to Jason's chin appeared confident at first glance, but his shaking hands and eyes glistening with tears gave him away.

Nice try.

"I have to tell you both that I'm so disappointed in you. No"—Stan rubbed his chin—"with *you*"—he pointed at Lilly—"I'm disappointed. But *you?*" He jerked his thumb at Jason. "You disgust me. You have an innocent young girl here. You know she's had trouble at home. You capitalize on that and position yourself as some kind of savior and then convince her to do things she shouldn't do." He turned to Lilly. "I'm going to let your mom talk to you about what happened here. But I'm hoping the fact that you called me means it didn't get too far."

"No. It didn't." Depended what he meant by too far. "Not as far as it could have, anyway."

"Good." Stan turned as though to leave, but something caught his eye. "Is that champagne?" He walked over to the kitchen counter and sniffed the empty bottle. "Did you two drink all of this?"

Lilly nodded.

"Ah, that's why you called me to come get you? Neither of you could drive?" Stan nodded. "Well, I'm thankful for that bit of common sense at least. Okay, let's go." He grabbed Lilly's things and held the door open for her.

Lilly stared out the window as the car sped toward home. What could she say to this man she'd hated for so long? He turned out be a decent guy, and now she'd gone and blown it. Would he forgive her, or would this make everything bad again? She'd finally given him reason to push her away for good—would he take the opportunity?

"Stan. . .I'm. . ." Lilly leaned her forehead against the cold window.

"I know." Stan silenced Lilly's attempts to speak with a fatherly pat on her leg. "We'll talk about it at home. It'll be okay."

When they pulled into the driveway, Lilly could see her mom standing at the kitchen sink looking out. "Mom's up."

"I'm sure she's concerned. She hasn't felt well today, though. Try to go easy on her." Stan pulled into the garage, turned off the car, then reached for his door handle. "Well? Shall we?"

They entered the kitchen through the garage door. "Where were you guys? Is everything okay?" Lilly's mom stood with her hands on her hips, her new blue robe wide open, exposing her swollen belly covered by a filmy nightgown.

"We're fine. We'll get to that in a minute." Stan went to her side. "How are you, Peg?" He took her hand.

"I'm okay. It must have been something I ate or just third-trimester blahs." Mom brushed off Stan's concern. "Tell me what's going on."

Lilly sat on a stool, cleared her throat, and started her story—leaving out no details—well, almost none. Mom didn't need to hear specifics about the make-out sessions—or maybe Lilly just couldn't bring herself to voice them. But she did tell her about the champagne. "I'm really sorry I lied to you. I'm so sorry that I got myself in such a mess."

Mom rubbed her temples and took a few deep breaths. She leaned against the counter and grabbed on for support. Stan brought her a chair and helped her sit down. "Don't worry about me. It just gets hard to stand up, and I'm kind of shocked by all this. I guess I shouldn't be, though." She shook her head and sighed. "Lill, we're going to have to talk about this tomorrow. There will be consequences, obviously—alcohol, lies, spending the night at your boyfriend's house. But there's more to all of this than consequences." She struggled to stand up. "I thought we'd made so much progress as a family." She bit her lip and gazed out the window.

"Mom. . ." *What have I done?*

Mom held up her hand. "Now's really not the time, Lilly. I'm too overwhelmed to think clearly. Maybe we'll wait and sort this out when we see Dr. Shepherd for our counseling session on Monday afternoon. I'll let her figure it out."

Huh? Lilly looked at Stan quizzically. Mom didn't want to talk to her about this until Monday? That was three days away.

Stan stepped up and supported Mom's arm. "I think that's a fine idea. For now, though, let's get some sleep. You need the rest." He helped his wife up the stairs and, once he got to the doorway to his bedroom, peered down across the railing to Lilly who still stood in the kitchen doorway. "Get some sleep. It'll be okay." He winked at her and shut the door to their room.

Lilly got herself a glass of milk, hoping it would settle her roiling stomach, and sat at the kitchen table. She fingered the fringe on the decorative cloth napkin as she thought back over the events of the evening. What was Jason thinking right now? Was he still mad at her? Was he lying in bed awake, worried if she was still mad at him? How could she restore things to the way they had been? It was too late to call him, but she'd try to reach him first thing the next morning. They needed to talk things through. Lilly took her glass to the sink and rinsed it out. She couldn't do anything else that night—or what remained of the night. She'd better get some sleep so she could tackle whatever tomorrow held.

❀

Third try, no answer. Lilly had been trying to reach Jason all morning, but he hadn't picked up his cell. She even tried his home phone—no answer. Maybe he hadn't gotten up yet. Lilly checked the time. One o'clock in the afternoon.

Unlikely he was still asleep. He must be avoiding her. Embarrassed? Yeah, maybe that was it. Maybe he regretted his behavior. Or maybe he was mad at her.

Lilly lumbered down the stairs and found her mom in the kitchen stirring the contents of a large stockpot. "Mmm, is that what I think it is? Homemade chicken-and-dumpling soup?"

"Sure is." Mom grinned at Lilly. "I think we could all use some comfort food. Don't you agree?" When Lilly nodded, she continued. "Lill, I'm so sorry about how I reacted last night. I shouldn't have walked out and not dealt with your troubles. I mean, I felt angry, hurt, confused, sure, but so were you. . .so *are* you, I'd imagine." She reached out to pull her daughter into an embrace. "I didn't feel good, and it all took me by surprise, so I handled the whole thing horribly. I'm here for you now, though. I love you, and we'll figure out how to fix this. . .somehow." She pulled back and tipped Lilly's chin up so they were eye to eye. "Okay?"

"I love you, too, Mom. And I understood, really. I mean, yeah, I was pretty confused last night—even more now—oh, I don't know. But I'm sure I'm in trouble. Where do you want to start?"

"Honestly, as far as any trouble you might be in, I think there's more to this than we can see on the surface. I think I'd rather wait and let Dr. Shepherd sort some of that out over the next couple of weeks. She has a way of getting to the heart of things, and I'm afraid I'll just make it worse. My radar seems to have been off-kilter for several years."

"Oh, it's probably not as bad as you think." Lilly gestured toward Stan sitting in the recliner and then smiled at her mom. They both laughed.

"Now. Tell me about Jason. What on earth happened?"

"Well. . ." Lilly sat down at the table and started fidgeting with the cloth napkin again. "I don't know. It's probably a simple case of girl looking for love turns to a friend who thinks he's God's gift to the female race."

"Jason? That doesn't sound like him." Mom narrowed her eyes.

"Believe me, I was shocked, too. I mean, I hope he comes around and realizes that I had the right to say no. But he seemed pretty mad last night."

"Sometimes boys have trouble getting past their physical desires. It's all they can think about when they get worked up. That's why we try to keep you from being in those situations—alone with a boy." Mom let out a deep sigh.

"I know. I get that now. I thought you were trying to control me—or let Stan control me, anyway. But really, you've tried to protect me from things."

"Right. . .me *and* Stan."

"Yeah. He was great last night. He really defended me." Lilly tilted her head toward the family room as Stan laughed out loud at something on TV. "He's really changed, Mom. I think it's for real."

"This is the Stan I married. He went through a tough time. But you're right, he's coming back." Mom rubbed her belly. "But what are we going to do about Jason? I assume you realize that your dating days are on hold now. Indefinitely."

Lilly chuckled. "Uh. Yeah. I figured that. It's for the best. As for Jason, I tried calling him a bunch of times—he won't answer. So he's either embarrassed or angry."

"Maybe both. It'll be okay, either way." Mom patted her hand. "You did the right thing, Lill. I'm so proud of you for standing up for yourself and what you knew was right even when the pressure was high—even when you really wanted to go the other way."

"Thanks, Mom. We can talk more about this later, but I'm going to go spend some time alone, if that's okay." She hugged her mom before she left the kitchen. "I love you."

"I love you, too, Lill."

Up in her bedroom, Lilly went into her closet like she used to do years ago when the fights between her mom and Stan started happening. She squeezed into the far corner and pulled the pants and skirts around her head. She pressed her head into the corner and closed her eyes. Silence. Solitude. She was all alone.

Now what?

Chapter 11

EXPOSED

Searching the grounds for signs of Jason, Lilly hurried into the school building. She wanted nothing more than to find him before class and make sure everything was okay between them. They'd hit a bump in the road, sure. But nothing true love couldn't overcome. She'd forgive him for pushing her too fast and let him know that she planned to wait until marriage for the kind of intimacy he wanted. Surely he'd understand. Right? What kind of man wouldn't want a pure bride on his wedding day? But was Jason a man at all? Only time would tell.

Lilly looked down the hallway toward the cafeteria. Students milled around in every direction—no Jason. She turned toward his locker, hoping to find him there. But no Jason.

Maybe he'd already gone to his first period classroom. Lilly grew frantic. What if she didn't find him until lunchtime? What if he hadn't even come to school that morning?

Almost time for the bell. Lilly reluctantly abandoned her search and went to collect her things. Her locker door squeaked open, and she bent to set her books on the lower shelf in order to select the ones she needed for study hall. Turning her head just slightly so she could reach a tad farther into the locker, Lilly noticed a note taped at eye level to the inside of the door.

Jason! He was the only other person who had the combination to her locker. He must have left the note that morning. Lilly tore the paper from the door and unfolded it to find one word printed in small capital letters in the middle of the page.

TEASE.

Lilly's stomach flip-flopped as that one word walloped her in the gut. Her chin fell to her chest, and tears sprang to her eyes as a new reality assailed her thoughts. Jason wasn't the man she thought. He was selfish. He didn't have her best interests at heart. He didn't care what she wanted. He. Didn't. Love. Her.

Looking at the note again—as though it

might somehow change—Lilly slumped against the row of lockers, deflating as she slid to the floor. The bell rang, but she didn't move. She'd be late for class, but so what? What mattered anymore? She'd lost the love of her life because she was too immature to do what it took to keep him.

No. That's not what happened.

Lilly shook her head and sat up a little straighter. She *had* done the right thing, the difficult thing—the mature thing. Jason acted like the immature one. More importantly, he proved he didn't deserve to be the love of her life. Surely God had someone already picked out for her who would honor her wishes and respect her body. Someone who would appreciate it when she wanted to do the godly thing rather than fight her about it. Someone who would be her one and only. Jason was not that person—obviously.

A realization slammed into her. She'd been headed down the same road her mom had walked. She had clung to Jason and almost given up her own values, just as her mom had clung to Stan and silenced her own voice in the process. Lilly had refused to see the wrong in any of her actions because she wanted so desperately to be loved and part of a whole.

She raised her knees up to her chest and hugged her legs as she put the pieces together. Lilly wished she could go back and change her reactions—say different things. She'd love to tell her mom she understood. It would be so great if she could tell Stan she respected him for his changes. Well. . .why couldn't she? Yep. That's what she had to do. She'd tell them how she felt.

Wait. Lilly looked up and down the deserted hallway. Where were all the students? She glanced at her watch. Twenty minutes late for class. Too late to just walk in, she'd need a pass from the office. She grabbed her books and strode toward the front of the school. Passing the hallway nearest the office, she sensed someone was watching her. She slowly turned— it felt like one of those movie moments when the slow motion signaled that something very important was about to happen—and locked eyes with Jason who sauntered toward her.

He held her gaze—not a flicker of a smile, not a nod of recognition. If anything, he smirked. Lilly focused on the coldness in his face for so long, she almost didn't notice the girl at his side who stared up at him with adoration and a private promise. He had his arm around her shoulders and gripped her upper arm tightly, possessively. Lily's heart trembled as the final reality hit her. Jason was a jerk.

With her hand on the office door, Lilly paused. *Thank You, Lord, for protecting me from myself and for showing me the truth.* Then she went inside and walked straight to the nurse—the students usually found her far more sympathetic than the secretary. "Um. Excuse me, Mrs. Thomas. I'm late for class, and I wondered if you could give me a pass."

"Are you sick, dear?" The nurse laid the back of her hand across Lilly's forehead.

Lilly shook her head. "No. My problem was more. . .um. . .personal."

"Oh." The nurse nodded and went to a metal cabinet. "Do you need some feminine products, then?"

"Oh. No. Not that." Lilly didn't want to lie to the nurse, but she didn't want to tell her everything, either. "I had some personal. . .um. . .relationship problems, and I kind of spaced out in the hallway for a little bit, thinking things through."

The nurse looked at Lilly for a few moments. She clucked her tongue. "Miss LeMure, I hope you know we can't have this kind of disregard for our school schedule. But since you don't make a habit of being late, I'm going to give you the pass this one time. In the future, you need to keep your personal troubles out of school. Okay?"

"I understand. Thanks so much." Lilly reached for the pass, but the nurse held on to it.

She smiled at Lilly. "I hope everything turns out okay with whatever was bothering you." She let go of the pass.

"Everything's going to be fine. Thanks." Lilly grinned and scurried off to class.

❀

"Mind if I join you?" Lilly smiled at Sam as she slid onto the metal bench beside her.

Sam slid her lunch down to make room. "'Course not." She smiled and popped a french fry into her mouth. "I heard you and Jason broke up. You okay?"

Lilly shrugged. "Wasn't really the best weekend of my life, but I'll live. Definitely for the best. Much rather find out who he really is now than after it's too late."

"Uh-oh. Sounds like there's a story there. Want to hang out after school?"

"That sounds good." Lilly took a drink of her Arizona Green Tea. "Oh wait. I can't. I forgot I have an appointment with my mom and da– Stan. How about I call you after dinner? If it's not too late, we can hang out— otherwise we'll chat on the phone."

"Sounds good." Sam's voice dropped to a whisper. "Looks like we have company." She tilted her head toward the space above Lilly's shoulder.

Lilly startled when she glanced up to find Jason standing there. *What did he want? Why didn't he say something?* She raised her eyebrows and waited.

"Can we talk?" Jason shifted his feet and shoved his hands into the pockets of his jeans.

"I guess." Lilly turned to Sam. "Can you scoot down a little bit?"

As Sam slid over, Jason shook his head. "No, let's go over there." He pointed at an empty bench along the far wall of the lunchroom.

Lilly rose and picked up her lunch tray. Having suddenly lost her appetite, she dumped the entire contents into the nearest trash can. Stepping over book bags and maneuvering around clusters of students, Lilly followed Jason over to the bench and sat down on the edge of the seat beside him. *Now what?*

He looked down at the tops of his shoes.

"Listen. I wanted to apologize for that note in your locker. My pride stung a little bit."

What did he expect her to say? Lilly forced herself not to respond, not even to flinch. If he thought the note was the big problem. . .

"I'm also sorry for having my arm around Stacie earlier. I only wanted to make you jealous."

I can't believe he's saying this. Lilly shook her head. *Digging a bigger hole for yourself, Jason.*

"I guess what I'm trying to say here is that I'm willing to give you a second chance."

Lilly sputtered as she tried to gain control of her laughter. "You'll. . .give *me*. . .a second chance?" Maybe she'd lost her mind, but she couldn't stop laughing.

Jason rolled his eyes. "Well, I can see you haven't grown up at all." He stood up to leave.

She swiped at the tears running down her cheeks. Hilarity mixed with relief—what a joyous combo.

Obviously flustered, Jason stormed off. Probably to go find Stacie or someone equally mature.

Lilly wiped her eyes with her sleeve and sat back to catch her breath. She surveyed the lunchroom like a general looking on a battlefield after a victory. Proud of herself.

Free.

Chapter 12

I DO

Dr. Shepherd tapped her pen on her teeth. "Let's try a little exercise. You've had a little over a week since *the incident* to sort things out. Now that you've had time to think, I'd like you each to tell me the one thing that disappoints you most about your own actions, and then tell me the one thing that upsets you most about what someone else did—someone who's here in this room. Stan, we'll start with you."

"Hmm." Stan appeared to be considering his words carefully. "What disappoints me most about myself is that I haven't been a good enough stepdad so Lilly would have known she could call me for help without being scared of my reaction. What makes me upset about someone else is that Jason—"

Dr. Shepherd held up a finger. "Nope. Someone in this room, remember?"

"Oh, right." He stared at the ceiling for several moments and then shook his head. "I'm sorry, I'm most mad at myself. I don't have an answer to this one."

"Okay, that's fair. How about you, Peggy?"

"I'm disappointed in myself that there was so much going on with Lilly that I was unaware of—out of touch. And what most upsets me about someone else is that Lilly lied to us. When I think of what could have happened that night. . ." She put her elbow on the armrest and rubbed her forehead.

"How about you, Lilly?"

"There are so many reasons why I'm disappointed with myself. I blew it. Big-time. There's so much I would change. I guess I'd go back to the beginning and not lie. That would have solved the whole thing." She bit a piece of dry skin off her lip. "Now, what am I most upset about in someone else?"

Dr. Shepherd nodded.

Mom's eyes traveled between Stan and Lilly.

Stan looked up and put his hands behind his head, exhaling deeply.

Lilly shook her head. "You know what? I

prefer not to answer this. We all know what I would have said six months ago. But that's history. If people change and ask for forgiveness, shouldn't we let that stay in the past?"

Mom grinned at Stan, who sighed in relief.

Dr. Shepherd sat back in satisfaction. "I think we've gotten somewhere here, folks. Lilly, how do you feel about relationships now? What do you think of when you consider marriage?"

"I used to think I didn't want to be married . . .ever. Jason made me feel like maybe I did. Then he changed, and the thought of marriage made me cringe again." Lilly rubbed her chin. "I guess I've learned that marriage can't be about someone else being perfect. It's kind of a choice you make—a commitment—and then you let God work out the rest. I mean, no one's ever going to be perfect right?"

Dr. Shepherd nodded. "Exactly—"

"Take my mom and Stan, for example. I used to use them as the what-not-to-do example for why I never wanted to marry. Now I sort of see them as an example of patience and commitment, and proof that anyone can change if they set their mind to it. But as for me, I guess I don't know if I ever want to get married." Lilly furrowed her eyebrows. "I don't need to know right now. Do I?"

"Absolutely not." Dr. Shepherd put down her pen and shook her head. "It really has nothing to do with your life right now. Your purpose right now is to be a daughter, soon a big sister, and a student. God will lead you where He wants you to go in your future if you let Him."

Dr. Shepherd looked at Stan. "I want to remind you all that the only place you'll find true unconditional love and acceptance is in the arms of Jesus." She moved her gaze to Mom. "Once you find fulfillment there, your needs and expectations of others will diminish and you won't suffer such disappointment when other people fail you." She turned to Lilly. "Then, when He chooses to, *He'll* love *you* through someone else, and He'll love that person *through* you. *That* is when you find out what true love *really* is."

Lilly nodded. It made perfect sense. Someday she'd know true love if God brought it to her. It wasn't something she had to search for. True love would come from God.

"Peg, you okay?" Stan sounded concerned.

"I'm not feeling too well. . ." Mom rubbed her belly. Her eyes widened, and she scooted forward on her chair and sat still for a few moments.

"Are you sick?" Stan's eyebrows furrowed.

"We can stop if we need to," Dr. Shepherd offered.

Mom shook her head, her body seeming to relax. "No, no. This is really good. I think we've made some great headway. I've been cramping throughout the day. It's part of the stretching that's going on to make room for our little guy." She smiled softly and patted her tummy.

"Okay then." Dr. Shepherd flipped a page in her notepad and continued. "I planned to help you recap the growth that you've all experienced as a way of remembering how far you've come these past few months."

"Oh boy." Mom's eyes grew wide, and she clutched her stomach.

"Or. . .not." Dr. Shepherd looked at her watch as she strode to her desk and picked up the phone. She punched in one number and waited. "Hi. Dr. Shepherd, here. It looks like I have a woman in labor."

Lilly's mouth fell open, and she dropped off the chair to her knees at her mom's feet. "Mom? Really? This is it?" Lilly looked up at Stan who broke into a grin.

"I wondered." Stan went to Dr. Shepherd. "Do we need to call an ambulance?"

Dr. Shepherd held up one finger to Stan. "I'm guessing about five minutes apart from the looks of things." She nodded. "Okay. We'll have her ready." Dr. Shepherd hung up the phone and hurried to Mom's side. "Okay. We're all set. Transport will come to get you and zip you over to the hospital. Your water hasn't broken, so you should have plenty of time."

Mom panted and clutched her stomach. She had paled, and her knuckles were white.

Lilly turned to Dr. Shepherd. "She doesn't look so good. Is something wrong?"

"Wrong? No." Dr. Shepherd laughed. "She's having a baby. It's hard work. Your mom will be fine."

Every minute or two, Mom started panting—slowly at first, then building to the point where she sucked the air in and blew it out with intense force every few seconds. Could she hyperventilate doing that? When it seemed like the pain reached a crescendo, Mom grabbed her belly and scrunched up into a ball—or at least what might have been a ball if her belly weren't in the way. The moans went right through Lilly. Could it really hurt *that* bad?

After a few seconds of what seemed like sheer agony, Mom let out a final moan, held her breath, and grabbed Stan's hand and squeezed until her eyes seemed to bug out of their sockets. That was the worst part for Lilly. What if Mom stopped breathing altogether?

Lilly grabbed her phone and punched out a text message to Grams. BABY. HOSPITAL. HURRY.

The van hit a pothole and everyone bounced a few inches off the seat. Mom groaned and clutched her belly. Her skin looked like paste.

"Hey! Can you be a little more careful?" Stan glared at the driver.

Mom squeezed Lilly's hand as another pain took hold. *Uh-oh—a big one.* Lilly winced and turned her face away so her mom wouldn't know she practically broke Lilly's fingers. It went on for a long time until, finally, her grip loosened and her gasps subsided. "That was a whopper, huh, Lill?" Mom offered a brave wink.

"Are you going to be okay?" Lilly leaned over so she could look right into her mom's eyes. "You're going to get pain medicine at the hospital, right?" She'd be crazy not to.

"What, and miss out on all the fun? Nah." Mom's grin wobbled at the corners. "I can take it." Another contraction started just as her words trailed off. "They're coming. . .faster," she grunted between breaths.

The van sped up, and the driver darted a glance in his rearview mirror. "Hang on. We're almost there. Keep breathing."

Stan rubbed Mom's shoulders.

Mom huffed and puffed.

Please, God. Get us there on time.

Finally, the transport van turned into the hospital's emergency bay and slowed to a stop. The driver gave three short horn blasts. Two nurses came out to meet them with a wheelchair. Mom motioned for them to wait until her contraction ended. The nurse in the panda scrubs shifted impatiently and looked at her watch. Finally, Mom lumbered from the van and squatted down to try to get into the wheelchair.

What if the baby fell out right on the sidewalk? Lilly shuddered at the thought as the nurses helped Mom lower into the seat. They wheeled her past the automatic doors and into the lobby. *Phew.* Lilly exhaled for what felt like the first time since they left Dr. Shepherd's office.

The group headed toward a set of swinging doors on which a big sign screamed: No

ADMITTANCE PAST THIS POINT. Nurse Panda turned around and put up a hand in front of Lilly. Peering over her half glasses, she pursed her lips and said, "You'll have to wait out here. Someone will come tell you if anything happens." *Swoosh.* The door swung shut behind them and Lilly stood there alone.

If anything happens? What had she meant by that?

Lilly sank down into one of the orange vinyl chairs in the waiting room and glanced at the television, her thoughts racing. What was happening to her mom? She would have a new little brother in a little while. But what if something went wrong? *Oh God. Please don't let anything go wrong.* Lilly jumped up and paced as she prayed. *You wouldn't take her from me now. Would You? Not when we were just getting things figured out. I need her, Lord. Stan needs her, too. And we all need the baby. Please, God.*

The sliding doors opened and someone came blustering in from outside. *Grams!* Lilly ran to her grandmother and threw her arms around her neck. "I haven't seen Mom since they took her back. We don't know anything. I don't even know if she's okay." Lilly sobbed on her grandma's shoulder. "What do we do?"

"Do? Well, we wait for this baby boy to come into the world." She chuckled and squeezed Lilly's shoulder. "Doll, people have babies every day. Just relax." Grams pulled back from Lilly's embrace and looked into her eyes. "It's going to be fine—great, even. Just have faith."

"Okay. I'll try." Lilly wiped her eyes and shook the tension from her arms.

"Come on." Grams jerked her head toward the elevators. "Let's go get some junk food."

Just then, Nurse Panda stepped up to them. "Are you here for Margaret Sanders?"

Why the formality? The nurse already knew Lilly. Something must be wrong. Lilly's mouth went dry.

Grams stepped forward. "Yep, I'm Peg's mother. This is her daughter."

"If you'll come with me, then." The nurse turned away without a word and led them to the elevators.

Why didn't she smile? Wouldn't a nurse be happy about the birth of a baby if everyone was fine? Lilly couldn't control her racing thoughts, but she knew she needed to get a grip before she saw her mom.

The nurse led them to the fourth floor, past the nurses' station, down the hall, and into a hospital room. In the middle of the room machines whizzed and beeped and medical-type people milled around. Lilly found Stan in the center of the melee—teary, but grinning. She followed his eyes as he proudly watched his wife, who looked exhausted but so very happy. In her arms lay a little bundle wrapped in blue with a pink and blue striped cap on his teeny head. The blanket rose and fell with the deep slumbering breaths of Lilly's little baby brother. Brother. *My brother.*

"Come here, Lill. He's beautiful. You've got to see him." Mom gazed down at her arms as if she held an angel. She tipped her elbow down and lifted the baby's head. "Meet your baby brother, Matthew—it means 'gift of God'. . .because he is." She grinned as she admired her son. Mom had never looked so beautiful.

Lilly stepped closer and peered over the folds of the blanket to see Matthew for the first time. She gasped as she gazed at the face of her baby brother. His perfect little rosebud lips were pursed in a kiss, and long, dark eyelashes rested on his chubby pink cheeks. The tiniest fingers she'd ever seen squeezed Stan's strong finger— they only reached halfway around.

To Lilly's surprise, her mom lifted the bundle and laid Matthew in her arms. When she looked into his eyes, she instantly understood what it meant to love someone so unconditionally it made her heart ache. This was what it meant to surrender and let God's perfect love flow through her to encapsulate another human being. Someday God might have another for her, but for now, Baby Matty was all she needed.

True love.

❀

The next three chapters tell the story of what happened to Lilly when she gave in to Jason's advances.

Chapter 10

WHAT HAVE I DONE?

Gazing into Jason's eyes, Lilly knew exactly what she wanted. She'd do anything to have his unconditional love and acceptance. "Don't worry, Jase. I'm not going to banish you to the couch." She smiled nervously. "Your place is right beside me. All night long. No matter what."

Jason grinned and jumped to his feet. "Now you're making sense. What're we waiting for?"

Lilly padded behind him toward his bedroom. *What's going to happen in there? This is so wrong.* She looked in every direction, hoping for a diversion. *But he loves me and I love him—true love—right?*

When they reached the doorway, Jason turned, his eyes crinkling at the corners as he smiled at Lilly. He took both of her hands and backed into the room without breaking eye contact with her.

Lilly willed her body to stop shaking. Could he hear the thumping of her heartbeat?

Jason guided her in and released her hands when they arrived at the bedside. He walked back to the door and closed it softly before turning to her.

She squeezed her eyes shut and took a deep breath while Jason approached.

"Everything's going to be fine, Lill. Look. . ." He reached down and pulled back the covers on the twin-sized bed. "We'll get in and cuddle." Jason brushed off some crumbs, climbed into the bed, and scooted all the way over until his back pressed against the wall. He smiled and patted the spot next to him.

Oh God. What am I doing?

Ignoring the cries of her heart, Lilly crawled into the bed. The springs squeaked as the rickety frame accepted her weight. She settled in next to him, her back pressed against his chest, and nuzzled her face into the pillow. Maybe she'd fall right to sleep and morning would come before anything happened. Maybe not.

Rustling of the covers gave way to the touch of his hand on her shoulder. He ran his fingertips down her arm to her wrist, sending sparks through her body.

"Mmm. Isn't this nice?" he whispered, leaning close enough that she could feel his hot breath. Then Jason feathered a series of light kisses on the nape of her neck.

Shivers shot up and down Lilly's body, and she trembled for a completely different reason than before. Her resolve melted into desire, and her self-control went out the window.

What am I doing?

Exactly what I want to do. Her body took charge as Lilly rolled over so she and Jason were face-to-face. They locked eyes in silent agreement; then Lilly moved a few inches until their faces touched.

Jason pressed his lips hard against hers, and electricity shot between them.

Decision made.

❀

Sunlight streamed through the vertical window blinds, leaving stripes on the wall like the bars of a jail cell. Lilly squinted, trying to grow accustomed to the light. Her eyes roved the room as memories from the night before trickled into her consciousness. She didn't want to lift her head or shift her position, because Jason would wake up, and then she'd have to face him.

What have I done? Lilly groaned in silence and mentally pounded her forehead—but remained still.

Wait a minute. They loved each other. She shouldn't be embarrassed. But what if she were pregnant? Could it happen that fast? From one time? Oh, there *was* that one girl from school. She had said it was *her* first time, but no one believed her. Most people had automatically assumed she slept around—Lilly had thought so, too. Would people think that of her if the same thing happened to her?

What if he doesn't want me now?

Lilly had expected to wake up feeling more connected to Jason—part of a whole. Instead, she felt alone, exposed, naked—and not only physically. Jason now knew her better than anyone else, but Lilly felt like she didn't know him at all. Could they go back to their old relationship?

No. Nothing would ever be the same. They'd taken a step that changed everything forever.

She'd given away her first time and could never, ever offer that to someone else—to her husband. Well, that settled it. She'd have to marry Jason—or no one.

Lilly reached out from the covers, stretching to pick up her sweatshirt from the floor near the bed. She pulled the shirt to her body, trying to move nothing but her arm. Still under the covers, she slipped her arms into the sleeves and got it ready to pull down over her head when she sat up, knowing the movement would probably wake Jason. *One. Two. Three. Now.*

In one motion, Lilly sat up and yanked her shirt down—without an instant to spare.

Jason groaned and rolled to his back. He stretched his arms over his head and smiled softly. He opened his eyes and saw Lilly sitting up beside him. "Hey, cutie. Where're you going?" He pulled her down for a kiss.

Eww. His breath smelled horrible. "I'm going to brush my teeth." *You probably should, too.*

"Okay. Then hurry back. We don't have much time." Jason wiggled his eyebrows up and down.

"Ha-ha. I don't think so. I'm going home to shower." Lilly moved from the bed, pulling one of the blankets around her exposed lower half. "We can talk later on, though. Maybe you can come over?"

"I don't know. . . . Will your parents be home?"

"Probably. Why? We can watch a movie or something." What was up with that? He wasn't interested in hanging out if her parents were around? Would their whole relationship be about sex now?

"We'll see." Jason propped up on an elbow. "I wish you wouldn't go so soon. We still have more time."

"No. I really have to go. I need to pull myself together." As if *that* were possible.

"All right. Make sure you lock the door when you leave." Jason lay down and pulled the covers up to his neck.

He wasn't even going to get up to see her out? Lilly blinked back tears and hurried to gather her things. She needed fresh air—and time to sort through what had happened.

❀

The hot water made her skin tingle. Lilly moved under the pulsating showerhead so the stream would cascade from the top of her head, down to her feet—cleansing, refreshing.

Not renewing, though. Lilly's tears mingled with the droplets and washed down the drain— like her innocence had the night before. *Why? Why did I do it?* She put her forearms on the ceramic tile and pressed her cheek against its cool surface.

Thirty minutes later, the hot water began to

turn cold. Lilly turned off the shower. She still didn't feel clean—but no shower could fix that. As she toweled off, she stared at the mirror, trying to find the changes. Were they visible on the outside? Would people know?

Lilly pulled the towel tight around her body and made her way to her bedroom, grateful no one else was home. A few minutes later, dressed in her baggiest and warmest sweat suit, Lilly crawled between the thick covers of her bed, curled into a ball, and squeezed her eyes shut.

Just let me sleep for an hour. Sleep—the only way to escape her thoughts, her regret, her shame.

❀

Please pick up. Please pick up. Lilly bounced her foot as she sat on the edge of her bed, waiting for the youth pastor's wife to answer her phone. She rubbed her eyes while she waited, still sleepy from her nap but a little less foggy.

"Hello?"

Oh, thank God. "Heather? It's Lilly. Do you have a minute?"

"Sure. What's up?" It sounded like she shut off a water faucet.

Lilly bit a piece of dry skin off her lip. "I'm not disturbing anything, am I?"

"Nope, just doing dishes—always glad to be pulled away from that." Heather chuckled. "Come on. Out with it. What's going on?"

"I did something—actually, Jason and I did something—and now I wish I could undo it, but I can't." Lilly started to cry.

"Oh, sweetie. I think I understand what you're saying." Heather sighed.

"Yeah. It's been a rough morning. I took a nap, and I feel somewhat better. But I can't get past the thought that I can't fix this. And. . .what if I'm pregnant?"

"Well, there's nothing you can do to change that now. You'll have to wait a few weeks to see. Try not to dwell on that, though. There's no point. . .until you know." Heather was silent for a few seconds. "Have you told your mom?"

"No way!" Lilly saw her wide-eyed, horrified expression in the mirror.

"Lilly, this is big. It's not like you watched a bad movie or said a swear word—what happened is life changing. You're going to need some help with this." Heather cleared her throat. "I really think you should give your mom a chance. Maybe Zach and I could talk to her with you."

Big mistake calling Heather. "Well, I'll think

about what you said. I have to go now."

"When you're ready, I have a group that I'd like to bring you to." Heather rushed her words. "It's for girls in situations just like you."

"Yeah. I'll think about it. Thanks. Gotta go." Lilly hung up and stared at the phone. Heather might have been right, but she could never tell Mom about what happened. Why had she even called her? This was private—what if Heather told someone?

Lilly groaned and flopped back on her bed. She pounded her forehead with her fist. How long would she feel this way? She wished she could crawl out of her skin. . .become someone else. . .start over. But sadly it was now crystal clear that life had no do-overs. She rolled to the side and clutched her blanket.

A soft knock sounded on her door. "Lill? You in there?"

Great. Just what she needed. "Yeah. Just a sec." Lilly jumped off the bed and smoothed her mussed-up hair. She took a deep breath and pasted a grin on her face before opening the door. She breezed right past her bewildered-looking Mom.

"Where are you go–"

"I'm starving—going down to the kitchen,"

Lilly shot over her shoulder as she hurried down the hall. "Want to join me?" *Natural enough, or over the top? Calm down a little.* Too much false energy was as bad as too little.

Mom had already started following—well, waddling—along behind her. "Stan and I just got back from lunch. I brought you a burger and fries."

"I can see we're still on the health-food kick," Lilly teased, hoping it didn't sound snide. Had Mom noticed a difference in her yet?

"Yeah. Hopefully the junk-food cravings stop when the baby comes." Mom smiled down at her belly and rubbed in gentle circles. "Only a few more weeks."

Oh right. Her shoulders relaxed. She needn't put on an act to convince them nothing was wrong—they wouldn't pick up on it even if she dissolved in tears right in front of them. She was invisible.

"Yep. A few more weeks." Talk about the baby. That would keep Mom distracted. Lilly took the foam carryout container from the refrigerator. "Can you hold out?" She peeked inside, suddenly famished.

Mom poured two glasses of milk while Lilly put her food in the microwave. "I don't have a whole lot of choice. This little guy will join us when he's good and ready."

"Are you nervous about the birth?" It had never crossed Lilly's mind to wonder about that before.

Mom tilted her head to the side. "Hmm. Nervous? I wouldn't exactly say that. I mean, I've done this before, and I pretty much know what to expect. I'm not looking forward to the pain, though." She laughed and brought the milk to the table. The chair creaked as Mom fell into it.

Lilly shuddered. "I don't know if I ever want to have kids." *Unless I'm already pregnant.* "The idea of knowing how bad it's going to hurt and that you kind of have to let things happen to you. . .I mean, the baby's got to come out. . . . Ewww." Lilly squeezed some ketchup onto her burger and into a mound next to the limp french fries. She took a big bite of her juicy burger. "No thanks," she mumbled through her full mouth.

"Oh, you'll feel differently about pregnancy and childbirth when you get older. You'll see." Mom swiped a fry and folded it into her mouth. "Remember when you used to think Jason was nothing but a gross boy? Things changed, didn't they?"

Why did she have to bring him up? "Yeah, I guess so." Lilly's appetite vanished. She moved the fries around and tried to take another bite. No use. "You want the rest of this, Mom?"

"Um. Sure. But why? I thought you were hungry." Mom reached across the table and pulled the container to her.

"I was. . .but not anymore."

Chapter 11

NOT ENOUGH

"You *what?*" Jason's eyes flashed as he stared Lilly down. "You can't decide to go back to the way things were. It doesn't work that way, little girl."

Lilly winced and covered her face with her hands, leaning her head against the brick wall of the school building. "I thought you loved me." Tears seeped between her fingers, and her shoulders shook. Surely he'd comfort her.

"I thought *you* loved *me*. But now you're trying to tell me you regret our time together?" Jason glared across the schoolyard as the students filed off their buses. "And you don't want it to happen again?" He lowered his voice to a hiss. "How can you even say that and expect it to be okay?"

"How can *I?* How can *you?*" Lilly dug in her

jacket pocket for a tissue. "You promised that if I got uncomfortable, we'd pull back. How can you be so"—she gestured at his crossed arms and angry facial expression—"mean?"

"I'm not being mean. I'm being realistic. You made your choice. There's no going back now." Jason raised his eyebrows. "So what's it going to be?"

"I don't even know you." Lilly sobbed, seeing but ignoring the stares of the students milling all around her.

Jason shrugged and grabbed his bag. He swaggered off to blend into the flow of people entering the building before the start of the school day.

Lilly watched him walk away looking casual, not a care in the world. Jason grinned as a friend approached him, and as they walked through the school entrance, Jason gave his a buddy a fist bump.

Lilly shuddered to think what that was about.

❀

How could such a busy lunchroom feel so empty? Lilly slid a tray along the cafeteria shelf and tried to select something to eat. Her stomach felt hollow, and nothing sounded good. She picked up half of a limp turkey sandwich and a little bowl of vanilla pudding, knowing she wouldn't eat any. Lilly searched for a seat, carefully keeping her eyes from wandering in the direction of the table where she and Jason used to sit.

In the middle of the room, Samantha Pruitt stood beside a table, waving. "Lilly. Come on over. I saved you a seat."

Phew. She hurried over to Sam and slid in beside her. "Thanks. You spared me several moments of agony."

Sam fingered her sandwich then popped a potato chip into her mouth. "So. . ." She held up a finger while she finished her bite. "I heard what happened. Are you okay?"

"You heard Jason and I broke up?" Hopefully that's all she heard.

"Well, yeah. But there are stories about the weekend floating around." Sam winced. "I hate being the bearer of bad news."

Ugh. Seriously? Three hours into the school day and news of the biggest mistake of her life was already being whispered up and down the hallways? "I don't even want to know. I'd rather crawl into a hole." Lilly put her head in her hands. "I feel like the biggest idiot on the planet. Ever."

"It'll pass. Sooner than you think. But are you okay?" Sam's eyebrows knitted together.

"Physically, I'm fine. Mentally, I'm exhausted. Emotionally—I'm destroyed. Any other questions?" Lilly dropped her head onto the table. "I can't believe he spread this around already."

Sam exhaled heavily. "Okay. I wasn't going to tell you this, but I think it might help." She took a sip of her Mountain Dew. "This summer I spent a month at my grandparents' house in West Virginia. I met some people and even dated this one guy, Chad. To make a long story short, I ended up having sex with him a week before I was due to head home."

Lilly's mouth dropped open. "Really? Did you regret doing it?"

"Oh yeah, totally. I think about that night all the time and wish I could take it back. But, as you know, it's too late." Sam shrugged.

"So what happened with Chad? Did you stay in touch?"

Sam shook her head. "Sadly, no. He turned out to be a deadbeat." She rolled her eyes and munched on another chip. "He bragged about his 'conquest' to all of his friends. Kind of like that." Sam gestured across the room to Jason who perched on a lunch table with five guys standing around, practically drooling over whatever he said. "Turned out he had a girlfriend who had been out of town at *her* grandparents' house while I was in town."

"Wow. That's terrible." Lilly lifted a spoonful of pudding and then watched it plop back into her bowl. "Guys are jerks."

"Some of them are." Sam's lip curled up in disgust as she surveyed the male options in the lunchroom. "We can only hope they get better with age."

❀

If time was supposed to heal wounds, five days sure hadn't made much noticeable difference to Lilly. She had stumbled through her days at school, made the motions to study, engaged in conversations—but she was numb. Whenever she stopped to think about what happ— *Shudder.*

Lilly pulled her car into the student parking lot and checked the time—7:50. She had study hall first hour on Wednesdays and didn't have to be in class until 8:10. Twenty minutes to mingle and chatter about useless things like parties and clothes? No thanks! She leaned her seat back as far as it could go and closed her eyes. She'd nap until she heard the bell. Who cared about all that stuff anyway? *Me, that's who. At least, I used to. . . .*

A few minutes later, she heard a whistle nearby. "You look hot, Stace." *Jason.* He must not have seen Lilly inside her car. She scrunched down even lower.

"C'mere, cutie."

Lilly cringed when Jason used *her* nickname on Stacie. How could he?

"Hey, Jason. How's it going?" Stacie tried to sound aloof, but Lilly knew her better than that. She visualized her sidling up to Jason and batting her eyelashes as she looked up at him.

Jason laughed. "It's all good now. Come on, the bell's about to ring. I'll walk you to class."

Lilly waited a few seconds to let them pass. She pulled on the steering wheel and raised her body so she could watch them retreat.

Jason smiled down at Stacie, who practically drooled over him as one of the straps to her book bag slipped off her shoulder. He reached around her and slid the strap up Stacie's arm until it rested in place. His fingers lingered on her shoulder, and he draped his arm across her back.

Slick.

That's it. Lilly threw open the car door, grabbed her books, and made her way into the school with her head held high. No more

ESSENCE OF LILLY

brooding in the car or hiding in the shadows. *He* was slime. *He* was wrong. Sure, she'd made a bad decision—and one she'd pay for, for the rest of her life—but she wasn't about to let him victimize her any longer.

❀

"Lilly, let's backtrack to the family session we had on Monday, okay?" Dr. Shepherd looked at her notes. "You really seemed out of sorts that day. You didn't want to participate."

Lilly shifted in her seat and chewed on her lip.

Dr. Shepherd lifted her eyes from her papers. "In fact, you seemed near tears several times."

She winced and raised her shoulders.

"Something was definitely bothering you, but I didn't want to call you out in front of the others. So what's going on?"

Should she tell her or not? "I don't know. I'm okay now." Lilly inspected a hangnail.

"Remember, our sessions are confidential. I can't really help you if you don't open up to me."

Lilly groaned and shook her head. "No offense. But I don't think even you can help with this one."

"Try me." Dr. Shepherd put her pen down and held Lilly's gaze while she waited.

Would she wait the whole session if she

355

didn't say anything? "All right." Lilly groaned. "It's really hard to say. It's about Jason. We. . .um. . .we broke up."

"I'm sorry to hear that. What happened?"

"Well. . .um. . .things went a little too. . .okay, a *lot* too far between us, and I wanted to pull back and he didn't." Lilly crossed and uncrossed her legs and bit her bottom lip until she tasted blood.

"How far is too far?" Dr. Shepherd leaned forward. "Please understand, I can only help you if I know what we're dealing with."

Lilly opened her mouth to speak but couldn't formulate the words. She could feel her cheeks growing red in her embarrassment.

Dr. Shepherd reached a hand out to Lilly's shoulder. "I'm assuming you two went all the way. Is that correct?"

Lilly nodded.

"And you have regrets, but he doesn't?"

Talk about an understatement. "Yeah, something like that." Lilly's eyes darted everywhere but at Dr. Shepherd.

Dr. Shepherd put her pen and papers on the floor under her chair and clasped her hands together. "Why don't you tell me what happened—what led up to it and how things got to that point?"

Lilly recounted the story, starting with their decision to go to church events in order to spend more time together, and ending with last Friday night—well, Saturday morning, actually.

"Okay. Right now we're not going to talk about what you should have done—something tells me you've figured that out. Let's talk about what to do now." She picked up her papers and wrote some things down. "Do your mom and Stan know?"

Lilly's heart sank. "No! You won't tell them, will you?" She touched her swollen lip with her tongue and tasted the blood.

"No, I won't tell them, Lilly. But I think you should." Dr. Shepherd waited.

"I don't want them to know. They'll be so disappointed in me."

"They love you—they both do—and they'll help you through this. This is big for anyone, but especially for young girls like you who had visions of remaining pure." Dr. Shepherd patted Lilly's arm.

She thought she'd cried her last over this, but telling the story, seeing Dr. Shepherd's concern, coming face-to-face with the magnitude of the situation again, unleashed the flood. Lilly's shoulders shook as she laid her head on her hands and sobbed. A wad of tissues appeared between her forearms, and she gratefully grabbed them.

It felt like hours but was probably only ten minutes later when Lilly lifted her head and found Dr. Shepherd sitting quietly with her eyes closed, moving her lips. Lilly cleared her throat and blew her nose.

Dr. Shepherd opened her eyes and smiled softly. "Feel better?"

"I guess so." Lilly shrugged. "Were you praying?"

"Yep. God is my counselor. I look to Him to help me help you." She grabbed Lilly's hand. "Our time is up, but think about what I said. I'll help you talk to them on Monday if you decide to."

"I'll give it some thought."

Chapter 12

REDEMPTION

Ten. Waiting for Dr. Shepherd to call them in for their family session, Lilly counted the days since *the incident.* Was ten days long enough to expect healing? Would twenty do it? How about thirty? *Sigh.* Lilly feared she might never find peace with her mistake.

Dr. Shepherd poked her head out into the waiting area. "Come on in, guys." She stood back and held the door open for them, then waited for everyone to have a seat. "I'm going to let Lilly start us off today. You can open up any topic you'd like, and when you need me to, I'll jump in."

Now what? Lilly looked from her mom to Stan and then over to Dr. Shepherd who nodded encouragingly. *Lord, what do I do?*

Trust Me.

She heard Him—felt Him—speak to
her spirit and knew without a doubt that she
needed to have this conversation. "Well, I do
have something I want to talk about." She took
a deep breath, sat up straight, and told her story.
She forced herself not to get sidetracked by the
sounds of her mom's sobs—didn't even look in
her direction.

I'm trusting You.

When she arrived at the part about Jason
and Stacie, Stan jumped to his feet and paced
the room like a lion in a cage.

Mom reached for a tissue from the box on
the coffee table in front of her. "I. . .I just don't
know what to say."

"What are you feeling right now, Peggy?"
Dr. Shepherd wrote on her notepad.

"What am I *feeling*?" Mom's eyes flashed.
"I feel angry at Lilly for lying to me and for
drinking alcohol. Angry at Jason for taking her
innocence. Disappointed in Lilly for giving in.
Confused why God let this all happen right
under my nose." She tried to stand but gave up
and sat back in the chair. "And mostly I am so
very mad at myself. I've been so wrapped up in
saving my marriage and preparing for this baby

that I've let Lilly take care of herself." The dark circles under her eyes glared in contrast with her pale skin. Her shoulders hung low, and heavy eyelashes veiled her dark eyes.

Lilly finally let go. The flood she'd been holding back since they started talking spilled out. She slid off her chair, crawled over to her mom, and put her head in her lap while she cried. "M–Mom, I'm s–s–so sorry."

"Sweetheart, we'll find a way to help you with what you've gone through—maybe Dr. Shepherd knows of a group or something." She chuckled. "Normally I'd have to punish the lying, the alcohol, and the overnighter, but I think we're beyond punishment with this. We need to figure out where to go from here."

"I think this is a good place for me to step in." Dr. Shepherd smiled. "First of all, let me say, you have all made such beautiful progress over the past few months. I see a loving family before me. Each of you has shown that you place the needs of your family members above yourself. It's wonderful."

Mom grinned. "You know what? You're right. This conversation would have gone much differently a few months ago."

Lilly returned to her chair. *Wow.* Mom was right.

Dr. Shepherd went to her desk and reached into a drawer. She pulled out a blue paper. "This is a group that meets at a local church." She handed the sheet to Lilly and then returned to her chair. "It's led by a pastor's wife who is also a counselor. The focus is to help girls like you reclaim their purity."

" 'Reclaim their purity?' " Lilly raised her eyebrows. "I don't know. Sounds kind of weird and. . .um. . .physically impossible." She read the paper and nodded. "The leader is Heather, my youth pastor's wife. She kind of started to tell me about the group."

"Great. You know, physically, some things can't be changed. But spiritually, it's another matter entirely." Dr. Shepherd leaned forward and put her elbows on her knees. "The Bible says that by changing your attitude to be like Christ, you can put off your old self that gets messed up by sin. Then you can take on the righteousness and holiness of God."

"Hmm." Lilly sat up a little straighter. Was there hope for her yet? "What do I need to do?"

"Lilly, I'm serious about this. It all comes down to your faith." Dr. Shepherd took her hand. "You see, the reason so many people struggle with defeat is that they don't believe they're worthy of God's grace, so they stay mired in their sin. He paid the price. He offered the forgiveness. He promised the renewal. So take it. It's a free gift for you. Once you have it, though, you have to believe you have it, or it won't help you get past this."

Lilly hung on every word. It made perfect sense. "I want that."

"I'd love to pray with you if you don't mind." Dr. Shepherd put down her papers.

"That would be great." *Wait.* "You know what? I think I'd like to pray myself if it's okay. I want to make this real." Pray in front of people? Lilly shuddered at the thought—but this was important. She would do whatever it took.

Mom cleared her throat. "I think that would be beautiful." Her voice cracked with emotion.

Stan walked back to his seat and sat on the edge. "I think it's a fantastic idea."

Here goes. Lilly took a deep breath and gathered her thoughts. She shut her eyes and lifted her face to the ceiling. "Dear Jesus. Please heal me." Her voice caught as she struggled to stay composed. "Forgive me for going against Your Word. I want to honor You with my actions and with my. . .um. . .body." She slid from the chair to her knees. "Please. I believe that You have the power to restore me. Please renew me so I can stay pure until I get married. I vow to You that I will. I believe in Your promise. Amen." Lilly knew God heard her disjointed prayer—even though it wasn't flowery and eloquent.

Dr. Shepherd wiped her eyes. "You will never know how much that meant to me, Lilly."

"Mom? You okay?" Lilly squinted through her tears to see her mom's white-knuckle grip on the arms of the chair. "What's wrong?"

"Oh nothing." She chuckled. "I think people have had babies before. Just keep going," she panted. "This is amazing."

"Peg! You're in labor? For how long?" Stan stood up and turned in a circle. "What do we do? Should we call someone?" His eyes pleaded with Dr. Shepherd who stared at Mom.

Mom scrunched her face and reached for Stan's hand. "No, no. I mean, yes, I'm in labor. But no. We don't need to call someone. I've got plenty of time. Keep talking." She huffed her breaths and struggled to push her words out. "I wouldn't want to interrupt this"—she released her grip and gestured to the group—"for anything." She clutched her belly and moaned.

"Uh, Peg. We might not have a choice."

Stan's eyes pleaded with Dr. Shepherd, the panic evident in his eyes. "Should these contractions be this strong so soon?"

"Yeah, I thought they were supposed to come and go." Lilly looked from Stan to Dr. Shepherd. "When will they let up?"

"Don't worry. Things are moving pretty quickly, but nothing about having a baby is standard. I'll call for an ambulance." She turned to speak into the phone while Lilly and Stan talked to Mom.

"Mom, you're going to be okay." *Oh God, please, please help my mom. Don't let anything happen to her. I need her—we all do.*

Stan held up Mom's sweaty hair and blew on the back of her neck.

Mom panted and gripped the chair. The contractions didn't seem to ease at all.

Dr. Shepherd returned with a cool washcloth and placed it on Mom's forehead. "I sure wish you'd told us sooner, Peg."

"I kn—know. I just didn't want to. . .inter-rupt what was. . .happening." She scrunched her face and squeezed her eyes closed.

The door burst open and two emergency medical technicians pushed a gurney into the room. "We heard someone wants to have a baby today." A chubby woman with red, curly hair approached Mom and took her pulse just as the contraction ended. "How long has this been going on?"

Stan stepped forward. "Not long—an hour maybe."

"How far apart are the contrac–"

Mom moaned again and clutched her belly.

The woman chuckled. "Oops. Never mind. I can see for myself." She turned to her partner—a beefy guy with a radio. "We need to get going, Mike."

"Breathe, honey." Stan sucked in air and then blew it out. "Like this, remember?"

Mike squatted down in front of her. "Mrs. Sanders, we're going to move you now. We'll get your vitals and the other information we need while we're on our way to the hospital, okay?"

Mom nodded. "Just hurry."

Grams! Lilly texted her a message to meet them at the hospital then watched in horror as they got Mom settled on the gurney and into the ambulance. Helpless. Her mom writhed on the little bed—what if she fell off? Those straps couldn't possibly hold her. Could they?

What if something happened on the way to the hospital? "Can I ride with her?"

Redhead turned to Lilly. "Sorry, hon. Just your dad. She's in good hands, I promise. Do you have a way to the hospital?"

"He's not my—" Who cared who Stan was? Get it together! "Yes. I can drive there. Hurry, though."

Mike stepped up. "Okay, but we're going to go fast and go through red lights. You make sure you drive the speed limit and pay attention to traffic signals. We don't want you in the ER tonight."

❀

Rushing through the sliding doors to the hospital, Lilly found Grams sitting in the waiting room. "Where's Mom? How is she?"

"She's upstairs in labor and delivery—I waited for you here so I could take you up. Come on. We'll go together." Grams put her arm around Lilly, squeezed her trembling shoulders, and guided her to the elevator. "It's going to be okay, doll."

The elevator beeped, and the doors slid open to the maternity floor. They stopped at the nurses' station, and a nurse looked up at Grams. "Can I help you?"

"We're looking for Peggy Sanders."

"Yes. You can have a seat in that waiting

room right there." She smiled and nodded toward the room. "Someone will come for you when we have news."

Lilly's heart sank. More waiting. What if something had gone wrong? "Please, is there anything you can tell us?" Lilly wanted to grab the nurse and shake the details out of her.

"No. I can't divulge information about patients." She looked around and dropped her voice to a whisper. "I will tell you this. If you listen really closely, you'll hear a lullaby from the overhead speakers. We play one every time a baby is born. The next time you hear that song, it will be because your baby brother or sister has come into the world."

Lilly nodded, her eyes glued on the speaker. *Come on. Play.* She walked into the waiting room and sank into a chair, never taking her eyes off the speaker.

Grams sat beside her and held her hand.

They waited.

And waited.

Finally, the softest twinkling sounds of Brahms' "Lullaby." Lilly jumped to her feet and turned to her grandmother. "They're okay! He's here." She jumped up and down and hugged Grams. "When do you think we can see them?"

"How about right now?" The nurse stood in the doorway, smiling. "They've asked me to bring you two to her room if you're ready."

"Lead the way." Grams held out her arm for Lilly to go first.

Lilly gritted her teeth as they walked toward the labor room. What if it was gross in there with blood and stuff everywhere?

The nurse stopped before a closed door and knocked softly before opening it. She held it for Lilly to enter first.

Lilly stepped into the bright room just as a nurse turned down the lights. An orderly wheeled a cart of soiled linens past them and out the door—no blood anywhere. Two nurses stepped away from the bedside, and Lilly finally saw her. They locked eyes. "Mom, are you okay?"

"I'm perfect. Come meet your baby brother." She smiled down at the bundle in her arms.

Lilly stood rooted to the spot. "He's here. . .right now?" Didn't they usually take the baby to the nursery or something?

"Yes, this is Matthew. His name means 'God's gift.' " Mom tilted her arm to raise his head. "Come on over."

Lilly took a few hesitant steps. Once she reached the bed, she peered over Mom's shoulder

369

at her brother. *My brother.* A single tear fell when she gazed into his huge eyes. She reached out a finger and touched his tiny hand, then gasped when his teeny fingers wrapped around one of hers. "He's amazing. You're amazing, Mom." Mom had never looked more beautiful.

Mom sat up a bit and lifted Matthew into Lilly's arms. As he nuzzled in, Lilly felt something she'd never experienced before. A complete and overwhelming sense of purpose—a reason for being who she was at that moment in her life. Suddenly, everything she'd been trying to figure out finally made sense. God's timing, relationships, sacrifice, obedience, unconditional love—all wrapped up in a tight little bundle right there in her arms.

Matthew. . .God's gift.

True love.

❀

Peeking through the window on the double doors, Lilly counted six girls and Heather. One rocked a blue baby carrier with her foot. One had a box of Twinkies in her lap and at least two empty wrappers on the floor by her feet. A girl about thirteen had her arms crossed on her chest and stared straight ahead. Two girls held Bibles. A very pregnant girl was crying. Heather passed her a box of tissues.

I can do this. Lilly took a deep breath and opened the door.

Heather's eyes brightened. "Lilly! I'm so glad you made it. Come on in and have a seat."

Lilly slid into an empty chair beside Twinkie Girl.

"I was just about to open the session with some news." Heather looked around the circle. "Kendra had her baby. She's fine and home from the hospital. The adoption went through as planned, but we'll let her share about that when she returns next week. She'd appreciate your prayers—this isn't easy."

The pregnant girl shook her head. "I think she did the right thing, but I couldn't give up my baby. No way."

Wow. Could I do that? Lilly shook her head. *I sure hope I don't have to find out.*

Heather smiled. "We all have to find our way with God's guidance. So let's support Kendra's choice."

"We have two new girls this week, so let's go around the circle and introduce ourselves. I'm Heather. My husband, Zach, is the youth pastor here at this church, and I lead this group because I've been where you all are." She looked at the pregnant girl to her left.

"I'm Paige. I'm about to pop, obviously." She grimaced and patted her belly. "I'm seventeen, and I'm keeping the baby—by myself. *Papa* isn't interested." She rolled her eyes and snapped her gum as she dabbed the corners of her eyes with the tissue. "What else is there to say?"

Heather patted her arm then turned to the next girl, who wore a nurse's uniform and seemed older than the rest of the group.

"I'm Beth." She held up her left hand and pointed to a delicate diamond ring. "My fiancé and I decided we wanted to reclaim our purity in God's eyes before we took our vows to each other in a few months. We were living together, but I moved out until after the wedding. It's been hard, but we both believe it's worth it."

As the girls told their stories, the image of Sam sitting at the lunch table describing her own experience flooded Lilly's mind. She'd invite Sam to the next group meeting—Sam needed it as much as Lilly.

"I'm Monica. This is my first time here. My boyfriend dumped me when he found out I was pregnant with his baby. I thought we'd get married—he had other ideas. So, I. . .um. . .had an abortion a month ago."

Lilly gasped involuntarily. Monica looked just like everyone else. She could be anyone's daughter, sister, friend. How many others were like her?

Monica looked down. "I really thought it was the best thing, but since then, I just can't stop crying. I throw up at least once a day. My doctor says it's post-traumatic stress something or other. My mom hopes that by hanging out with some girls who are going through what I am, I'll get better."

"Welcome, Monica. I'm very sorry for your loss. We'll talk more about seeking forgiveness and forgiving yourself as we go on." Heather turned to Twinkie Girl. "Debbie?"

The next girl wiped the crumbs off her baggy sweatpants and tightened her ponytail before speaking. "I'm Debbie. I. . .um. . .I was raped. Well, I guess it's called molested—it was my uncle." Her eyes darted around the circle, and she unwrapped another Twinkie. "I can't stop eating junk food. My therapist says it's because I want to gain weight so men won't find me attractive. I don't think that's it. . .but"—she broke the snack cake in half and stuffed a piece into her mouth—"maybe." She shrugged.

My turn. "I'm Lilly—sixteen. I. . .uh. . . had

sex with my boyfriend a few weeks ago. It was my first time."

Several girls rolled their eyes.

Lilly sighed. "I know. You've all heard that before, right? But it really was my first time. I had wanted to wait until marriage, but I messed up. Then, when I wanted to go back to the way things were before we went all the way, my boyfriend dumped me. And now I don't even know if I'm pregnant or not." More tears. Where did they keep coming from?

Monica clucked her tongue and shook her head. "Giiiirl. Why do they *do* that?"

"I hear you about the waiting. It's the not knowing that's the hardest." The young angry girl practically whispered. "I'm waiting for the results of my HIV test. There's a good chance they won't be good."

Oh God. HIV?

Heather cleared her throat. "Carrie, will you stay after for a few minutes? I'd like to talk to you about that and pray for you if it's okay." She smiled at each of them. "I'm so glad that each one of you has decided to be a part of this group. Every single one of us has pain involved with our stories. So, over the coming weeks, we're going to spend a lot of time talking about forgiveness and identity."

"Identity?" Monica's eyebrow furrowed.

"Yep. How do you see yourself? How do you think others view you? How do other people *really* see you? And most important, how does God see you?" Heather looked up as though choosing her words. "Often, the reason behind an improper sexual relationship stems from a lack of self-confidence. Girls either don't think highly enough of themselves to protect their bodies, or they just want love and acceptance from anyone so badly they'll do whatever it takes." She reached for her Bible. "Understanding how God sees you is the first step toward a proper self-image."

"Can I ask a question?" Lilly raised her hand about shoulder height.

Heather leaned forward. "Please do."

How do I phrase this without sounding crazy? "Well, my counselor helped me pray to reclaim my purity. I believe that God sees me as whole. . .pure. However, nothing will change the fact that I'm not a virgin physically. I can't fix that for a future husband. . .can I?"

Beth nodded. "That's true—I'm in the same boat. We all are."

Heather nodded sadly. "Unfortunately, the

physical effects of some choices cannot be undone. God has an order for things, and we can only get back on His path where we veered off. We can't go back to the beginning."

"But it's still *His* path for us, right? Even though we messed up?" Lilly's voice raised in hope.

"Absolutely. It might be a different path than it would have been had you made a different choice. But that no longer matters to Him." Heather grinned excitedly, shaking her head. "Don't you see? He meets you where you are right now, sets a new course before you, and calls you to walk with Him. From this moment on is all that matters."

Soaking in every word, no one spoke.

Heather smiled. "You girls are so blessed to be here together. You have each other, and you're getting it right. Many girls just continue down the path toward a lifetime of low self-esteem and sexual relationships, never finding true love."

Lilly nodded. There it was again—true love.

"Together," Heather continued, "we're going to find out what true love is. We'll know it so well that no boyfriend, no relationship, will ever come close to measuring up to the true love of God." She smiled at each girl.

"Sound okay, Lilly?"

"Sounds great to me." Lilly relaxed in her chair. It was over. She forgave herself—the final hump toward complete healing. *Thank You for bringing me here. Thank You for forgiving me.*

Thank You for true love.

My Decision

I, *(include your name here)*, have read the story of Lilly LeMure and have learned from her experiences. I promise to place my purity above any physical desires or pressure I might face to have a sexual relationship before marriage. I believe in God's plan for a husband and wife, and I commit to uphold that standard in my own life.

Please pray the following prayer:

Father God, I am weak, and sometimes I take a wrong turn. I realize that my purity must be guarded above all else. Please let the lessons I learned as I read about Lilly imprint onto my heart, that I might remember to uphold these standards I've committed to. Help me to be strong in the face of pressure and able to withstand even my own physical desires. Help me to place honor and godliness above a boyfriend, the desire for love and acceptance, and anything else the world might dangle before me. I know that You love me and accept me for who I am. Thank You for Your true love. Amen.

Congratulations on your decision! Please sign this contract signifying your commitment. Have someone you trust, like a parent or a pastor, witness your choice.

_____

Signed

_____

Witnessed by

CHECK IT OUT

For information on the latest
Scenarios books, great giveways, girl talk,
and more, visit scenariosforgirls.com!

Find Scenarios author
Nicole O'Dell on the Web:

Web site: www.nicoleodell.com
Facebook: facebook.com/nicoleodell
Twitter: twitter.com/Nicole_Odell
Blog: nicoleodell.blogspot.com

Teen Talk Radio, with host Nicole O'Dell,
airs on www.choicesradio.com.

SCENARIOS FOR GIRLS

DARE TO BE DIFFERENT

Lindsay Martin and her friends begin playing a game at sleepovers, and it all starts as harmless fun. . .until the dares become more and more risky. Drew Daniels wants to be as different from her twin sister as possible—new haircut, new clothes, new friends. . .and a boyfriend. What happens when Lindsay and Drew are faced with making difficult choices? Will they dare to be different?

RISKY BUSINESS

Molly Jacobs gets hired at the ultimate girls' clothing store and her friends—even the popular girls in school—are envious. Kate Walker secures a spot on her school's swim team but soon becomes obsessed—with practice and making it through the championships with flying colors. What happens when Molly and Kate are faced with making difficult choices? How will they handle the risky business?

Available wherever books are sold.